Murder
in the Dark

Books by Kerry Greenwood

The Phryne Fisher Series
Cocaine Blues
Flying Too High
Murder on the Ballarat Train
Death at Victoria Dock
The Green Mill Murder
Blood and Circuses
Ruddy Gore
Urn Burial
Raisins and Almonds
Death Before Wicket
Away With the Fairies
Murder in Montparnasse
The Castlemaine Murders
Queen of the Flowers
Death by Water
Murder in the Dark

The Corinna Chapman Series
Earthly Delights
Heavenly Pleasures
Devil's Food
Trick or Treat

Short Story Anthology
A Question of Death:
An Illustrated Phryne Fisher Treasury

Murder in the Dark

A Phryne Fisher Mystery

Kerry Greenwood

Poisoned Pen Press

Copyright © 2006 by Kerry Greenwood

First U.S. Edition 2009

10 9 8 7 6 5 4 3 2 1

Library of Congress Catalog Card Number: 2008931501

ISBN: 978-1-59058-439-2 Hardcover

Poisoned Pen Press
6962 E. First Ave., Ste. 103
Scottsdale, AZ 85251
www.poisonedpenpress.com
info@poisonedpenpress.com

Printed in the United States of America

This book is dedicated to Miz Cindy Brown and Phoenix of Port Townsend. Cuter than a little white pup sitting under a shade tree and sweeter than a pound of molasses poured over a kitten.

Acknowledgments

With thanks to so many people. The friends who have forgiven me lost lunches, forgotten birthdays, missed appointments, errant dinners. All my singers: my fellow folkies from the old days at the Three Drunken Maidens, my MUCS and MO-NUCS, my IV and Scratch and R.A.G. choirs. My Ars Nova and my Society for Creative Anachronism, dancers and musicians.

To Jean Greenwood, the researcher every author should have, and David Greagg, whose patience ought to gain him sainthood. Samantha of Dragonfly, who healed me. All the Pryors. And Belladonna my cat, who by gently tapping the caps lock key every two hours and suggesting a little exercise and some cat treats, managed, devotedly, to get me through this book uncrippled. For Michael Warby's advice on medieval games and in loving homage to the master of us all, PG Wodehouse. For Adina Hamilton, who made a marzipan boar's head. And for Tom Lane, who wanted me to save Gatsby.

Possession is nine points of the law.
—Blackstone Laws of England

A bird in the hand is worth two in the bush.

Chapter One

Deck the halls with boughs of holly,
Fa la la la la la la la la,'
Tis the season to be jolly,
Fa la la la la la la la la.

Trad.

Monday, 24th December 1928

Very few people turned Phryne Fisher down. She wasn't used to it. With her looks, which were those of the cinema star Louise Brooks, her wealth, which was that of Croesus, her élan, which was remarkable, and her appetites, which were reputed to be those of an unusually broadminded nymph, she didn't hear 'No' a lot. Mostly people said nothing but a correctly phrased 'Yes, please.' It was therefore with some astonishment that she realised her beloved Lin Chung was, indeed, turning her down as flat as the linenfold panelling of her boudoir.

'No,' he said patiently. 'I really can't, Phryne.'

'Can't?' she asked, rolling over with a flash of thighs and sitting up to consider his strange, uncooperative attitude. 'Or won't?'

'Both, really.' Lin Chung buttoned his loose blue shirt over his admirably smooth torso. 'I have to preside over my old Great Great Uncle's funeral. I liked him, Phryne. He was a brave old man. I would not skimp on his ceremonies. Grandmamma is ill. Camellia needs my presence. I cannot justify neglecting the venerable dead and taking a week off from my business in order to play cowboys and Indians in Werribee with the Templars, Phryne.'

'Aha,' she said, observing him closely. 'You don't like them, do you?'

Lin shrugged his collar around his neck and stabbed the fastening closed. He reached for his light blazer.

'No, I do not like them. I do not approve of them, either. Those bright young things burn far too bright for me.'

'There's something behind this attitude,' she commented, dragging a dressing gown on and belting it tightly.

'Probably. I am influenced by a number of things,' admitted Lin. 'But the conclusion of it is, I cannot accompany you to the Last Best Party of 1928, and I hope you are not too grievously disappointed.'

'Surprised more than disappointed,' she said. 'You won't change your mind?'

'I regret,' he said, giving her that sidelong glance which she thought of as quintessentially Chinese.

'Then I shall find my own company,' she declared.

'As you wish,' he agreed.

The boudoir was silent for a moment, as Ember the cat arose from his silken nest and paused at the closed door, mouth open in a plaintive but entirely unvoiced meow. Phryne jumped up and let him out.

'A drink,' she said, and escorted her lover onto the landing.

The bijou residence of the Hon. Miss Phryne Fisher, located in the desirable if a little scruffy suburb of St. Kilda in the town of Melbourne, was home to the said Miss Fisher, her maid and constant companion Miss Dorothy Williams, her adopted daughters Jane and Ruth, home from school for the holidays, her cat Ember, the girls' dog Molly, a shrill but persistent canary which Dot was minding while her sister was making other arrangements for it, and Mr. and Mrs. Butler, the bulwarks of the establishment. Phryne had secured their services by offering a very good salary with very good conditions and never interfering in the manner in which they ran the house. Mr. Butler buttled, orchestrated cocktails which would have made him a deity in any alcohol based religion and drove the Hispano-Suiza whenever Phryne would let him. Mrs. Butler cooked and kept the house. Other functionaries came in by the day to dust and polish, and the laundry, of course, went to the Chinese, who understood about starch and never lost so much as a pillowcase.

One of the perks of the Fisher household was that apart from their own bedroom and parlour, Mr. Butler had a small cubbyhole called a butler's pantry in which to entertain his own intimates. It was just big enough for a sink and the tasting glasses, a couple of chairs and a window that looked out into the fernery, which was full of orchids. The window was open. A scent of jasmine floated in. The afternoon was at three, the port was remarkably fragrant, and Mr. Butler was content with the world. Especially since Dot had volunteered to do the refreshments should Phryne decide that she wanted any. A jug of Pimm's Number One Cup was already mixed and in the new, huge, American Ice-maker and Refrigerator.

Mr. Butler filled his guest's glass and said comfortingly, 'Don't take on so, Tom.'

'Oh, it's all very well for you,' said Tom Ventura, pettishly. 'You and your Miss Fisher and your cellar full of port. You're comfortable enough, I dare say. You don't have a house party which is going to take as much organising as a small war only half done and you, and I say this for your ears only, Tobias, you don't have an employer who's half off his head all the time. And her head. They're both bloody mad.'

'My Miss Fisher can be a bit excitable,' said Mr. Butler judiciously. 'But she's very reasonable.'

'Not so the Templars,' groaned Mr. Ventura.

'They can't be that bad,' soothed Mr. Butler. His guest choked on the good port and would have leapt up, eyes flaming, if he had not been so tired. Besides, the dog Molly was asleep on his feet. Mr. Ventura liked dogs. His voice, however, rose to a cracked shriek.

'Eleven times the whole plan has been changed! Eleven! Each time I have had to recalculate all the accommodations, the staff, the hampers, the amounts of drink and food, the timing of deliveries—the difficulties would make a devil weep!'

'Now, now, Tom, where are those drops the doctor gave you? Here,' said Mr. Butler, sloshing some into a clean glass and adding water. 'Take these and just sit quiet for a little. I didn't mean to upset you.'

Molly rose from her couch and licked Mr. Ventura's hand. She was a compassionate dog and, besides, she loved the taste of valerian. Mrs. Butler opened the door and offered a small tray on which a coffee pot reposed. Mr. Butler took it. Amazing woman, his Aurelia. Always understood what was going on.

He poured a demitasse for Mr. Ventura and observed, 'I know that my Miss Fisher is going to your party, Tom. And I know that your twins—the Golden Twins, the paper called them—your Gerald and Isabella Templar have hired the old Chirnside place at Werribee from the Catholics for this house party. Called the Last Best Party of 1928, reputed to be costing a fortune, and all the guests to be housed in tents on the grounds for the whole five days, full of fun and sensation and the Lord knows what goings-on. Not like my Miss Fisher to stay in a tent,' mused the butler, taking another sip of port and observing that his guest seemed to be recovering. 'And I know that the weather is going to be hot and the police have been taking a dim view.'

'Then,' said Tom Ventura, 'you know a lot. I've been chasing down ice-making machines for the Palace of Glass all day. Do you know how many ice-making machines you need for that much ice? It's like staging the Great Exhibition. And I don't think I'm going to get a knighthood out of it, I really don't.' He contemplated the dregs in his coffee cup. Mr. Butler refilled it. 'And just as likely when I get back he'll say he's changed his mind and we don't need the Palace of Glass anyway—or not where I've put it—and perhaps we could have a Gothic castle instead. Then she'll egg him on and…I don't know how long I can stand this,' he said plaintively.

'Why did you take them on?' asked Mr. Butler, a little censoriously. He had conducted careful enquiries into the character of Miss Fisher before he accepted a place in her household.

'Oh, I thought they would be exciting,' said Tom Ventura, patting Molly. 'I was bored. I remember being bored,' he added. 'It was nice. I didn't appreciate it at the time.'

The bell rang. Mr. Butler heard Dot get up from her seat at the kitchen table, where she and Mrs. Butler had been amiably shelling one hundred chestnuts for stuffing the Christmas goose. Removing two strongly adherent shells from the annoying nuts was a job best done in company. He heard Dot say, as she laid her chestnut down with a click, 'That's ninety-three, Mrs. Butler.'

In her parlour, Phryne noted the approach of the jug of Pimm's Number One Cup, with its slices of cucumber and sprigs of mint, with pleasure. She liked the burned-sugar flavour of the gin-based cup, but required it to be double-diluted and the glass jug packed with ice, preferably rasped. This jug was so cold that it was breathing little chilly clouds into the tepid air.

'Mr. Butler still in conclave?' she asked. Dot nodded, put down her plate of cheese straws and poured out two glasses of Pimm's.

'That poor man is having a terrible time with those Templars,' she commented. 'But me and Mrs. B have almost finished the chestnuts. Are you sure you can manage tomorrow, Miss?' she asked. Dot yielded to no one in her opinion of her employer's daring and courage, but took a very poor view of her domestic talents, which even Phryne admitted were negligible.

'My sister Eliza and her friend Lady Alice Harborough will manage. They used to run soup kitchens for the poor and apparently they are managing very well in that nice little house Bert found for them. Eliza has been having cooking lessons and they have bought their very own copy of Mrs. Beeton,' Phryne replied, sipping with delight. 'Perfectly freezing! This new ice refrigeration machine was a good investment. Won't you have a glass, Dot dear?'

'Too cold for me,' said Dot. 'Makes my teeth ache. Miss? I really don't like you being without me and the Butlers for so long.'

'Nonsense,' said Phryne bracingly. 'You will like seeing all your relatives, the Butlers want to see their married daughter's new child, and all I have to do is go to church and supervise the lunch—and if all goes totally disastrous there is a nice collection of canned things and plenty to drink. My sister and the girls and I are old campaigners, Dot dear; unless we burn down the house I don't see how it can go very wrong. Just pack up your hampers. Don't forget the sweets and the crackers and the crystallised fruits and the chocolates and Mrs. B's mince pies, and I've put out a bottle or two of the good port for your father. He'll probably get a case of the old Fisher gout, but we can't have everything.'

Dot was a plain young woman with a long brown plait, coiled into a bun at the back of her neck. She always dressed in earth colours. Even her apron was beige. She had a fresh complexion and very kind eyes, but no one would have called her beautiful until they saw her smile, and she smiled now, dazzling Lin Chung. Dot was suddenly overwhelmed with gratitude and Christmas spirit. She leaned down and kissed Phryne's blooming cheek, and then hurried herself back to the chestnuts. Miss Fisher might hand over this gem of a goose to her sister's uncertain handling and it might turn out tough, but it would not lack its *purée de marrons* if Dot had anything to do with it.

'She seems happy,' commented Lin Chung, sipping his drink and freezing his tongue. Miss Fisher, his concubine, did tend to extremes. Her chosen vindaloo made him weep and gulp from the water jug and this drink was colder than the Nether Hells. But he liked her extremes, so he set the glass down to melt.

'Dot has a talent for being happy,' said Phryne, refilling her glass.

'So, how are the preparations for Christmas coming along?' he asked easily.

'Without undue difficulty. All the presents are assembled, the crackers ready, the menu planned, the food bought. The girls are in their room working on the finishing touches to their presents, I believe, at this moment. Dot has bought a sack of gifts for her own family. It's my first Christmas here. It really doesn't seem right, the sun shining and the birds singing at Christmas, which is in the heart of winter at home. Still, we can walk to midnight mass without slipping on the ice on the way. And I can leave the atheists here to mind the stove while I go to a nice, rousing, Christmas carol service in the morning.'

'Sounds very pleasant,' said Lin, unwisely relaxing.

'And what did the Templars do to you?' she asked.

'Their hearties played a game of "fling the Chinaman" with my young cousin. Very amusing, no doubt, but they might have ascertained if he could swim before they threw him into the Thames. They stood on the bank and watched him struggle, and they laughed. A boatman and I managed to drag him out before he actually succumbed to the water and the cold.'

'How horrible,' said Phryne, without emphasis, watching him closely.

'So I owe the Templars—oh, undying loathing, and they owe me two rather good tailored suits. Not to mention spending a week talking my cousin out of quitting university and going to be a monk.'

'How did you talk him out of it?'

'I turned him over to Li Pen and told him to keep the boy to his own spare vegetarian diet and to make him do martial arts exercises all day. After a week, he confessed that he preferred the fleshpots and went back to university. He is a very good doctor. It would have been a pity to waste him.'

Lin took a gulp of his drink and gasped. All of his teeth shrieked for mercy.

'Detestable,' said Phryne. 'But they throw a wonderful party.'

'Yes, and I don't mind you going to it—much,' said Lin honestly. 'But I really can't do it myself. Every time I see that Gerald's golden laughing face I get an irresistible urge to hit it with a brick.'

'Understood,' said Phryne.

They imbibed gently for a while.

The afternoon post was carried in by Jane and Ruth, who were allowed a sip of Mr. Lin's drink as a reward. While investigating a gruesome murder on the Ballarat train, Phryne had acquired the pale, studious Jane, whose destiny was to be a doctor, provided someone made her catch the right tram and turn up to her exams and meals on time. This person was Ruth, darker and plumper, who had been rescued from grim domestic slavery by Phryne's commie mates Bert and Cec and who could not be left behind. Phryne had never meant to have daughters but found them interesting and rewarding. Jane was sucking her finger.

'Sewing wounds?' asked Phryne, sympathetically.

'Yes, but it's all done now,' said Jane. 'What a lot of cards! Can I open some?'

'By all means, here is the letter knife. Make sure that you keep the envelopes together until we can list who sent them. Lin will help,' said Phryne, volunteering him heartlessly.

Ruth, whose interests were culinary, had slipped away to the kitchen to watch Mrs. Butler stuff the goose. She had seen chickens, pigeons, quail, pheasant, spatchcock, duck and turkey stuffed, but never goose. It might prove different and Mrs. Butler's accompanying lecture was always worth hearing.

Mr. Butler was showing his companion out as Ruth came into the kitchen.

'It will be all right on the night, you'll see,' he murmured soothingly.

Mr. Ventura laughed bitterly. Ruth gave him a sympathetic smile and he patted her on the head in passing. She did not like being patted on the head, but if it made this harassed man feel better she was willing to put up with it. Tom Ventura had been a frequent visitor over the last week and Ruth was sorry for him.

'Hello, little Miss Ruth,' he said. 'You still want to be a cook?'

'Yes, sir,' she said.

'Stick with it,' he advised, and went on into the hall.

'Ah, Ruth, catch hold of this wing, will you?' said Mrs. Butler. 'We need to truss it close, or all the stuffing will burst out.'

They struggled with the anointed, slippery, dead bird for a moment, before Mrs. Butler flipped it onto its back and subdued any possibility of escape by looping string around both wings and securing it with a parcel knot. 'Good,' she said, pushing forward a bowl of a palish brown substance. 'Have a morsel. That's *purée de marrons*, it's taken Dot and me all morning to peel the dratted things, but it tastes good, eh?'

Ruth rolled herself a little ball of the forcemeat, put it into her mouth, considered, and grinned. Mrs. Butler grinned back. No faddy appetites in Miss Fisher's house. Mrs. Butler and Ruth continued operations on the goose. When it was stuffed and slicked and larded and wrapped and back in the American Ice-maker and Refrigerator, Mrs. Butler put her plump, clean cook's hand on Ruth's shoulder and spoke very solemnly.

'I'm leaving you with the luncheon, Ruth. I know Miss Fisher's sister used to run a soup kitchen but that's no recommendation to a lady's house. You've been with me all year and you've learned a lot. I wouldn't trust many young girls with it, but I'm trusting you. I know you won't disappoint me.'

Ruth's adolescent breast swelled with pride and she covered Mrs. Butler's hand with one just as clean.

'I won't let you down,' she vowed, as transported as the young Saint Joan.

'Good girl.' Mrs. Butler bent backwards and stretched. 'Now there's just time before we start lunch for a sit-down, a nice cuppa and one of those mince pies. The mince pies worked out very well this year. You never know with them, it all depends on the quality of the dried fruit…'

Ruth put on the kettle and bustled about, listening with infinite pleasure to cook's chorus or kitchen shop, which covers all the vagaries of the human appetite and the natural world, and goes on forever.

In the parlour, Lin was sorting envelopes by size and passing them to Jane, who was sitting on the hearthrug surrounded by pretty scenes of robins and snow and Father Christmas. Phryne was filling out late cards for the people to whom she hadn't sent a card. A distressingly large number, it seemed. Fortunately there were three postal deliveries a day at this time of the year and plenty of time. Her own Christmas card consisted of a very pretty photograph of the Fisher ménage with 'compliments of the season' scrolled underneath in silver-gilt. The photographer's name, Forrester, appeared in little letters on the back.

'And there we all are,' said Phryne to herself, contemplating the group. Posed in a pretty garden under a jasmine bower were, front, sitting on a picnic rug, Jane and Ruth, with Molly. Ember the black cat had declined to cooperate. Then, seated, Eliza and Phryne, flanked by (standing) Lady Alice and Dot. Dot had never been photographed before. She wore an expression of grim determination which was very comical. Behind them were Mrs. and Mrs. Butler.

The card was useful for all of the family, though Lin Chung, like Ember, had resolutely declined to be reproduced on a three-inch by five-inch card. Its lack of Christian symbolism meant that Lady Alice and Eliza could send it to their Fabian Socialist friends. Mr. and Mrs. Butler were tickled at being included on a card and Mrs. Butler considered that her best hat had come out very well. The girls were relieved at not having to choose Christmas cards for their few friends at their public school, as the form and nature of the very cards them-selves seemed to be a quagmire of fashionable danger. Phryne was pleased to have such a presentable family and the quiet design of the card was in the best of taste.

Which could not be said for the rest of them spilling out of their envelopes onto the rug, but they were cheerful and the senders meant well, and Phryne had always rather liked Christmas. In her impoverished childhood it had marked the beginning of a new year. Then, after the grand dislocation caused by her father's unexpected accession to the baronetcy, wealth and tedium. In her father's manor, it was marked with huge meals, dances, more huge meals, and the infliction of compulsory goodwill on the innocent tenantry, who just wanted to get on with their dinner in peace. Phryne had ensured that she was always welcomed with open arms in the cottages by staying for less than ten minutes, always bearing bottles of port, and passing small amounts of cash to the mothers and copious sweets to the children. Here in Australia she was free of social duties. Which reminded her to send a cheque to Edward Dunne, a Quaker who did useful work amongst the poor. While she was writing it, she heard Jane exclaim and drop the letter knife.

'What's the matter, did you cut yourself?' asked Lin Chung, concerned. Except when it came to dissection, Jane was a butterfingers.

'No,' said Jane. 'It's this card. Miss Phryne, look!'

She turned over a card which depicted the usual snow and robin. Inside it bore a carefully drawn skull and crossbones.

'Not very Christmassy,' commented Phryne as it was handed to her. 'Good drawing, though. "Don't go near the Last Best Party",' she read aloud, '"or it will be your Last Party of All". Well, well. Signed, "A Well-Wisher".'

'How curious,' said Jane.

'Curious indeed,' said Phryne. 'That decides me. I hadn't sent in my invitation card. I'll do it directly.'

'But someone doesn't want you to go to that party,' Lin pointed out. He had shuddered a little at the sight of the Jolly Roger. Pirates were something of a delicate topic for Lin Chung. They were, for example, the reason why he was missing an ear.

'Yes, and won't it be interesting to find out who and why?' she answered sweetly, and he watched her sign the gold embossed invitation to the Last Best Party of 1928, to be held from December 27th to the 1st of January at Werribee. She folded it into a plain envelope addressed to Gerald and Isabella Templar, care of the Windsor Hotel, Melbourne.

'*Alea jacta est,*' said Phryne, and rang for a gin and tonic.

Lin sighed. The die was, indeed, cast.

The Joker fanned the cards. The movement was practised and deft. They were hand-painted Italian playing cards from the eighteenth century, when decoration was arcane and whimsical. He smiled as he looked at their faces. They were all jokers.

Chapter Two

Now bring us some figgy pudding,
Now bring us some figgy pudding,
Now bring us some figgy pudding,
and bring some out here.
For we all like figgy pudding,
For we all like figgy pudding,
For we all like figgy pudding,
so bring some out here.

Trad.

Tuesday, 25th December

Ruth usually slept like a small, plump cat, neatly and easily. She and Jane had gone to bed early in their jazz coloured bedroom in order to wake up earlier. Jane had read three pages of her copy of *Origin of Species* before sighing, putting out her light and folding her hands. Ruth had laid aside *Carême on Cuisine*, with its hard French words, and closed her eyes. She did not fall asleep. She tried counting sheep leaping over a fence. She got to three thousand one hundred and eleven before she gave up. Then she tried recollecting every recipe she knew and found that she really knew a lot of recipes. But it was no good. She was excited about Christmas, a foreign concept in her previously mean and straitened history.

Her previous guardian had made a watery fruit pudding for her lodgers, it is true, and scorched the smallest chicken she could find in the market. But none of that provender had come the way of Jane or Ruth, the scullions. This was fortunate, because Ruth had never been very good at the Christian virtue of gratitude and had copped many a belting for not saying thank you sincerely enough for some noxious tidbit. Life with Phryne had been so full of treats that Ruth feared she might be becoming spoiled.

Then there was the lunch, which was her responsibility and hers alone, and Ruth gave up. She was not going to get any sleep. She rolled and sighed and bounced in a way that made the springs of her mattress squeak, and finally Jane awoke and asked, 'Can't you sleep?'

'No,' said Ruth.

'Well, come into my bed and we can tell stories,' offered Jane, who always considered sleeping a bit of a waste. She might miss something. 'I heard a new one today about a queen called Hecuba...'

◇◇◇

Christmas Day 1928 dawned clear and cool, with a breath of north wind which might turn hot later. Jane and Ruth had waited, tucked up in Jane's bed, watching the sky for the very first hint of light before they left their bed, stubbed a toe on Molly, apologised, banged into the door, finally found the electric light switch, chided each other to be quiet several times in ascending tones and at last made it into the hall.

They had almost managed to tiptoe into the parlour without another sound until Molly, for some reason, let out a loud wuff. Ruth suppressed her with a hand around her muzzle and the dog allowed herself to be shut outside. Jane and Ruth had never had what Phryne called a 'proper' Christmas, with a tree and presents and far too much to eat. They were determined to enjoy every scrap of it.

Gaily wrapped presents of intriguing shape were piled up under Phryne's beautiful silver and gold tree, but they were for later. Ruth collared the two holly-decked football socks from the mantelpiece and they ran back into their own room. Molly joined them, leaping onto Jane's bed. She was not ordinarily allowed on anyone's bed but she shrewdly suspected that the two young ladies were not going to object just this once.

Not only did they not object, they didn't appear to notice. And when they did, they didn't remove her but fed her black jelly beans.

Molly licked hands. She was altogether in favour of Christmas.

'What's this?' asked Jane, as Ruth popped a tidbit into her mouth. 'Mmm! Crystallised pineapple! I didn't know you could crystallise pineapple. And this is a cherry,' she added, rummaging. 'A chocolate cherry. And some ginger. Boiled lollies. Musk sticks. What have you got there?'

'A purse,' said Ruth. 'With five shillings in it. A pair of real stockings—*real* ones, Jane. A comb. Some honeysuckle soap. And some more lollies.' She bit thoughtfully into a crystallised cherry. 'You know, Jane, I really don't think I have ever been this happy. You?'

'No,' said Jane, after some thought. 'No, this is the happiest I have ever been.'

She kissed her foster sister on the cheek. Molly licked her, in case any trace of sweetness lingered. They truffled through the wrappings together, looking for more jelly beans.

'I hope everyone else is having a day as good as ours,' said Ruth, who was feeling generous after her third piece of crystallised ginger. Jane gave the matter her full consideration.

'Mr. Lin doesn't have Christmas, of course. Mr. Bert and Mr. Cec are going to be with their families,' said Jane. 'So it depends on how they get on with them. Some families are not at all nice,' she added, shuddering slightly.

'But we're fine,' said Ruth, and fed her sister another chocolate cherry.

Bert raised his glass and looked through it at a happily distorted view of his auntie's pub. Closed to the patrons, of course, open to the family. Auntie Joan always cooked a turkey for Christmas, and Bert and his dad were delighted to accept her invitation to lunch.

Bert's father said one of the things he invariably said as he sat down in the cool, darkened parlour: 'She'll be a hot one today with that wind.'

Bert nodded and sipped his beer. Three small children raced past, firing cap guns. Bert drank some more beer, unmoved. The bar parlour reassumed its serenity as the cries of 'I got yer! I did! You have to lie down! You didn't! I won't! It's not fair!' died away with the kiddiewinks into the kitchen, to be swatted at by overheated women.

Then Bert's father said the other thing he always said: 'Joanie puts on a good spread, but it ain't a patch on what your mother used to do.'

Bert nodded again and poured his father another beer. Conventions had been observed. It was now Christmas in Bert's world. All other events, like turkey and pudding and mottoes and silly hats and Bert's uncle Les dancing the tango with a hat-stand, would now follow inevitably.

Bert raised his glass to his father. 'Cheers,' he said.

Cecil Yates, invariable companion of Bert, was engaged in a fierce game of cricket with the smaller members of the Yates clan. There seemed to be hundreds of them. Cec's grandmother had taken to heart the biblical injunction to increase and multiply and, of her sixteen children, eleven had lived to marry and produce children of their own. This meant that in any country town in Victoria there would be at least one Yates cousin, and the Yates children were constrained to behave because, wherever they went, there was no chance that they would escape notice if they were naughty.

Cec underarmed a gentle throw to a pint-sized wicket-keeper, watched him take off the bails with dashing enthusiasm, and declared himself out for the moment. The wind was picking up. It was going to be a hot day. The Yates family Christmas party was taking place on a large property in Hoppers Crossing belonging to Zephaniah Yates, who farmed it with his brothers Hezekiah and Ishmael. The farmhouse was stuffed with women of the Yates clan, managing the last minute cooking and arranging, though the early work had been done by Hezekiah's wife, Betty.

The Yates women were at present, Cec knew, admiring the engagement ring he had bought for his intended, Alice Greenham. Miss Fisher had got him a real good price on that diamond. Cec had brought Alice along even though she was desperately shy about meeting his family. 'Might as well get it all over at once,' said Cec cheerfully. But he had been worried. What if they didn't like Alice? For if he couldn't have Alice, there was no one else for Cecil Yates.

Fortunately, after one long, raking study which took in her neat dress, her shy demeanour and the excellent-looking short-bread she had brought—such a useful present, you can always use more shortbread—all of them, including Cec's strong-minded mother Rosalita, decided to like Alice. And when the Yates clan decided to like you, there was no use kicking against the pricks. They were planning her wedding dress as Cec crossed the dusty yard.

Wiping his forehead, he went up onto the verandah to join his brothers Aubrey and Trevelyan and his cousins Hez and Ish.

'Take the weight off, King of the Kids,' said Trev. 'Here's my Terebintha with a beer for you.'

'She's an angel,' said Cec gratefully. He sat down. Immediately, three dogs and a cat joined him on the swinging seat. A standard Yates maiden—tall, slim and blonde—produced a jug. Cec swigged and Terebintha refilled.

'So how's tricks?' asked Cec.

'No worse than usual,' said Ish. 'Got a lot of green feed stored from that wet spring, might last us through the dry. How's things in the city?'

'Not bad,' said Cec. 'Still working the taxi lark with Bert. Do some rough work for Miss Fisher, sometimes.'

'That's the lady detective that Mel's Lisbet met on the cruise ship? She sounds like a cracker,' said Hez.

'Oh, she is,' said Cec, thinking of bright colours and noise and sparks and explosions. 'She's that, all right.'

He tickled the big ginger cat behind the ears and wondered how Miss Fisher's Christmas Day was going.

Mrs. Butler joggled her grandchild. A nice piece of work, she thought critically, well formed, solid, with the blue Butler eyes and the rosy Butler complexion. Already the strong little legs were flexing and pushing, eager to grow, to crawl, to walk. None of those pasty-faced weaklings for her daughter Sally. Then the baby—Phryne—smiled an adorable gummy smile and Mrs. Butler melted.

'Oo's an ickle pretty den?' she cooed.

For once, she herself was not working. She spared a worried thought for Ruth left with Miss Phryne's goose, then resolutely turned her thoughts away. Just for today, she said to herself, I'm not cooking and Tobias isn't waiting on people, and I'm not going to say a word about how Sally is mistreating that pair of chickens. Not one word. I shall eat it and be grateful.

She accepted a cooling sherry cobbler and smiled on her son-in-law, who was a grocer.

'So, Bill,' she said. 'How's business?'

Dorothy Williams surveyed the table and pushed back her hair. It looked lovely. She had twined long strings of jasmine around everything, in the way she had seen in one of Miss Fisher's *Home*

Beautiful magazines. The scent was heavy in the air. Everything was prepared, the plates and glasses gleaming, the array of cutlery set out next to the head of the table where her father would presently carve the turkey. Any moment now everyone would be back from church and the feast would be ready for them. Dot had said her rosary while she was decorating. She was in a perfect state of grace as she embraced her sister Joan and her two small children, come down from Sydney for the festivities. Everything was in order in Dot's world.

Phryne Fisher rose betimes and bathed, remembering just in time not to ring for breakfast. She had been aware of some surreptitious activity and a few barks early in the morning, but what else was five am on Christmas morning for? She remembered creeping into her family's English parlour in freezing darkness, feeling for the filled stockings and running back to bed before her feet froze. She also remembered the entirely disproportionate value, in her impoverished childhood, of a tin bangle, a packet of boiled lollies and an orange. Phryne's daughters were going to do better than that.

She dressed in a bright red suit and went down to find that Ruth was in charge of breakfast. Both her daughters were wearing, for the very first time, silk stockings, and were terribly aware of snags, edges and Ember, who knew what a threat he posed and was standing over them as neat as a Fitzroy Street bully for more than his fair share of bacon. Phryne picked him up and put him in the garden, along with a whole rasher for his very own in case he should feel affronted. He was affronted, but he ate the bacon. Molly sat alertly under the kitchen table, humbly waiting for largesse.

'Oh, thank you!' gasped Ruth. 'I was so scared he'd stick a claw into my new stockings! Coffee in the pot, Miss Phryne, and toast in just a jiff. Would you like eggs and bacon?'

'No, thank you,' said Phryne. 'But keep frying, here comes Eliza and Lady Alice, and I bet they haven't eaten.'

Phryne answered the bell and admitted her sister, in a flow-
ered frock and hat, and her companion Lady Alice, in shabby
brown with a beige felt hat which had seen better centuries.
But Phryne gave her points for trying. She had pinned a sprig
of holly to the front and resembled a rather vague and elderly
member of Santa's gnomes.

'Oh, Phryne dear, how nice,' she said. 'Is that bacon cooking? We had a bit of an emergency with some of the girls and
haven't eaten a crumb.'

'Sit down,' said Jane, delivering Phryne's toast. 'Tea in that
pot, Lady Alice. Merry Christmas!'

'And a merry Christmas to you too,' said Lady Alice, which
went against all her Socialist principles. But one could not disappoint this nice child.

Eliza threw her hat onto the dresser and kissed Phryne as the
latter helped herself to Oxford marmalade. 'This is a change
from the old country, eh? No frost! No sad little dead birds! No
compulsory visits to those poor cottagers! And best of all...'

Phryne raised her coffee cup in salute and agreement. 'We
are eleven thousand miles from Papa.'

'Indeed,' said Eliza fervently, and poured tea for herself and
her lover in the most devout of familial spirits.

Ruth had successfully made breakfast and stacked the dishes
for later washing. Now she was about to face the greatest challenge of her life to date, and she was anxious to get as many
people out of the house as she could.

'I'll stay,' offered Eliza. 'I've got up to page five of Mrs. Beeton,
you know.'

'And I do not care to attend the shop-worn conventions
of an outmoded religion,' declared Lady Alice. Jane tugged at
Phryne's sleeve and she looked up in time to intercept Ruth's
agonised appeal.

'No you don't, you pair of atheists,' she said to her sister
and Lady Alice. 'You're coming along with me to a nice rousing
singsong. Do your souls good. But first, it's Ruth's turn with
the Advent book.'

Propped up in a stand on the mantelpiece in the parlour was the Advent book, which had entrancing, brightly painted pictures, all concealed behind little windows which folded out or down. Phryne's household had alternated in opening them, page by page, and most excitingly there were more after the birth of the baby Jesus, which would be today's picture.

It was. The mother cradled the child in her arms, and a suspiciously clean collection of shepherds knelt at her feet. Their animals had obviously been freshly rinsed as well.

'Lovely donkey,' commented Lady Alice.

'Nice baby,' agreed Eliza. 'Well, if we have to go to this antique ritual, let's go.'

Phryne winked at Ruth and walked her family out of the house and into the dead quiet of Christmas morning. No buses. No trucks. No vans. Almost no traffic. Phryne was relieved to see a few of the gentlemen of the street, over-full of Christmas spirits, asleep on the bench by the church. St. Kilda was itself, after all.

'Oh come, all ye faithful,' sang the choir, and the Fisher family went into church.

Ruth went back to her room and removed her prized silk stockings. She put on her old lisle ones and her stout boots. Mrs. Butler was firm about bare feet in her kitchen. Too dangerous, she said, with scalds and dropped pots. She returned to the kitchen—all hers now—and wrapped herself up in one of Mrs. Butler's aprons. She tied back her plaits and consulted her list. It seemed very long and daunting.

'Light stove,' murmured Ruth, and found the long matches.

An hour later she was wiping her forehead and licking her pencil for the thirtieth time. The list was almost at an end. The shelled peas were in their colander, waiting to be cooked. The brussels sprouts likewise. Ruth had yet to be convinced that brussels sprouts were food, the bitter morsels having been a mainstay of her scullery days, but the cookbooks said that with chestnut purée they were superb, and Ruth was not about to start second-guessing *Ma Cuisine*. The potatoes were in the oven, basted in goose fat. To her probing skewer they were already tender. The pudding was on the stove, steaming, next to a singing kettle which would resupply the pot with boiling water. The washed and dried salad and the iced fruit sorbets were cooling in the American refrigerator. There remained only cream to whip and a few small matters to adjust.

Ruth pushed back her hair and laughed at the last item on Mrs. Butler's list: 'Now make yourself a cup of really strong tea and take it into the garden. Ginger biscuits in the tin.' Hers not to reason why, Ruth made her tea, spiked it with four sugars and carried it and the biscuits out into the garden. She sat down under the jasmine bower, where she could see the kitchen door and hear if the pudding began to boil dry.

She was exhausted and exhilarated. Molly wandered into the garden and slumped down on her feet with a sigh. The scent of that cooking goose was a heavy burden for a small starving dog to bear, she conveyed. Ember was at large in the kitchen but he could hardly hook the goose out of the oven with only his own four paws. Birds sang in the Christmas quiet. Ruth drank her tea, listening to a group of magpies chortle their water music, sweeter, Miss Phryne said, than nightingales.

She had just rinsed her cup and saucer when the bell rang and she went to the front door, wondering who would call on Christmas morning. No one was there, but a bright parcel lay on the step, directed to The Hon. Miss Phryne Fisher. Ruth turned it around, shook it experimentally, and then took it inside and put it under the tree. Miss Phryne had a lot of admirers.

She heard an ominous boiling-dry noise and ran back to the kitchen.

'Well,' said Phryne expansively, taking another slice of breast, 'that was the best goose in all the world.'

'Never tasted better,' beamed Miss Eliza.

'Delicious,' agreed Lady Alice, holding out her plate for more goose, brussels sprouts (and who would have thought they did taste that good with chestnuts? Even Jane had eaten some, Ruth marvelled, resolving never to doubt her texts again), potatoes, gravy, chestnut stuffing and peas. Ruth was delighted. Not by the spoken compliments, though they were very nice, but by the second and even third helpings for which everyone was asking.

'There's pudding to follow,' she warned. 'And iced sorbets.'

'In due course,' said Phryne. 'Just a little more gravy, please.'

The party relaxed and nibbled their favourite tidbits. Phryne and Eliza began to reminisce about the ceremonies taking place even now in their father's house and how glad they were not to be witnessing them.

'He'll be on his third bottle by now,' said Eliza, smothering a giggle at her daring in criticising the Patriarch.

'Drunk as a lord and bellowing at the butler,' said Phryne, pouring another glass of the moselle which the Barossa Valley was making so competently.

'Mother will be scuttling along, protesting,' continued Eliza.

'And he will not take a blind bit of notice. He will invade the kitchen and dismiss the cook for insubordination, and she will fling a gravy ladle into his face and stalk out, leaving mother, who cannot boil an egg to save her life, to cook dinner for twenty-five.'

'So she will rush after the offended cook.'

'And perhaps James might manage to get the master into the parlour to amuse the guests,' said Eliza. 'Oh, such a fuss! It's lovely to have this feast just laid out without any panic and hysteria, though we do appreciate how hard Ruth must have worked to produce it.'

'No, really, I just followed the instructions,' said Ruth modestly. She and Jane had changed into their summer frocks, skimpy cool things with short skirts and scooped necklines, pale mauve for Ruth and pale green for Jane, who was blonder. Ruth had decanted the pudding and left it to drain and seethe before she had dared replace her boots with sandals.

She accompanied Jane into the kitchen as they began to clear the table. Just the pudding, cream, brandy sauce and sorbets to go. Jane scraped each plate into the greasy baking dish and stacked them for washing. She was careful, because when she lost concentration she had a tendency to drop things and this was Miss Phryne's Clarice Cliff dinnerware. Molly lurked under the table, knowing that as soon as the plates were cleared, that baking dish piled high with leftovers was her Christmas dinner. She salivated and licked her chops loudly.

Jane carried the baking dish out into the garden and Molly leapt to follow, tail whirring. When Jane came back she found Ruth transfixed with horror.

Ember had become bored waiting for his treat, or had possibly lacked sufficient trust in humans to be sure that it would eventuate. He had decided to reward himself and was whiskers deep in the bowl of whipped cream, purring like a dynamo.

'Oh, Jane! What shall we do?' whispered the hitherto redoubtable Ruth, wringing her hands. 'I can't serve whipped cream with cat fur in it! And I haven't got time to whip more cream!'

'You get Ember,' said Jane. 'I'll get a big spoon.'

Ruth grasped Ember around the middle. Jane scooped out a generous amount of cream around where he had been licking. She placed spoon, cream and cat on the floor of the scullery and shut the door on the furry, purring thief.

'There,' said Jane, patting Ruth's trembling shoulder. 'It's all right. No one will know. I've seen Mrs. Butler do similar things. Now you take the pudding and I'll take the cream and the sauce and off we go.'

She gave her foster sister a push and Ruth bore the pudding into the dining room.

The pudding cloth had peeled perfectly. The pudding squatted, spherical and smooth, without a blemish. Ruth accepted the company's compliments. Phryne gave her a shrewd look and a glass of sweet muscat, instructing her to drink up and recruit her strength after such hard work. Ruth did so, gasped, and shook herself. Of course it would be all right. She didn't even wince when Lady Alice took whipped cream and brandy sauce with her pudding.

The feast trailed off into spoonfuls of iced lemon sorbet, strong coffee, mince pies and little chocolates. Then Phryne betook herself to the kitchen and sent her guests to their rooms to have a siesta.

'I washed dishes for a living,' she told Ruth, who protested. 'Before I made more money as a model. You and Jane go and lie down for a couple of hours. Then we shall have tea and crackers and carols and presents,' she promised.

Ruth waited until she saw Miss Phryne fill both sinks in a no-nonsense fashion and begin on the glasses before she allowed herself to be persuaded away. Jane flung herself down to read some more Darwin and Ruth fell asleep instantly, her tired feet elevated on a pillow. Miss Eliza led Lady Alice to the guest bedroom for a little nap. Phryne washed dishes.

She rather liked washing dishes, if she didn't have to do it for a living. And provided there were gallons of fresh hot water and soda and soap. When she had got to the pots, she left them to soak for a while and brewed herself some more coffee. She became aware of a mewing noise in the scullery.

'Ah, she said, opening the door and taking in the licked clean spoon and the offended cat. 'So you like whipped cream, eh? I might have guessed it. If you come out,' she hinted, 'there is a plate of carefully cut-up goose scraps for you which some kind girl has prepared and which you do not deserve in the slightest.'

Ember emerged, gave himself a fast once-over wash to demonstrate how he felt about being deprived of a bowl of cream which he had personally hunted down, and addressed himself to the goose. Molly came in, having demolished her mountain of scraps, and flopped down under the table, full to satiety for the first time in her deprived life. And Phryne scrubbed and drained pots, finding that the baking dish had been admirably nibbled clean by the dog. She finished the task and took her coffee into the garden.

The salt wind from the sea, which burned all vegetation in summer, was in Phryne's garden foiled by large screens of bamboo, unkillable by any earthly force. The delicate trailers and vines sheltered behind the bamboo, able to grow higher than the fence without being blighted instantly. The jasmine was in bloom. The sun was not too hot and Phryne basked a little, very happy in her own house and her own company.

Then she mounted the stairs for a little nap before tea, and presents, and carols.

Christmas carols were playing on the gramophone. The tea tray was prepared. Phryne, in a loose gown, presided as Ruth and Jane alternated in taking parcels from under the glorious gold and silver tree.

'Miss Phryne,' said Jane anxiously. Phryne opened it. Inside was a small, cambric handkerchief with a slightly wobbly orchid embroidered on the corner. Blood spots had not quite washed out of it.

'Jane,' said Phryne warmly, 'how lovely. What a good choice of flower.' She tucked it into her pocket so that the orchid showed. Jane let out her held breath.

'Jane,' said Ruth. Jane unwrapped a book. '*Gray's Anatomy*,' said Phryne. Jane gave a small cry of joy as she reverently opened it and displayed a flayed human form, all muscles marked and numbered. Ruth shuddered slightly and opened her present, a proper starched cook's cap and apron. Lady Alice and Miss Eliza had also provided books for their friends. Phryne had *London Labour and the London Poor* by Henry Mayhew, in three volumes. Jane had Beatrice and Sidney Webb on the economics of poverty and Ruth *Plain Recipes for Poor People* by Soyer. Phryne commended her sister on not starting the girls on *Das Kapital* too soon.

'Oh, it's central, of course, but it's so dull,' said Eliza. 'Thank you for the shortbread, Ruth. And the pen wiper, Jane. That will come in very useful. And the writing things, Phryne. Purple, my favourite colour too, and such good cream-laid paper. I always think I write better on really good paper.'

'And here is a box of biscuits for Molly,' said Ruth.

'And a pair of gloves from Lin Chung. How very beautiful,' said Phryne. The gloves were Florentine angel's skin, thinner than kid and as scarlet as sin.

'And what's in this one?' asked Lady Alice.

'Oh yes, it was left on the porch,' said Ruth. 'This morning.'

Phryne cut the string. Molly came to her side, gave a profound sniff and began to bark. Ember, who had been catching forty winks on the arm of Phryne's chair, woke up cross and spat.

'Molly, what's the matter?' exclaimed Jane, as Phryne lifted the lid of a small box, disclosing an arm ring in the shape of a brightly enamelled serpent. It was coral and brown and ivory, so beautifully coloured that it might have been alive.

'What a pretty thing,' said Phryne, and reached for it. It lifted its head and hissed.

Her life was preserved only because the snake was unsure whom to bite first, the barking dog or the moving hand. It streaked up to half its length, aiming at a point between Phryne and Molly. But it had not counted on there being a cat within easy reach.

Ember had not had a good day. His cream had been taken away from him. He had been locked in the scullery. Then just when he had been adequately regaled and was taking a well deserved nap, he was woken by barking dogs and importunate snakes. It was too much.

With a skilled, clawed, faster than light right hook, he slapped the snake out of the box and onto the carpet. As it fell, he leapt beside it, his black body flowing through the air, seized its neck in his jaws, and bit as hard as he could. Then he spat out the dead body and batted it a little as it writhed and twisted its coloured corpse. There might be some amusement to be gained out of this, he thought, swatting it again. Come along, little snakey, want to play?

It just lay there. He threw it into the air a couple of times but it came down as unresponsive as a rubber band. Bored, he left the snake and retired to the arm of the chair again, from whence he was removed by a distracted Miss Eliza, who poured him a whole saucer of cream. Humans were odd. First they took the cream away, then they brought it back. Still, cream was cream, thought Ember, and licked and licked at this bounty while it lasted. Lady Alice, who loathed serpents, joined Eliza on the floor with the cream jug, hastily revising her previously hardline views on the uselessness of cats.

'That's a coral snake,' said Jane through numb lips. 'It's in my natural history book. It's really, really venomous. One bite…'

She leaned on Ruth, who embraced her.

'It's dead now,' said her sister, feeding ginger biscuits to Molly, who was still barking at the dead snake. 'Do shut up, Moll, it really is dead.'

'But who sent it?' asked Miss Eliza. 'There's a good, clever, alert, brave, beautiful, intelligent cat,' she added, replenishing the cream.

'Well,' said Phryne, 'let's see.' She took up the coral snake with the fire tongs and placed it on a saucer. Then she probed the box and a small card fell out. It had a jolly scene of robins in snow on one side. The other said, 'Stay away from the Last Best Party or it will be your Last'.

'From a well-wisher, I expect,' commented Phryne. 'Lady Alice, break out the liqueur tray, will you? We all need a drink. Isn't it lucky Dot wasn't here? She hates snakes. Mind you, I'm rapidly going off them myself. What a very nasty trick. Someone is going to be sorry that they played it. Jane? Can you get a glass jar and some metho? And just pop our specimen in. I might need to exhibit it.'

'Yes, I'll fetch them,' said Jane, and hurried off to raid Mrs. Butler's cleaning materials. Lady Alice got up off the floor and poured liberal doses for all: muscat for the girls and High-land

Park whisky for the ladies. They sipped, watching Ember lap cream and Jane bottle the coral snake in a metho-filled jam jar. Jane screwed on the lid very firmly. The creature looked totally improbable. Bottling it had the effect, however, of convincing Molly to stop barking, which was a relief. The dog wagged her tail and accepted another biscuit from her Christmas box.

'Are you going to call the police?' asked Miss Eliza. 'That was an attempted murder, you know, only foiled because of this valiant, beautiful, skilled, clever cat.'

Ember purred as more cream was vouchsafed to him. Miss Eliza wondered distractedly how much cream one cat could hold. Ember had always wondered the same thing, and was willing to experiment.

'No need to bother the police,' replied Phryne. 'The trickster will be at the party. And when I find him,' she bared her teeth, 'then he shall learn that I know a few tricks of my own.'

The Joker considered his disguises. The lady's dress with the high heeled shoes always attracted the right sort of attention. If anyone had been there to see him, they would have seen his mouth—always a little dry, like a serpent's mouth—curve.

Chapter Three

White Lady

2 parts gin
1 part Cointreau
1 part lemon juice

Shake with a dash of egg white.

Wednesday, 26th December

Boxing Day was notable for returns. Dot came back delighted but rather fatigued by her large family, glad to be home in the relative peace of Phryne's house. Mr. and Mrs. Butler returned pleased to have their own space again and noting that they had lost the knack of ignoring a crying infant. After a fast review of her kitchen, Mrs. Butler was delighted to congratulate Ruth on her cooking and Miss Fisher on her dishwashing. ('Who would have thought?' she said privately to her husband.) Nothing had been broken and when Ruth, in dead secrecy, confided the tale of the whipped cream, Mrs. Butler laughed and said she would have done the same herself. 'What the eye doesn't see, the heart doesn't grieve over,' she told Ruth. 'And least said, soonest mended.' This was a great relief to Ruth's mind.

Boxing Day was also the day when Mrs. Butler made up baskets of Christmas cheer, including her incomparable mince pies, for the domestic workers, who arrived on and off all day to receive their basket and Miss Fisher's Christmas card and bonus. Miss Fisher's generosity was well known so there was a stream of visitors all day, from the window washer to the knife sharpener to the ladies who obliged with rough scrubbing and polishing.

Jane read her *Anatomy*, occasionally raising her eyes from a diagram to consider any human within sight in a dissecting sort of way which, Dot said, gave her the willies. Phryne read her detective stories. Dot did the same. Ruth helped in the kitchen wearing her new cook's apron. It was a quiet, sleepy day, always notable for rissoles made of yesterday's poultry and a sense of comfortable inertia. Phryne played more Christmas carols because she liked Christmas carols and the pudding tasted just as good cold with chilled brandy sauce. The Advent picture which Dot uncovered showed a sky full of angels singing.

At three in the afternoon a special messenger delivered an unexpected package, and Phryne took it into the jasmine bower to open it. Dot, who had been shown the bottled coral snake, stood beside Phryne with a broom, ready to repel reptiles.

The string was removed and the leaves of the box were opened gingerly with the tongs. Nothing lethal was disclosed within. Phryne tipped the box on its side and a cascade of coloured leaflets, books and party favours spilled onto the table.

'It's my guide to the party,' she told Dot. 'The Last Best Party. Let's see. Here we have a room key, the Iris Room, sounds nice. A map of the grounds. A ticket to park the car. A rather detailed guide to events and personalities. A mask for the *bal masqué*. Lots of stuff. But none of it dangerous, Dot dear.'

'This party…' Dot began.

'Yes?' Phryne looked at her through a cat mask.

'You're taking me, aren't you, Miss Phryne?'

'I don't think so,' said Phryne candidly. 'It might be danger-ous and it will certainly shock you. And I might want to be shocking myself, you know. I really don't think your young man would approve of you being within a hundred miles of this party, Dot.'

'No sin except in intention,' argued Dot. 'A saint sat on the steps of a brothel for days and she was unstained. My Hugh knows I'm a good girl, and if he doubts me then he's not the man I thought him—and not worth having. Anyway, who's going to look after your clothes?'

'I'll tell you what. Drive down with me tomorrow, and we'll have a look at the situation. If it's too, too vile for a nice girl, Mr. B shall take you home and bring you back each morning with clean clothes and so on. That will mean that I don't have to leave the car where one of those hearties might steal it. Besides, I shall be working. Someone doesn't want me to come to this party, and I want to know who they are, and why, and many other useful things. Cheer up, Dot. You know you don't like wickedness.'

'No,' said Dot. 'If you're sure, Miss Phryne.'

'I'm sure.' Phryne repacked the box and carried it inside. Dot followed, relieved at not having to preside over too much sin, and a little wistful at losing so much interesting gossip to share with her sister Joan. Joan taught deportment to Tilly Devine's girls in Sydney, and always had such a lot of highly coloured things to tell.

Phryne sat down in her boudoir and examined the printed book. Bound in limp purple leather, very tasty, with gold embossings. It purported to be a complete guide to the Last Best Party, which had been meticulously planned, down to the finest detail, probably by poor, overworked Mr. Ventura.

First day: arrival of guests after lunch. Cocktails at five in the Great Marquee. Dress: optional. That was irritating. One ran the risk of being over- or underdressed. Of the two, Phryne always preferred overdressed. Dinner and dancing on the lawns, boating on the lake. Phryne considered a moment. What was the blight of all outside entertainment anywhere near water? Mosquitoes. She made a note to replenish her supplies of citronella oil. On the one hand one smelt like a slightly chemical lemon grove.

On the other hand, one was not covered in large itchy bumps. Phryne decided on a couple of stronger perfumes which might combine well with the citronella and read on.

Oh, my. Each day was themed and costumed, probably from the Victorian Opera. A Day at the Court of the Mikado of Japan. One Thousand and One Nights with Sultan Al-Jabira. The Feast of Fools with the Lord of Misrule. Lord have mercy. No way to prepare for all that, thought Phryne and decided on minimal clothes, a shady hat or so, and her wits, which had been reliable in the past. Who didn't want her to go to this bash? And why?

'Someone who doesn't know you very well,' said Jane, when Phryne proposed the question to the table at dinner.

'How so?' asked Phryne.

'Well, Miss, the best way of getting you to do something is to forbid you to do it. You're contrary,' said Dot, then blushed. 'I mean...'

'Yes, you're right, I am contrary,' agreed Phryne.

'Tell us about these golden twins,' urged Jane. 'I've just been reading about twins. They are fraternal, of course, not identical.'

'How do you know that?' asked Ruth, with her mouth full of shortbread.

'Because one's male and one's female, silly,' said Jane.

'So they are,' said Phryne, intervening before they could bicker any more. 'Gerald and Isabella Templar, both tall and slim and blond and blue-eyed. They took Paris by storm with a series of astonishing parties.'

'What sort of parties?' asked Dot suspiciously.

'Well, there was the *fête du clochards*, a beggar's ball, where everyone had to dress like a tramp. There was the Festival of Virgins, where everyone had to wear white and tell the story of how they lost their virginity. It is a measure of their social importance that the Princesse de Cleves turned up to that party dressed in red and they sent her home to change. And she went, *etonnant!*'

'And are they fabulously wealthy?' asked Ruth, captivated.

'Tolerably fabulously, I believe. They are the very last of a rather illustrious English family. Their father and both their brothers were killed in the Great War, and their mother expired of grief not long after—which left them alone, in possession of a huge fortune. They are running through it at a rate, though. There can't be a lot of it left. That may explain what they are doing in Australia. This might be the Templars' last best party, too.'

'And you don't think they're going to settle down to life in the suburbs, do you?' asked Lin Chung in a low voice, waving away a refill of soft Rhine wine.

'Not likely,' said Phryne, making a shushing gesture. 'How are your obsequies going?'

'Very well. Everyone has visited, old people hobbling along who knew the ancestor when he was a child on the goldfields. I had no idea so many of them were still alive. Grandmamma has been most gratified. Are you still determined on this party, Phryne?'

'Yes,' said Phryne, and that was the end of the discussion.

Thursday, 27th December

After lunch Mr. Butler started the Hispano-Suiza with his usual facility and pleasure. The big car, its coachwork buffed to a gleaming finish, squatted redly by the kerb. It purred, he declared, like a tiger. Miss Phryne and Dot climbed aboard.

'Werribee ho,' directed Phryne, and Mr. Butler engaged the gears. The big car slid out into the traffic like a shark into tropical waters.

It did not take long to leave the city behind and soon they were looking at a flat treeless waste of thistles and boulders. Milestones flew past.

'Ugly country,' commented Dot.

'Might have looked better before they chopped all the trees down. If it ever had trees. And, of course, it would be prettier if it was green.'

'I suppose,' said Dot. She did not like the countryside at all. It was undisciplined, spiky, and might harbour snakes. Dot always felt that picnics were best enjoyed inside a nice house with tables and chairs and a reliable stone flagged floor.

'Here's the government farm—and there's the sign,' said Phryne.

Mr. Butler indicated to other road users that he was intending to turn. Majestically, the Hispano-Suiza slid across the road, only to halt with a shriek of brakes as an impudent Austin dived under its bonnet. It kept going down the carriage drive to the house with a cheery braying of klaxons and Mr. Butler so forgot himself as to swear. Phryne heartily agreed with him.

'Quite so,' she said. 'Let's hope we can arrive alive. You stay with the car, Mr. Butler, and defend it with someone else's life. I'll send Dot back to you as soon as I can. Hello! Livestock.'

A string of polo ponies trotted behind an escort on a stock-horse. Mr. Butler slowed down to walking pace to pass them and the rider tipped his hat. He looked like a standard bushman—oilskin, boots, leather hat—until the car's inhabitants realised that 'he' was a woman, riding as easily as if she was sitting in an armchair. Phryne grinned at her and was rewarded with a smile, white teeth in a tanned face.

Then the car swept around a further curve and the house was revealed.

It was a true, proper, stately home, Phryne thought. It had a portico. It had a tower. It had a huge sanded area in front for carriages to turn around. It had a superb formal garden and swathes of greensward. The said greensward was dotted with white marquees. But there was room here to bivouac an army.

The front of the house was congested with vehicles, including the cheeky blue Austin, Phryne noticed. There was a lot of shouting going on. Phryne directed Mr. Butler to turn the big car for an instant getaway and alighted, savouring the gravel with her soft shoes. Dot and the baggage could stay where they were for the moment.

Phryne sauntered through the expostulating throng and saw that the front door of the mansion was being held, at the risk of his life, by a single white-gloved entity whose patience was evidently growing ragged. He was assailed by a collection of public school boys who had clearly lunched far too well.

'You must go and report to the red tent,' insisted the butler for the thousandth time. 'You cannot come into the house, gentlemen!'

'Where's old Gerald?' asked one beery voice. 'Ought to be here to greet us, he ought.' He surged forward, or would have had not an unaccountably strong lady's hand caught hold of his shoulder. He desisted from making any move, amazed.

'Gentlemen,' said Phryne sweetly. 'The red tent,' she said. 'See? Just over there. You don't want to cause trouble on such a nice afternoon,' she told them. 'You don't want to be thrown out of the Last Best Party for 1928,' she added, thinking, you horrible little worms. 'Off you go, now,' she said and, subdued by her governess-nanny-mother-knows-best tone, they went, shouldering each other like young bulls.

The butler sagged a little and mopped his brow.

'They should never have left you out here on your own,' said Phryne sympathetically. 'Can I lend you my chauffeur? Or perhaps I can summon a couple of footmen.'

'They've just gone off for their tea,' he said. 'Thank you, Miss. They'll be back soon. How can I help you?'

Phryne exhibited her invitation.

'Oh yes, you're in the house,' said the butler, ticking her off on his list. 'Just up the stairs and to the right, Miss Fisher. And your baggage…?'

'My maid and I can carry it,' said Phryne. 'Ah, here come your henchmen.' Two large footmen were approaching from around the corner of the house, wiping their mouths. 'They ought to suppress any further riot. Dot? Come along,' she called, and Dot appeared with Phryne's suitcase and one small bag.

'Up the stairs and to the right,' said Phryne as the butler opened the front door.

It had been a very beautiful house. The hall was high, the proportions grand without being grandiose. The graceful stair-case bisected a good-sized entrance, which had once been elaborately decorated. There were niches for tall Chinese vases and little sconces which had once illuminated specially treasured paintings of ancestors. The floor was meant to have a carpet, probably commissioned to be woven for the pleasing dimensions of the rooms. The windows with their restrained etchings were meant to be clean and the brass rails were meant to be polished. The whole was meant to be lit by a big, heavy, glittering chandelier dripping with candles, originally, then fuelled by gas, scattering diamonds of light over the pink of the painted plaster roses and the green of the vines.

All that was gone, suppressed, violated. The plaster had been whitewashed a dead chalk. The floor was bare but for a scrubby strip of American cloth. The walls had been wounded by bicycles and hockey sticks and the only light came from meagre electric bulbs, bare, on long snaking cables which hung down like hangman's nooses. Someone had stuffed arm-loads of fresh flowers into a miscellany of pots, buckets and vases, but the underlying smell of wet woollens, unwashed boys, footy boots and good wholesome cabbage boiled for three hours rose above the floral scents like a vile miasma in some fetid English slum.

Phryne was so taken aback that she cried out: 'Oh, Lord! What has happened to you, poor house?'

An elderly woman carrying an armload of towels was stopped dead in her tracks by this cry and turned to stare.

'It's whitewash,' said Dot, horrified. 'All over them plaster flowers and pretty things. Who'd do such a thing?'

'The present owners,' said Phryne, mounting a fine stair-case whose gracious contours could not be marred by lack of polish. 'I suppose they consider flowers frivolous. Oh well, Dot, let's find my room. They all have flower names along this corridor. Fuchsia, Sweet Pea, Rose, Violet—aha! Iris.'

Phryne applied her key and the door opened. It was a small room, hung with iris chintz. A tall vase of irises decorated the plain dresser. There was a wardrobe, a double bed hung with iris patterned curtains, a jug and basin on the washstand and not much else. The chintz, Phryne ascertained, had been folded and then nailed or stapled to a wall which still showed pale patches where the owner's paintings had been removed. Draping the room in printed fabric was a good way of changing its appearance if there was no time or inclination to repaint and refurnish. Mr. Ventura was a clever man.

'A bit bare,' commented Dot, hanging up Phryne's meagre wardrobe. 'Here's the bag for your laundry, Miss, your stockings are in this drawer and your underwear in this. The emergency rations are in the picnic basket. Are you sure you're all right to be left, Miss?'

'Yes,' said Phryne. 'I just wanted you to know where I will be sleeping so you can find it again tomorrow. Let's have a look around, Dot. Despite the whitewash, this is a lovely house.'

'Yes, it's a nice shape,' agreed Dot. 'Not too huge, like a church.'

'Human-sized,' said Phryne, locking her door and putting the key into her petticoat pocket. This was a fashion of her grandmother's which Phryne had resurrected as a remedy for the sad lack of pockets in female attire. She led the way out onto the balcony, which ran the full length of the house. It was edged with marble pillars. Phryne looked down and saw bright blue tesserae winking at her from the floor. The Church had not uglified the mosaics, then. Probably through lack of time. No doubt they would get around to them with that tin of whitewash.

Neither had they destroyed the gardens, which were extensive and beautiful and filled with people, tents, horses, wagons and large trucks.

'Look, a monkey puzzle,' said Dot, who loved these odd shaped trees.

'Yes, there's another—no, three,' said Phryne. 'And we have a knot garden, a parterre, a vegie garden—look at the size of those tomatoes!—and over there must be a lake. And a polo ground. Do you feel better about leaving me here now, Dot dear?'

'Yes,' said Dot. 'If all else fails, you can climb a tree.'

'True,' said Phryne.

Dot took her leave. Phryne walked her back to the car and waved as they drew away. It was now getting on for five o'clock, and the directory to the party told Phryne that cocktails would be served in the purple marquee from five. A nice cold drink would be bracing, she thought, and glided through the throng of giggling girls and hearty young men towards a distant glimpse of purple.

The red tent, which she reached first, was efficiently handing out tickets for places in marquees. A peep into one of the decorated bell tents showed it lined with camp beds, each draped with mosquito netting. This would be needed, Phryne knew. Even now she could sense the hum as the bloodsuckers exercised their wings and whetted their beaks for human prey.

She was not looking where she was going and thus was surprised when she caught her foot on a trailing rope and almost fell over a goat. The goat made a bleating protest and Phryne, saving herself from falling by grabbing a handy tent pole, patted it soothingly between the horns.

'Quite, my dear sir or nanny. Nanny, I perceive. I wasn't watching where I was going. On the other hand, you don't precisely look as though you belong in this tent either. Shall we go outside and find your owner? I observe that you have chewed through your tether,' she said chattily, taking the end of the frayed rope and leading the goat out into the sunlight, 'so presumably you had somewhere that you wanted to go.'

The goat, which was mostly white and quite large, with floppy ears, went biddably as she was led. Phryne, blithely unconcerned as to the picture she presented to the assembled partygoers, went towards the purple tent. Just because she had acquired a goat didn't mean that she didn't get a drink. And perhaps the goat would like one as well.

'Pornutopia,' commented a young man with a studied forelock.

'Nonsense, that was a pig,' replied Phryne, leading the goat past him. It made an experimental snatch at the book he was reading, and he fled with a squeak.

'Not books,' Phryne told the goat reprovingly. 'You might start small, just a little poetry, limp covers only, then you get a taste for it and move on to the major playwrights, and pretty soon you'll find yourself tucking into the complete works of George Bernard Shaw and that would give you indigestion. Come along—I want a drink. And so do you, I expect.'

The purple tent was hung with long banners of purple silk. There was a bar set up in the middle which seemed blessedly uncrowded and Phryne went straight for it.

It was very well equipped. Nestling in huge tubs of ice Phryne saw capped bottles of beer. In chilled compartments in a humming machine Phryne saw jugs of cocktails, all ready for pouring and decorating. Behind the rank of personable attendants were assistants seated at a long table, cutting up fruit and squeezing juices. The air smelt of pineapples. Exquisite.

Phryne leaned up against the bar, next to a woman in a shimmering green evening dress. She had a mass of black curls cascading down her bare back almost to her waist, where her dress began again after a long absence. She was addressing the barman in a slow, sweet drawl which could only have come from the more Southern parts of America. South Carolina, Phryne considered. Georgia, perhaps. A voice that had been dipped in blackstrap molasses.

'Honey, y'all want to mash that mint real good,' she instructed.

The goat suddenly made her move. She nudged the woman aside and reared, so that her front hoofs were on the bar. Then she made a strong and loud bleating demand, right into the barman's face.

He jumped, retaining his hold on his cocktail shaker only by the barman's strict training and adherence to his code.

'I'm so sorry,' apologised Phryne, hauling on the rope. 'Do forgive me. Could I have a White Lady and a bunch of mint, please? When you have finished that julep.'

'Phryne?' asked the lady in the evening dress, tottering for a moment and then recovering her balance. 'Phryne, honey, is that you?'

'Nerine,' said Phryne, embracing her. 'How very nice to see you.' As always, hugging Nerine was a sensual experience not to be missed. 'Are you singing here?'

Phryne was not insulted that Nerine hadn't noticed her until now. It was well known that the singer was perfect of pitch, of heart-wringing Bessie Smith like talent, supple as a snake, shameless as Josephine Baker in her banana skirt and very acute of hearing, but only found her way to the front of the stage by feeling with one foot. She was, everyone agreed, as short-sighted as an owl.

'Sure am,' said Nerine. 'I'm with a new band, they're waiting for me outside.'

The barman had completed the julep and compounded Miss Fisher's White Lady, of gin, Cointreau and lemon juice with a dash of egg white, at record speed. He wasn't used to goats in his bar and this one, he feared, was giving him the evil eye.

Phryne took her drink and the mint and led Nerine out into the garden, where three young people were waiting to escort her to the jazz venue. They were well supplied with beer. Jazz, Phryne knew, ran on beer.

'The band,' said Nerine proudly. 'Three T's—Thomas, Terence and Tab. That's Tabitha, she plays the clarinet real good for a li'l bitty mite, and Tommy—he blows a mean horn—and ol' Terry, that ol' boy he plays anythin' with strings, piano to banjo. This is my ol' fren' the Lady Phryne,' she told the band. 'She once—no, twice—got me out of the tightest spot I ever been in in all my natural born days. She's a fine lady. We gonna play real good for her, y'hear?'

They heard. The band members were all about the same height, chestnut of hair and haggard of complexion, very young, perhaps skimming twenty-one, and they all grinned rather shyly at Phryne. She was not used to shy jazz musicians and was delighted.

'Y'all liquored up to last?' asked Nerine, extending a hand confidently. Terry took it and tucked it under his elbow. 'We gotta go find some rehearsal time. You come hear us tonight, Phryne, we'll play real good for you.'

'I promise,' said Phryne, and kissed Nerine's scented satiny cheek once again for the pleasure of it. Nerine always reminded Phryne of a big, plump cat—a leopard, perhaps. It would have been a pleasure and an honour to be stalked and eaten by her. The band grinned again and led Nerine away, seeking whom she might devour. Provided she ran into it nose-first, of course.

Feeling a little bereft, Phryne wandered over to a garden seat to sip her drink and feed mint leaves to her goat. The goat sat down on her haunches like a dog. Mint was what she had gone out in quest of, mint was what she now had. The goat glowed with self righteousness.

Phryne sipped her White Lady and waited for events to overtake her. It was that sort of day.

Presently someone said, 'May I?' and Phryne waved a hand. Breeches and a loose shirt—a young woman, it seemed, with a bottle of beer in one hand and a puzzled expression on her weatherworn face.

'That your goat?' she asked, in a strong Australian accent.

'For the moment,' said Phryne equably. 'Phryne,' she said, holding out a hand. The young woman shook it heartily.

'Ann,' she said. 'I like goats. But we're here with horses. Polo, you know. Gunna show them la-di-da boys how to play the game.'

'And I'm sure you will,' said Phryne. She had never seen better riders than Australian stockmen, and that reminded her of the girl at the gate.

'Are all your team female?'

'Nah, just me and Jill. Y'see, not so many of the boys came back from the Great War, and when they needed a polo team they sort of had to let us play. We got big money on us,' said Ann, taking a swig of beer.

'I shall venture a small wager myself,' said Phryne. The goat nudged her for the last leaf of mint. Passing gentlemen laughed. Ann drank more beer. Then a rasping voice breathed in Phryne's ear, 'You got me goat!'

'I assure you, it was mutual,' said Phryne, considerably startled but suppressing her reaction. 'Who are you?'

'Call me Madge the Goat Lady', said the apparition, half emerging from the bush behind the wooden seat. She was dressed in cast-offs, with broken canvas bathing shoes on her bunioned feet and a wide hat which must have been straw, because why else would the goats have been chewing it? Phryne hauled her goat to her hoofs and presented the tether to the goat lady.

'Here you are. Large as life and twice as natural.'

'What you been feeding Mintie?' asked the old voice with intense suspicion.

'Mint. It was what she had in mind,' explained Phryne.

'Hmph,' said the goat lady, and woman and goat vanished abruptly, leaving but a gamy effluvium behind.

'Mad,' commented Ann, after a pause for thought. 'Oh, there's Jill. Can you talk to her for a moment, while I go get more beer? And can I get you another drink?'

'Thank you,' said Phryne, relieved to have respectably disposed of her goat. 'Get me another White Lady, if you please. Hello,' she said to the other young woman in moleskins and white shirt, 'I'm Phryne. Your friend Ann has gone for more beer.'

'Bonzer,' said Jill. She was taller, older and heavier than Ann and flushed with heat and exercise. 'Nice to meet yer. Drink'd go down good. We been eatin' dust all day. But they got the horse lines well arranged, say that for 'em.'

'When is the game?'

'Monday. We're playing an exhibition tomorrow, though. You want to come and watch. We're not bad at all.'

'And your opponents?'

'They're some city team,' she said dismissively. 'Lots of money and four remounts. They could wear us down. We mostly only got one neddy each, though I've got two ponies. But we're pretty tough,' she added.

'Where are you from?'

'High Plains, Gippsland,' said Jill. 'We're called the Won-nangatta Tigers.'

Ann returned with an armload of beer bottles and a White Lady for Phryne. Jill levered the tops off two of the bottles with her teeth and spat out the crown seals. Ann giggled. Phryne was impressed and reminded herself to put a wad of cash on the Tigers for the polo cup. She took a gulp of her drink. It was delicious.

The crowds had been ebbing and flowing through the red tent, and now Phryne could see that the marquees were mostly occupied and a lot of the cars and conveyances had gone. Now the purple tent was buzzing with thirsty partygoers. She thought of proposing a walk to the riders. The area was getting very crowded.

'You Phryne Fisher?' asked a high voice. The method of address was so very impolite, especially coming from a younger person to an older one of higher estate, that Phryne did not speak. The demand came from a young boy, dressed in jerkin and hose of cloth of gold. He had a gold cap with wings on his curly dark head and little shoes with wings on his heels. Eros, perhaps, or Hermes. His pretty face was curdled with contempt.

'And who is asking?' said Phryne curiously.

'Tarquin Southam,' snapped the boy. 'Only the master wants Phryne Fisher and he sent me out to find her. Is it you?' he demanded again. 'Only they said you liked low company so I came here.'

Phryne grabbed Jill's wrist to forestall the clip over the ear that she was about to deliver to this pouting slipgibbet who was so clearly in need of just such personal attention. And might, indeed, be the better for it.

'My name is Phryne Fisher,' she said, getting up. 'When you address me again, Master Tarquin, you will add an Hon. and a

Miss to it. Clearly Gerald likes you mannerless or he would not employ you, but I don't. See to it.'

'Yes, Hon. Miss Fisher,' said Tarquin insolently.

'Better than nothing,' said Phryne. 'Good luck with the game, Jill, Ann. I'll see you there.'

Tarquin turned on his winged heel and she followed his stiff, offended, golden back through the throng to a tent of special magnificence. It had streamers all over it. It had hangings. It had decorations on its tasselled decorations and frescoes all along its sides.

Tarquin stood by the door and announced, 'The Hon. Miss Phryne Fisher!'

Phryne pushed aside the hanging bamboo curtain and went in.

◇◇◇

'Saint Stephen,' announced Dot, opening the book. The girls and Molly settled down obediently. Jane found the anatomical details of martyrdom interesting. Ruth just liked stories, and Molly just liked company. 'Stephen had a revelation of the birth of the baby Jesus. He was Herod's serving man, and he said to Herod, "There is a child born in Bethlehem who will save us all." But Herod scorned him, saying, "That is just as likely as this cooked capon—"'

'What's a capon?' asked Jane.

'It's a chicken,' said Ruth, who didn't feel that she fully understood the term 'castrated cock' and that Miss Dot would definitely not want her to explain it if she did.

'As likely as this cooked chicken rising up and crowing.'

'And did it?' asked Ruth.

'It rose up in the dish and flapped its wings and crowed "*Christus natus est!*" Which means "Christ is born",' said Dot triumphantly. Jane was about to comment on the unlikelihood of this but Molly trod heavily on her lap in an endeavour to steal a biscuit and the moment passed.

'Then what happened to Stephen?' asked Ruth.

'They took him out and stoned him to death,' said Dot. 'And his soul ascended to join the Father in heavenly bliss.'

Ruth accepted this. Jane began to calculate. How many stones of, say, a pound each would you need to lethally disable an average saint?

Dot sighed. She feared that the girls were growing up to be heathens, like Miss Phryne.

Chapter Four

Queen and huntress, chaste and fair,
Now the sun is laid to sleep,
Seated in thy silver chair,
State in wonted manner keep;
Hesperus entreats thy light,
Goddess excellently bright.

Ben Jonson 'Hymn to Diana'

She stood still, allowing her eyes to get used to the dimness. Oddly enough, she felt sure that she could hear running water. The air was cool and scented with sandalwood, a bracing, masculine scent. There was an overscent of hashish. The acolytes had started smoking early this evening. The flooring was soft under her hot feet. In the dim light she could see a figure occupying one of a pair of carved, throne-like chairs at the far end. She went towards him, suppressing the urge to genuflect.

Tarquin raced ahead of her and threw himself at Gerald Templar's feet. The seated man's hand came down and rested gently on his curly head with its winged cap.

'Good boy,' he said. 'Phryne, my dear.'

'Gerald,' said Phryne evenly. This took an effort. Gerald Templar's beauty struck her afresh each time she saw him, and it was extreme enough to take the breath away. He was not just made like a Greek boy, all long limbs and light muscles. It was not just that his face had the fine-cut purity of a marble by Michelangelo, though others spoke of a Canova Eros in Venice. His eyes, admittedly, were like sapphires and his hair—a little too long, reaching his collarbones—like spun gold. He was a veritable masterpiece of the Divine art. But mere beauty alone would not have been enough to enchant a sceptical, irreligious city like Paris, as he had done. Gerald rose and came to take her hand, and Phryne felt it again. A flood of love, of attention, a focused wave of empathy. His charisma preceded his person by at least ten paces in every direction. Gerald could have led an army to free Jerusalem.

'How kind of you to come to my little party,' said Gerald. He led Phryne forward, through a collection of semi-recumbent bodies. Their faces turned towards him as he moved, as fish turn towards a spring of fresh water in a stagnant pond.

The source of the coolness was now revealed. A fountain had been set up, spraying cold water into the humid air. Gerald's acolytes were all dressed in white cotton shifts called, as Phryne remembered, caftans, embroidered round the neck and sleeves with pale arabesques. There were always thirty of them in the Unchanging Ones. When one died, dropped out, found marriage or God, or inherited his father's hog-slaughtering business or just got bored with adoring Gerald, he or she was instantly replaced. There had never been a dearth of devoted admirers of Gerald Templar.

To balance the Unchanging Ones, there were the Lady's Own, presently all spread out to provide a constant stream of cool air over the flawless body of Isabella Templar. She was lying supine in a string hammock, supported at each end by two of her admirers, and fanned by three others with Cecil B DeMille peacock fans. And she was surpassingly beautiful, this sister of the aureate Gerald, in quite an opposite way. Where he glowed as golden as Apollo, she was as icy and severe as Artemis. His hair was Hyacinthine ringlets of precious metal; hers was as colourless as flax, hip length, perfectly straight and shining like the moon. Her eyes were the colour of a cold Scandinavian sky. Her skin was as pale as pearl and in the half-light she seemed to glow like an undersea creature, edged with phosphorescence. Phryne noticed that even her feet were perfect—high arched, glossy, with pinkly glowing rounded nails and not a scar or a bunion to deform their elegant shape.

It would be pointless to feel envy, Phryne thought, and didn't. As well envy a Botticelli madonna. Isabella waved a languid hand at Phryne and turned her face to the cool air again.

'Tarquin, a chair for Miss Fisher,' said Gerald. Making a fearful face, the boy fetched a chair and slammed it down at the foot of Gerald's throne. 'Naughty,' said Gerald.

'And if the wind changes your only prospect of employment will be as a gargoyle,' agreed Phryne. Tarquin scowled at her. Gerald patted the boy on the shoulder.

'You should listen to Miss Fisher,' he told him. 'She's certainly the wisest person I know. Well, perhaps not the wisest,' he added, 'but the cleverest.'

Tarquin scowled again but did not demur.

'So, you've imported the whole circus?' asked Phryne, observing the Unchanging Ones as they lay, half slain by heat and hashish.

'Unkind,' chided Gerald. 'You always were unkind.'

'But clever,' put in Phryne. 'Why did you come to Australia, Gerald? Not for the climate,' she said. 'Isabella hates the heat. Some trouble in Paris, was there?'

'You are acute, and unkind, as I mentioned before,' said Gerald ruefully. 'Let us just say that we felt we needed some fresh woods and pastures new. Here, I suspect, there is great scope for us, and also living is less expensive. But the Unchanging came with me of their own free will.'

'And the Lady's Own of theirs,' scoffed Phryne gently. 'Let us have less talk of free will in that context! I hope you brought enough hash for all of them.'

'Suitable supplies have been organised,' said Gerald blandly. 'Will you smoke?'

'Just cigarettes,' said Phryne. 'I prefer my own.'

Tarquin, nudged by Gerald's bare foot, rose and lit Phryne's Virginian cigarette without setting fire to her hair or garments, much as she felt the little monster desired to see her burn. She had never felt such jealousy radiating off a human.

'And Tarquin?'

'He is an orphan,' said Gerald. 'I found him in the Infants Home in Melbourne on my first day here. He is my boy now, eh, Tarquin?'

Tarquin flung himself at Gerald's feet and embraced his legs. Phryne watched, a little uncomfortable at such a lavish display of devotion.

'I never suspected you of sentiment,' was all she said.

'I am many things which you have never suspected,' said Gerald grandly. 'My sister is still not speaking to me. She got a little girl at the same place, one Marigold, a sweet little thing, but she ran away as soon as we got here. Now Isabella grudges me my Tarquin.'

'Because she has lost her girl?' asked Phryne.

'Because Tarquin loves me,' said Gerald. 'Now, to business.'

'Business, Gerald?' she asked, astonished. 'You?'

'Go down to the kitchen,' Gerald instructed Tarquin, untangling him gently. 'Stay there until the housekeeper can give you her word that the menu will be strictly adhered to, then come back as quickly as you can. I am trusting you, Tarquin.'

'The Lady Isabella has already talked to the old bidd—the old chook—the old…woman,' protested Tarquin.

'Even so,' said Gerald. Tarquin poised on one foot, like the Eros of his costume, half inclined to argue some more and half inclined to show Gerald how fast he could run. Finally he took to his heels with no more noise than a large bird taking off, and was gone through the bamboo curtains in a breath.

'He's fast,' commented Phryne.

'Good thing too, or he might not have been able to outrun his alcoholic father or his beastly mother,' said a voice close to her ear.

'My dear,' said Phryne, patting a fat cheek with an affectionate hand. 'My dear old Sylvanus, I should have known that you would be here.'

'Just going to get a refill, darling girl. Can I get one for you, too? Gerald? Not smoking that vile weed, you see, I get terribly thirsty.' Sylvanus posed briefly, hand in waistcoat pocket, mouth drawn down, other hand extended in a begging gesture.

No one doubted that Sylvanus had modelled himself on his hero, Oscar Wilde. He had run to fat as Wilde had, concealing the fact in loose robes or well cut gentleman's sporting waistcoats. Rumours that he wore a corset had never been disproved. Or proved, of course, Phryne conceded. He had less hair than Oscar, it was true, but more head to put it on. His eyes were almost black, and could be very penetrating. Most of the time he affected a lazy grace which competent critics might have thought overdone in a hibernating sloth.

Sylvanus Leigh was witty, acerbic, considerably older than the company's average age of twenty-five, and one of the kindest men Phryne had ever met—provided that he was not detected in his good deeds. When asked once why he was carrying two miserable Parisian kittens, rescued from a dog's jaws, in his pocket, he had taken them out, examined them carefully, and said, 'Mittens,' before returning them to their sanctuary. Phryne happened to know that they now ruled his tiny Montparnasse flat as royalty, but no one else ever suspected it. She smiled at him with real affection as he bowed elaborately over her hand.

'Sweet and adorable Miss Fisher, you walk in beauty like the night, though not this vile hot one,' he told her. 'I fly for some more nectar before the hearties wreck the tent.'

He ambled away.

Gerald sighed. 'It's like this,' he started the story again.

'Phryne!' squealed four female voices, and Phryne went down under an avalanche of Sapphic kisses. Sabine, Marie-Louise,

Minou and Sad Alison. They were just as Phryne remembered, though Alison seemed to have got sadder. In that bright company she stood out like a blown bulb in a string of fairy lights. The girls from the Tea Shop of Sybaris, Rue de la Chat Qui Peche, Quartier Latin, Paris, stroked and hugged and pecked while peppering Phryne with questions—wasn't this a strange country, what on earth was she wearing under that silk shirt, was it always this hot, wasn't Gerald looking divine, had she seen that there were two girl riders in the polo team, how deliciously decadent!?

'Not now,' said Gerald, shedding an atom of his carefully cultivated serenity. 'I want Phryne to myself for a moment.'

'Oh,' lips pouted and quivered. 'As long as you give her back later. Still, it is your party, isn't it, darling?'

'It is,' said Gerald, and the girls, arms around each other, dawdled back to the company of the Lady's Own, reclaimed their feathers and resumed fanning. Phryne put Gerald back on his throne and perched herself comfortably on the wide, padded arm.

'Now, look straight ahead, try not to move your lips and talk fast,' she instructed. 'We can ride out the next interruption as it comes. What is biting you, Gerald Templar?'

'Someone is threatening to kill me,' he said, obeying her to the syllable. In men, this always had an ameliorating effect on Phryne. She allowed her chin to rest on his magnificent chest for a moment.

'Who?'

'Don't know.'

'Why?'

'Don't know that either. Started in Paris. Got letters.'

'Kept letters?'

'All of them,' he said, confounding Phryne's detective-story narrative reflexes. In such novels the victim had always burned the letters, adding a degree of difficulty to the detective's task, in case the author thought that he or she was having too easy a life.

'Good. Go on,' she instructed him.

'Tried to poison me,' said Gerald. 'Arsenic in the sugar on Turkish delight. I didn't eat the stuff. But Tillie Mayer did and was taken to hospital. Tried again, a toadstool in the *potage automne*. Three people in the ambulance that time. Tried to ruin me. Wrote to "Faits Divers" in *Paris Jour* and said that we held black masses and orgies like in that *À rebours* book.'

'But, Gerald—' said Phryne. He held up his hand and she subsided. Time was, indeed, of the essence. She could see a boy with a tray being chivvied by Sylvanus Leigh into crossing the tent and not stepping on any important parts of the recumbent bodies.

'Police investigation,' he said. 'Cleared us. Paper printed a retraction. Mud sticks, though.'

'So it does,' said Phryne.

'Then he began stealing from us,' said Gerald. 'Money went missing. Suppliers' cheques vanished. Jewellery, too. Thought I'd left him behind in France. Now he's here. I invited you to my party, Phryne, and now I want you to save my life.'

'You're exaggerating,' she told him. 'No one is dead yet. How do you know he's here?'

'Got note,' said Gerald. Phryne saw with admiration that he really had the hang of prisoners' lingo, which was spoken without moving the lips and was hell on plosives. But Gerald always had been the clever twin.

'Here's Sylvanus,' she said. 'Have someone put the notes in my room disguised as a hat in a locked hatbox. You should not be seen giving them to me. But I have to tell you, my dear, that someone has already made two determined attempts to keep me away from your little gathering, so I am disposed to believe you.'

Gerald sagged a little. 'I thought it would take much more to convince you,' he admitted. 'Very well. Sylvanus, you are a lifesaver,' he said in his usual baritone as the older man came puffing to the dais. 'What have you brought us?'

'No point in messing about in this climate,' said Sylvanus, nodding to the boy to put the jug down into its ice bucket and allowing him to hand out glasses. 'You have a superlative barman, Gerald, and a very tasty one as well. Arms like a wrestler. Just the gentlest beading of honest sweat upon his manly bosom. Said bosom, half bared, was at lickable height and I almost swooned while waiting. He concocted them for me. Singapore slings just like Raffles used to make. Bottoms up,' he encouraged, and drank down his glass.

Phryne sipped. Cherry brandy, gin, lemon juice? Tonic water certainly. A sure preventative against the malaria which she might catch from a citronella loving mosquito. Should an anopheles stray her way south from tropic climes where malaria lived…

Her mind was definitely wandering under the influence of all that hash smoke. She shook herself briskly. That had been adroit of Sylvanus, bringing not individual glasses but a big jug of the drink—and drinking it first to prove it harmless. Assuming he knew about the poisoning of the soup and the Turkish delight. She eyed Sylvanus narrowly and he smiled at her with his neglected teeth.

'Oh for a beaker full of the warm South…' he began. 'The true, the blushful Hippocrene…'

'I am happy about the beaded bubbles winking at the brim,' Phryne said, 'but I worry about the purple-stained mouth. Generally I find wine which stains the mouth also destroys the digestive system.'

'Oh Lord, yes,' agreed Sylvanus, slumping ungracefully down to sit on the dais, contriving thus to be at both Gerald and Phryne's feet. 'I can recall a 1915 chianti which tasted just like red ink flavoured with engraving acid. I only had the one glass, though. My concierge pinched the rest for cleaning sinks. Still, nothing was going to do poor Keats any more harm, so he might as well have drunk bad wine.'

'True,' agreed Phryne. 'Talk to me, Sylvanus. How was your voyage?'

'Oh, pleasant, very pleasant,' he said. 'Never travelled so far before—not ever, really. Your Australia is about as far away as you can get from anywhere at all, isn't it?'

'Almost far enough from my father,' said Phryne, sipping. She would have to watch how many of these she drank. They were sweetish and sourish and very, very moreish.

'Ah, yes, I saw your unesteemed progenitor in Paris on the way through,' said Sylvanus, chuckling. 'He was yelling at a porter, who was not carrying his baggage in a respectful enough manner. You know what those railway porters are like, Phryne. Tough as old railway sleepers and able to carry just about anything—including a medium-sized bistro—on that strap arrangement across their forehead.'

'So, what happened with Papa?' asked Phryne.

'He yelled louder, because it is well known to English people that foreigners only pretend to speak those nasty foreign tongues but really understand English if it is shouted loudly enough. Then the porter unlatched the strap, dumped all the baggage on the platform and began, very deliberately, to throw it, piece by piece, into the path of the oncoming Train Bleu.'

'No!' exclaimed Phryne, delighted. 'What did the old buffalo do?'

'Stormed off to get a gendarme. Meanwhile, your mother produced money and apologies and really much better French than she thinks she speaks and by the time the policeman arrived the baggage had all been carried to a taxi and no one knew what the trouble was about...I do like your Papa, you know,' he mused. 'He is perfect, in his way.'

'As a viper is a perfect viper or a tarantula a perfect tarantula,' Phryne riposted. 'You want Papa, Sylvanus dear, he is all yours.'

'He would look good stuffed, in some decent museum.'

'On that we can certainly agree,' Phryne laughed. 'You still tell a very funny story, my dear old thing.'

'Well, to get into the best society nowadays you have to either feed people or amuse people or shock people,' he replied seriously. 'She feeds them, he shocks them and I amuse them. It's a fair bargain.'

'Sylvanus?' said Gerald.

'Yes, my dear?'

'Can you go and find Tarquin? He ought to have been back by now.'

'I don't know what you see in that horrible child,' said Sylvanus, brushing aside his thinning forelock. The gesture belonged to a time when he had more hair, and now just looked clumsy.

'Myself when young,' said Gerald.

'Surely not,' protested Phryne.

'I only sent him to the kitchen and he always skimps kitchen visits—can't see the point of aspiring to culinary perfection. Mind you, the poor little scrap only got bread and dripping on birthdays and Christmas so he hasn't actually got any standards.'

'You sent him away half an hour ago,' Phryne reminded Gerald. 'And you told him to stay until the housekeeper person-ally swore that your menu would go onto the table un-changed. He might not appreciate haute cuisine but he adores you and if you told him to stay until he had the old lady's word, then I believe he would stay.'

'Yes, probably. The thing I told you is making me more con-cerned than I usually am about people and their sad fates.'

'Sad fates,' mused Sylvanus. 'What I could tell you about sad fates. There are so many more of them than happy fates.'

'Only because a happy fate doesn't make a good story,' objected Phryne. 'For every student who runs away with her teacher and lives happily ever after outside Montpellier with their five children and pet rabbit called Max, there is one dreadful tragedy involving nunneries and sharp knives.'

Sylvanus evidently disliked her reasoning. 'Oh come, Phryne, that's like saying for every young man who kills a stranger at a crossroads and then goes on to merrily marry an older woman as his queen and rules happily ever after there is one tragedy involving torn-out eyes and a noose made of a girdle. Some things are just bad, bad from the very beginning.'

'Indeed,' said Gerald. He was looking across the tent at his sister, utterly relaxed on her hammock, turning her delicate face into the cool air from the fountain, a movement very like a baby seeking its mother's breast.

'All right, given that you can have things bad *ab initio*,' argued Phryne. 'Oedipus, for instance, initiated his terrible fate by losing his temper at the place where three roads met and killing an older man. That, I agree, is not a good beginning. Bad deeds breed other bad deeds. Murder requires recompense, blood, as they say in Greece, calls out for blood. But if the deed which sparks off the terrible fate is as simple and benign a one as falling in love, then there have to be other possibilities.'

'Do you really think that falling in love is a benign action?' asked Sylvanus wearily. Suddenly he looked old. His cheeks sagged. 'Th' expense of spirit in a waste of shame is lust in action.'

'Thank you, Mr. Shakespeare,' said Phryne tartly.

'Jonathan, Sylvanus and Phryne shall be our reciters tonight,' said Gerald. 'Subject: evil. That ought to settle the point, and it will also delay the nine thousandth repetition of Chesterton's "Lepanto" by our dear friend Nicholas. Just lately I've come over all unnecessary at the line "dim drums throbbing".'

'It just shows your innate good taste is reasserting itself,' said Sylvanus indulgently, 'after all that time contemplating the sort of second rate modern French drivel to which I would not give library room.'

'Such as?' bristled Phryne, who was fond of modern French poetry.

'"Flowers of Evil",' sneered Sylvanus. 'Pretentious windy rubbish.'

'Oh dear,' said Phryne. 'I fear we are going to differ very markedly in our recital, Syl.'

'I would have been astounded if we did not,' he replied courteously.

Phryne put her hand over her glass as he offered to refill it. Poetry recitals—yes, a feature of the Templar court was recitals. No one was allowed to merely read a poem, they had to know it by heart. Phryne, having a memory as sticky as flypaper, sorted through her repertoire. What would amuse this gathering?

Elbowing her imp of the perverse firmly aside and turning down flat her suggestion—'Daddy wouldn't buy me a bow wow'—Phryne took her leave to perform her ablutions, don her own evening clothes and see how much poetry she could, in fact, remember well enough to perform. A sonnet, perhaps? A piece of the *Inferno*? Verlaine or Rimbaud to annoy Sylvanus? Or what about her old friend Villon?

The heat outside the tent took her by surprise. That fountain really had been effective in cooling the air. Outside there was nothing to cool it. Groups of young men lay about on the parched sward, drinking far too much beer because they were thirsty. There would be some suicidal hangovers tomorrow whatever the weather. The north wind was picking up. By tomorrow it might be the full dragon's breath which withered trees and started bushfires and always gave Phryne a headache. She slipped past the lazy groups, heading towards the house.

There was a flash of gold and Tarquin sped past her, his mission completed. So that was all right. Phryne wondered what was in those notes that Gerald had carefully preserved. She quickened her pace. The country house rule about bathing—he who bathes first, bathes fast—was a good one but she did not mean to comply with it.

Phryne was gritty, sweaty and a little intoxicated and what she wanted was a lush, full, hot, foamy bath in which she could recline.

She ran lightly up the stairs and gathered all her bathing things, locked herself into the bathroom as the taps roared, and sank into a strong scent of lemon blossom, which went well with citronella. The house might have been vandalised and its spirit broken, but its hot water system worked just as superbly as it ever had, when Governor La Trobe was expected to dinner and all of the guests wanted a bath at once.

She closed her eyes, just for a moment.

He remembered when he had acquired his new name, the Joker. He had played cards for a living for a while, skinning the high rollers on the trans-Atlantic boats. When he had discovered his vocation, he had laid a playing card joker on the breast of his first victim. From that moment, he knew his title.

Chapter Five

If you don't like my peaches
why do you shake my tree?

'St. Louis Blues'

Phryne only opened her eyes again when someone began banging hard on the door and she was reminded of her surroundings.

'Drat,' she said. 'All right! I'll be out directly!' she added, rising from the scented bath and wrapping herself in her soft towelling gown. She opened the door to a young man in a tunic who sniffed delightedly.

'Ooh, lovely! Leave me your bathwater, Miss Fisher? Smells like a whole Sicilian lemon grove.'

One of the hashishim, Phryne thought, rummaging for a name. Gilbert, that was it. Nice boy, only interested in other nice boys. She sailed past him, assenting to his use of her bathwater with an inclination of her Dutch-doll head. An unusual request but not, she thought, objectionable.

Regaining her own room, she dried and arrayed herself in suitable evening dress, a loose Poitou tunic and trousers of old rose silk. She slicked herself with citronella under her lemon perfume and sat brushing her hair in front of the small mirror. One hundred strokes, every day. Except when she forgot. Or didn't feel like it. Or Dot wasn't there to do it for her. Phryne didn't believe in rigid routines. They robbed the day of spontaneity. But at the moment she liked the bob of her shiny hair and the movement of the brush and the soothing caress of the bristles.

The little room was hot, but Phryne did not open her window. It gave onto the balcony, and that faced into the shafts of the setting sun. She would not be cool, she was convinced, until she was home again and swimming in the St. Kilda sea, or lying in her own room with a fan blowing over a basin of ice. Until then, anywhere was probably cooler than her room, so she secured her petticoat pocket around her waist, decorated her sleek head with a garland of dusty pink roses, took up a fan on which she had written selected cues for her performance and, lighting a conscious gasper, sauntered out of the room called Iris and into the main house, where a buzz of conversation, the tuning noises of a string quartet and the scent of cooking revealed to her the location of the dining room.

The original owners had wanted this room to be sombre and impressive but not overwhelming, and although their decorations and even their colour scheme had been obliterated by a severe Church, the proportions were still charming and Gerald's hangings of bright Morris cloth ameliorated the vandalism and covered up most of the whitewash. Phryne knew that she would never think of whitewash in the same way again. She walked boldly into the room where she was greeted as a sister by the Sapphic girls and hauled into their company, where she was always pleased to be.

'Cruel what they've done to the house, eh?' asked Sabine, who, when she spoke English, spoke the soft Border Scots of her nurse, an accent that later educators had not been able to eradicate. She designed silks for fashion houses when she wasn't chasing big strong girls. Sabine was small and delicate and quite implacable in her *amours*. At present, Phryne saw, she was half reclining on the stalwart bosom of Pamela English, a jolly hockey lass straight out of a girls' boarding school story. She had butter yellow hair cut short and a high complexion, enhanced by her habit of running five miles before breakfast. Phryne reflected that she and Sabine were a match made in heaven and said so as she sat down and reached for some hors d'oeuvres. Stuffed eggs, very tasty.

'Quite so,' agreed Sabine, giggling. 'And I hardly had to chase her at all, which was lucky, because she could outrun me any day.'

Pam blushed and offered Phryne a plate of devils on horse-back. 'Nice place, though,' she said, referring to the house. 'Got a tennis court. I've lined up a few partners for tomorrow. Do you play, Phryne?'

'Occasionally,' said Phryne through a mouthful of prune and bacon. 'But not in such hot weather. Can one swim in the lake?'

'Oh yes, it's spring fed and quite cold. I took a dip this after-noon. The hearties hadn't arrived then. I expect it will be full of boys by the morning,' said Pam sadly. She loathed any-thing in masculine form except Gerald Templar. Sad Alison, who sat on the other side of Sabine, hauled back her lank hair and sighed.

'Some of them are quite good-looking, though,' she said.

Sadly. With her spotty skin and despondent air, she was unlikely to attract any of them.

Phryne reflected that she could probably manage the boys and ate a piece of toast with something vulcanised on it—fish paste, perhaps? She hoped that this dinner was going to be mostly cold, or it would be unbearable.

'So, have you come alone?' asked Sabine.

'Yes,' said Phryne. 'But since I've been here I've met several interesting people. One jazz singer who can tear the heart out of your breast, two girl polo players and one goat.'

The story about the goat lasted through the soup, which was vichyssoise, and the fish, which was a cold mousse concocted of crabmeat and prawns. A discussion of Erik Satie and the modernist school of music beguiled the roast, which was cold baron of beef with all the trimmings. That accounted for civility and culture. The girls began to gossip along with the fruit salad and ice cream.

'They say that they are coming to the end of their fortune at last,' whispered Amelia, biting a piece of pineapple as though she had a grudge against pineapples and all their race.

'Do you think so?' asked Phryne.

'It might be,' said Pam slowly. 'Why else come to Australia, which is about as far as anyone can run from Paris? No one can afford to spend like they've been spending for the last three years. I reckon the carnival ride might be coming to an end. It's been a great ride, though,' she sighed.

'What will you do if it does all come to an end?' asked Phryne.

'Stay here, I think. Sabine likes Melbourne. I can find a job and I've got a little income of my own, and so has Sabine. We'll manage.'

'And I wouldn't have missed it,' said Sabine. 'As Pam says, we'll manage. But I don't know about some of the others. The hash smokers are pretty out of it. It was probably cruel to bring them all this way. Some of them haven't the wit of a dormouse and they'll never get home, even assuming they can remember where home is.'

'Sabine!' exclaimed Pam, shocked at this blasphemy, and Sabine waved an apologetic hand. 'No, I didn't mean that Gerald was cruel, or the Lady either. But perhaps they didn't think.'

'Would anyone want to harm Gerald?' asked Phryne. 'Someone, perhaps, who knows that it is all coming to an end and blames him for stranding them in Australia?'

'No,' said Pam and Sabine together. 'No one would want to hurt Gerald. You just have to be near him to feel how he loves us.'

'Yet each man kills the thing he loves,' quoted a rich voice. 'By each let it be heard. Some do it with a bitter look, some with a flattering word. The coward does it with a kiss, the brave man with a sword…'

'Really, Sylvanus,' reproved Sabine. 'One day you'll go too far!'

'Oh, I intend to,' he told her, taking a vacant chair at Phryne's side. 'I can resist anything except temptation.' He helped himself to ice cream, which was melting rapidly in the heat. Phryne sipped her chilled hock and wondered how long dinner would last.

'Have you decided what you are going to recite, Phryne?' asked Sylvanus, giving her a smile which indicated clearly that he understood just how uncomfortable she was. He mopped his brow with a purple silk handkerchief.

'I have,' she answered. 'Coffee, please,' she said to the servitor over her shoulder.

'And for me,' added Sylvanus. 'Well, are you going to tell us which poet has your esteemed patronage tonight?'

'No,' said Phryne. 'But I'm willing to bet you will never guess, and also that this poet has never been recited at a Templar gathering before.'

'How intriguing,' said Sylvanus, as Phryne had hoped he would. Then he began guessing, which freed Phryne to think about the Templars while coffee was drunk and the company was at last released from the dining oven. Phryne gladly followed the Templars into the grounds and back into the cool pavilion, where the fountain had got into its stride and it was almost cold.

Cold drinks were distributed. Phryne was allotted one which was vividly green and found it was a strange mixture of lemon juice and crème de menthe. Not what she might have chosen for herself but blessedly tinkling with real ice. Phryne's father had always held that the best drinks were free drinks and there was something in what that detestable old lush the pater said, she thought. The mint flavour grew on her as she sipped, remembering Nerine and her julep.

The reciter from the other side, Jonathan, stood up and, at Gerald's signal, began to deal with the matter of evil by means of a Swinburne poem—a man who thought a great deal about evil, it was true, though it was clear that he was a fan.

'Cold eyelids that hid like a jewel
'Her eyes that grow soft for an hour
'The heavy white limbs and the cruel
'Red mouth like a venomous flower…
'O mystic and sombre Dolores
'Our Lady of Pain…'

He spoke on, of 'limbs too delicious for death', in praise of
Dolores, the 'pallid and poisonous Queen'. The melodious verses
swung past, larded and heavy with internal rhymes as Dolores
moved 'to the music of passion with lithe and lascivious regret'.
He made a good performance out of the poem, only losing his
place once and projecting his voice so that it carried across the
still air in the tent. Actor's training, perhaps, or was this an errant
clergyman? Phryne thought so as she heard the achingly sincere
regret in his delivery of the last lines.

'What ailed us O Gods to desert you
'For ones that refuse and refrain?
'Come down and redeem us from virtue
'Our Lady of Pain.'

Then Phryne stood up. She walked to stand by Gerald's feet and
started to recite, and Sylvanus, having failed to guess, spat 'Blake,
by the Gods! How you dare, Phryne!' as she began to speak.

'To see a World in a Grain of Sand
'And a Heaven in a Wild Flower
'Hold Infinity in the palm of your hand
'And Eternity in an hour

'A Robin Redbreast in a Cage
'Puts all Heaven in a Rage.

'A Dove house fill'd with Doves & Pigeons
'Shudders Hell thro' all its regions.'

The couplets were delivered in the measured, tranced voice of a seeress. Gerald Templar, listening hard, forgot the cheery Victorian voice of his nanny who had originally read them to him. In Phryne's performance, the auguries became prophecies again, as Blake had intended. He shivered. Phryne was just visible in the drifting smoke as a rose-crowned, epicene figure, quite as uninvolved with her prophecies as the Angel who came to Tobias.

'A Dog starv'd at his Master's Gate
'Predicts the ruin of the State

'A Horse misus'd upon the Road
'Calls to Heaven for Human blood.

'He who shall hurt the little Wren
'Shall never be belov'd by Men

'He who the Ox to wrath has mov'd
'Shall never be by Woman lov'd

'The Wanton Boy that kills the Fly
'Shall feel the Spider's enmity

'The Poison of the Honey Bee
'Is the Artist's Jealousy…'

'Kill not the Moth nor Butterfly,' concluded Phryne into dead, impressed silence, 'For the Last Judgment draweth nigh.'

She sat down and gulped the rest of her crème de menthe as the applause began.

'Another drink for the hetaera Phryne!' shouted Sylvanus. 'Melt down a dozen pearls in red wine!'

'Thank you, plain gin and tonic will be most welcome,' said Phryne.

'Tarquin, get the lady a drink,' ordered Gerald.

Scowling, the gold-clad boy sped out of the tent. Sylvanus engulfed Phryne in a highly scented hug.

'What possessed you to think of Blake?' he asked. 'He is just too, *too* passé!'

'So passé as to be back in fashion,' replied Phryne, releasing herself gently. Sylvanus used altogether too much freesia perfume. He smelt like a slightly rancid flower garden. 'I have always liked Blake, such of him as I could understand, which isn't a lot.'

'Ah, but he knew about evil,' said Sylvanus. 'What about "London"? How the chimney sweeper's sigh, ev'ry black'ning church appals, how the hapless soldier's sigh...'

'Runs in blood down palace walls,' concluded Phryne. 'Exactly so. But Jonathan delivered that Swinburne very well. Such solid verse, I always think.'

'But hard to forget,' said Jonathan, who had ventured closer to join the discussion. 'Swinburne sort of glues itself to the surface of the mind like toffee to the palate.'

'How poor Swinburne would have hated to be compared to anything sweet,' mused Sylvanus. 'Where is that boy with the drinks? My tongue's hanging out. Shall I go and hurry him along, Gerald?'

'Yes, do,' said Gerald, allowing a look of worry to crease his perfect forehead.

Phryne engaged Jonathan in a discussion of the more obscure of the romantic poets. A tray of drinks was brought in by a servitor from the purple tent. No Sylvanus. No Tarquin. Phryne was already halfway through her gin and tonic when the Oscar Wilde figure returned.

'I'm sorry, Gerald,' he said, 'but I can't find the little beast anywhere. He's probably flounced off in a tantrum.'

'Well, I'll just have this drink,' said Phryne, 'and then I'm going to the jazz singers. I'll call by afterwards and make sure that Tarquin has come back.'

She was glad to collect the Sapphic girls and leave. Soon the kissing and caressing would begin, and she had not thought to have someone make her a new set of karez drawers, which prevented unintended consequences to the Templar Feast of Love.

Phryne and the girls went to the jazz tent, where Nerine and the three T's would soon be playing. The jazz tent was not so much a tent as a pavilion. There was a sky-shade in case of rain and a curtain behind the stage, otherwise it was open to the elements—and, regrettably, the mosquitoes and the heat. In deference to the total lack of what any musician would have recognised as acoustics, the singer had a microphone. Nerine always did well with a microphone. Because she was so short-sighted she held it close to her mouth and the visions conjured up by the sight of Nerine singing into the microphone at close range were enough to quite overcome some gentlemen, who felt the need to go and take a midnight swim in rather a hurry. In some cases, in their clothes.

Tabitha caught sight of Phryne as she came in and nudged the singer. Nerine finished 'St. Louis Blues' and said, 'This song is for my ol' fren' Lady Phryne. You lissen up good now,' she told the audience, and they listened up good as Nerine began the aching lament: 'I went down to St. James Infirmary, and I saw my baby there.'

'The singer—you know her?' asked Pam, blushing.

'Certainly. She is an old friend. Shall I introduce you, girls?'

The girls nodded. Even if Nerine was not of their sub-species, she was gorgeous beyond belief—just looking at her was almost enough.

'Let him go, let him go, God bless him,' sang Nerine, undulating so close to the edge of the dais that Phryne's heart was in her mouth. 'He never did love me!'

Phryne did not leave the jazz pavilion until Nerine and the three T's had taken a well-earned break and the Jubilee Jazz Band was on, playing quicksteps and bunny hugs for such patrons as could still both find their feet and stand on them. She bade the girls goodnight after introducing them to Nerine and went back to the Templar tent, wondering if that bad boy Tarquin had reappeared. The karez hour was over and most of the disciples had departed to their virtuous beds. Only Gerald and Sylvanus sat together, drinking another G and T and trying to play chess. They both looked up hopefully as she came in. By the way their faces fell, Phryne had her answer.

'So he hasn't come back,' she said, glad for an excuse to leave the leftover hash smoke, which was making her giddy. 'I'll just go along and have a little look at the scene.'

'Would you, Phryne? I'd be so grateful,' said Gerald. Sylvanus patted his shoulder. Phryne went out again into the hot night.

It was not hard to trace the gold-clad child's progress as far as the drinks tent. The barman reported that he had made up a tray, jug and glasses, and had personally seen Tarquin safely to the door with them, as the hearties had thought his gold tunic risible and might have tripped him. 'In fun, of course, Miss Fisher.'

From the drinks tent Tarquin's path back to Gerald would have been straightforward enough. Phryne stepped carefully in and out of the light of tall electric standards, which lit the ground under them and left a pool of ebony darkness between. In one such she felt glass crunch beneath her sandalled feet and stopped abruptly. The ground was wet underfoot and a scent of gin rose all about her, as unmistakable as eau-de-cologne.

'Still, it might just be a broken bottle,' she mused, scraping the ground with careful fingertips to estimate the amount of glass. Far too much for one bottle and, anyway, the glass was thinner and curved: wine glass shapes had been broken on this spot.

She saw a white flicker of paper on the nearest standard and carefully peeled it away from the iron. The lamplight was too dim to read by and she didn't want to attract attention. She placed the paper in her bosom for future reference and cast around for further clues. She found nothing but one of the winged shoes, caught in a box thorn hedge. The full search would have to wait for daylight. Beyond the lights the night was as dark as nights ever got in summer in these parts. Which was very dark indeed.

Carrying the shoe, she went sadly back to the Templar tent to report to Gerald that someone seemed to have ravished his fairy child away as cleanly as Ganymede was kidnapped by Hermes. It was only then that she remembered the piece of paper and extracted it from her bosom. It was a common luggage label, stiff white paper with blue borders, gummed on the back to be attached to a trunk. Someone had given it an inadequate lick when gluing it to the lamp post.

'It's a riddle,' she said, displeased. In the middle of the label, in neat clerkly script, was written: 'It flies, it wastes, it drags, it goes,/And like the River Thames it flows.'

'A riddle? Could it have something to do with Tarquin?' demanded Gerald.

'No idea,' said Phryne. 'But it was on the post near where he dropped the tray. We can easily find it by daylight, the ground is covered with broken glass. You like parlour games, Gerald. Can you guess the riddle?'

'No,' said Gerald forlornly. 'I'm no good at riddles.'

'Well, there's one person who wanted Tarquin,' said Sylvanus with great daring, echoing Phryne's thought.

'Who?'

'Why,' said Sylvanus, 'your sister, Isabella. Hadn't you better ask her if she knows where the imp is before you raise the camp by night?'

'How dare you!' Gerald leapt to his feet.

Phryne found the subsequent scene exhausting. Finally she dragged herself away and headed for the great house, wanting nothing more than a wash and a bed of some kind. In pursuit of this modest ambition, she skirted a band of howling boys, who apparently thought they were wolves, and just avoided tripping over a pair of lovers who had miscalculated how far the shadow of their tent extended. Nerine's voice echoed in Phryne's mind: 'So cold, so blue, so bare…'

Where was that pestilential small boy? Had he really run away in a pet? It was possible. But Phryne had a bad feeling about the event. She didn't think that Tarquin would sacrifice one of his winged shoes, however cross he was with Gerald and however jealous of Phryne.

She undressed, washed briefly, and sat down at her impromptu dressing table to remove her make-up. The room seemed untouched. The locked hatbox which presumably contained Gerald's threatening letters was on her bed. Gerald had put the key into her hand earlier in the evening.

She reached for the cold cream and swiped a gob of it across a scratch on her wrist, which instantly began to bleed. 'Ouch,' said Phryne, fascinated. The cold cream had felt like sandpaper. She staunched her wrist with a handkerchief and smeared a sample of the cold cream across a piece of paper. She held it up to the light and saw minute glittering specks in it.

'What a nasty trick,' she said to herself. 'Ground glass in the cold cream. I could have gouged my face with it if I had just plonked it on and given it a good rub as I usually do. That was the idea, of course. I wonder what else he has prepared for me? Scorpions in my slippers? Snakes in my bed?'

Never one to ignore a sensible precaution if she had time to comply with it, Phryne carefully banged both slippers upside down on the floor before putting them on. No scorpions or spiders. She threw back the covers on her bed and revealed nothing but a small bag with ribbons which smelt of lavender. She put it on the windowsill, just in case. She searched the room for other lethal traps and found nothing. Not an attempt to kill, just to mutilate.

'Oh, what fun,' said Phryne, now thoroughly awake. She had a sudden idea and scrabbled for the key to the hatbox in which reposed Gerald's threatening letters. But when she opened it, it was entirely empty.

'Damn,' said Phryne, and donned her negligee. She put her cigarettes and lighter in her petticoat pocket and secured her little gun in her long medieval sleeve. The camp had settled down to sleep, except for the hardy souls still dancing to the Jubilee Jazz Band. But there was a light on in the back of the house, and thence Phryne went, keeping to the shadows, making no noise that an unusually alert leopard would have heard. She needed some answers. And some coffee.

◇◇◇

'John the Evangelist,' announced Dot, opening the book. 'He was the son of Zebedee, one of the apostles. He wrote a book of the Bible.'

The girls' attention wandered. John hadn't done much, they considered. He was a writer. He was there when Lazarus was raised, but so were all the others. He hadn't cut off any ears, or denied Christ, or even got himself martyred in an interesting way…

'He was thrown into a huge pot of boiling oil,' said Dot.

They stopped playing with Molly.

'Ooh!' said Ruth.

'How big?' asked Jane.

'Huge,' said Dot. 'And he came out of it without a blister. So they let him go.'

Jane's mind raced. How much oil, and what sort of oil, would she need to boil a saint? And what temperature would really hot oil attain?

Dot was pleased with their attention, and handed out a good conduct chocolate each.

Chapter Six

With cat-like tread upon our prey we steal,
In silence dread our cautious way we feel.
No sound at all, we never speak a word.
A fly's footfall would be distinctly heard.

W.S. Gilbert
The Pirates of Penzance

Creeping through a dark house was, Phryne would be the first to admit, not easy, especially if it wasn't your house. Fortunately, though probably in favour of nocturnal visitors, the stern Fathers had removed almost every whatnot, plant stand, vase, stool, decorative fire screen and set of Benares images which had made Victorian decor such a nightmare to dust. Phryne drifted through the darkness, feeling her way, not hurrying. She found the green baize door by touch and opened it without a creak. Then she stood blinking in bright light.

She had always heard that things were different below stairs. Upstairs and in the tents outside, the guests were falling asleep. Here all the preparations for a huge breakfast for two hundred were being made. A butcher was slicing rashers from a whole side of bacon. A young woman was bringing in baskets of eggs packed in straw. An elderly lady was slicing a harvest of loaves, brown and white. Porridge cauldrons were being scoured in the back kitchen beyond and potatoes and white fish were being cooked and eggs hard-boiled for kedgeree. A huge array of sauces were being strained, checked and decanted into serving jugs.

As Phryne stood amazed a girl, pleating her apron, asked the elderly lady, 'Can't Tommy go out into the scullery?' And she snapped, 'Oh, Elsie, surely you haven't been listening to those stories about a ghost!' when the butcher saw Phryne and the whole active kitchen ground slowly to a halt.

If Phryne had not anticipated the kitchen staff, the kitchen staff were astonished to see Phryne, clearly a lady, and in her nightclothes, in their kitchen. They were a tableau from Ford Madox Ford for a moment, until the elderly lady settled her apron and cap and bustled forward.

'Yes, Miss? How may we serve you? I'm Mrs. Truebody, the housekeeper. You others get on, get on! We've got two hundred breakfasts to prepare and it's already past midnight. Come this way, Miss. You must be the Hon. Miss Fisher,' said Mrs. Truebody, leading Phryne aside into a small room furnished with an easy chair, a very professional roll-top desk and the usual accoutrements of an office. Phryne sat down composedly in the visitor's chair, which was straight backed but well padded. Something in the housekeeper's tone had been familiar. Deferential but not overawed.

'And I'm not the first titled person you have had in your kitchen, am I?' she asked affably.

'God bless you no, Miss Phryne!' The housekeeper allowed herself a small, strictly controlled smile. Getting her title correct, Phryne noticed. Phryne was an Hon., as her father occasionally pointed out, and therefore not entitled to be called 'Lady'. Especially when she behaved as Phryne behaved, he usually added.

'The governor used to dine here, regular as regular. Princes, too, we've entertained. Royal princes,' she explained, as if Phryne might mistake for real British royalty that raffish Russian and

Polish strain about whom Mrs. Truebody had doubts. 'But what can I do for you, Miss Phryne?'

'I need a cup of coffee and some answers,' said Phryne frankly.

'A cup of coffee you shall have,' said Mrs. Truebody, making a gesture at Minnie, a young woman in a linen apron so white that by the carbon light she seemed wrapped in acetylene flame. 'Answers, if I have them, certainly.'

'How long have you worked here?' asked Phryne.

'Forty years,' said Mrs. Truebody, sinking down into her padded chair. 'Last of the family died and the others sold the house to the Church, and they—well, they didn't need a house-keeper. I retired. I had a good salary while I worked and a good pension, and I saved a lot. I have my own little house in Werribee near my two young brothers' families. But not in them, if you see what I mean.'

'I do,' said Phryne. 'Young children can be so exhausting.'

'Quite. But when the Templars made me such a generous offer, saying that only I understood how the old house worked, I agreed to come back just for this party. Actually I dealt with their man Mr. Ventura. Such a fuss budget! I never knew a man to be—forgive me, Miss—such an old woman. I gave him a room in the servants' quarters because he would not leave my people to get on with their work, but would keep meddling. If he wants to behave like a servant he can stay with the servants, I said.'

'And you were right,' said Phryne. Mrs. Truebody settled her considerable bosom. She was a plump lady with white hair in a bun, spectacles on a long black tape and a comfortable figure under stern control. Her corsetry creaked a little if she made a sudden movement. Her eyes were blue and her colour high without the aid of rouge. Her dress was dove grey and her apron white and she was as wholesome a creature as Phryne had seen in a long day. When the coffee came, clear, strong and hot in its own copper pot with a jug of hot milk and some ginger snaps beside it, Phryne was happy to drink and nibble and listen to the history of the mansion.

'In the 1840s there were two brothers, Thomas and Andrew Chirnside, who bought the land and built the house,' she said. 'On a visit back home, Thomas fell in love with their cousin, Mary Begbie, but her parents wouldn't let him have her. So when Thomas came back here he sent Andrew and begged him to fetch Mary to Australia any way he could. And he did—oh yes, he did.'

Phryne scented a rat. 'Married her himself?' she guessed.

'Yes,' said the housekeeper. 'But they must have forgiven each other because Thomas had this house built to be her domain—serene, he wanted it to be, and dignified. Such times as they had! All the notables to dine, and picnics and race meetings and polo tournaments and cricket games. They prospered.

'At one time, old Mrs. Davies told me—she was house-keeper before me—they supplied the house entirely from the estate: home killed meat, home smoked ham and bacon, home grown fruit and vegetables, home baked bread, and butter, cream and cheese from the cheese factory out on the Geelong road. Grain and flour from their own mill. Now we get our eggs and chickens from Mr. Cullen, our vegetables from Gar-field's and our milk from the dairy college, and that's all very satisfactory, but it must have been like living in one of those old manor houses, in the old days. Of course, then, you couldn't just send a boy down to the shop if you ran out of cream.'

'Indeed not,' said Phryne. 'So what happened to the brothers?'

'They died within a couple of years of each other,' said Mrs. Truebody. 'Then the sons divided up the land and that was the beginning of the end. Prices sank, costs and taxes rose. Oh, and the old mistress, a terrible thing, died when her hair caught on fire from a spilled bedside candle—terrible burns. An awful death.'

There was silence for a moment, and Phryne heard the kitchen noises: chopping of herbs, slicing of bread, a seething of pots on the range. And an 'ouch' as a bread cutter cut her finger instead. Then Mrs. Truebody resumed.

'They sold out in 1922 and the Church bought the house and land in '23. They built that extra wing last year. And they whitewashed the house, making it look like a ruin. But no use repining,' said Mrs. Truebody bracingly. 'The house had its day and now is something else, and very good sort of people they must be, of course. They get up at five in the morning to pray, I am told.'

'Indeed,' said Phryne, and took another ginger snap.

'Yes, such is the nature of human life, as the vicar says. We come up and are cut down like the grass. Oh dear, yes. When my young man was lost to that wicked African war I thought I'd die of grief, but I didn't die. And I'm glad I didn't, on the whole. But I'm running on like an old gossip. What was it you wanted to ask me, Miss Phryne?'

'Several things. They concern small boys, ghosts, and time. You've seen the little pest whom Gerald has adopted, a little ratbag dressed in gold?'

'Yes, and a more ill-conditioned boy I never saw. I would have had him across my knee if he hadn't been the master's favourite,' responded Mrs. Truebody.

'He's missing. Do you think he has run away?'

The immaculate head bent over Mrs. Truebody's competent hands. She inspected a thumbnail as she gave the matter suitable consideration. Finally she looked up, having made up her mind.

'I wouldn't have thought so. Pest that the little runt is, he adores the master. Adores him. After all, Mr. Templar did rescue him from an orphanage, or so they say. Tarquin—what a name for a boy!—really loves him, jumps to it as soon as Mr. Templar speaks. Only sign of decent gratitude I've seen in the brat.'

'My feeling entirely,' agreed Phryne. 'Now the next question. In the old days, did the household play parlour games? Riddles, perhaps?'

Mrs. Truebody smiled reminiscently. 'Oh yes, dear, and charades. I was always handing out aprons and caps and tea towels for charade costumes.'

'Would any of the family's parlour games books still be around?'

'I doubt it, Miss Phryne, all the movable goods, the pictures and plate and so on, were sold at auction, and the rest the Church has sold—even the stair carpets, for the Lord's sake. Woven specially for the house, they were, and ripped up and sold for a song. It's a wicked world,' said Mrs. Truebody sadly.

'No argument here,' said Phryne. 'When did you last see Tarquin?'

'When he came in to enquire about the master's orders for dinner. I swore to him that it would all be done as Miss and Mr. Templar ordered, and then he ran away—back to Mr. Templar, I assume. Last I saw of him. But I shall ask the staff presently. Anything else, Miss Fisher?'

'How do you manage to get such clear coffee? Not a ground in it,' said Phryne.

'It's clarified with crushed eggshell,' said the housekeeper. 'Takes up all the loose grounds and when the coffee is strained, the grounds go with the eggshells. Also, it is something to do with the eggshells. I hate wasting them but the head gardener does not like them in his compost and they really aren't edible.'

'No, I suppose not,' agreed Phryne. 'What would you understand by "time"? As a clue in a riddle, I mean?'

'Oh, a clock, I suppose. There are several of them here. Has something really happened to that poor little scrap?' she asked suddenly, laying a hand on Phryne's arm.

'I'm afraid it has,' said Phryne.

'Well, we can't have that,' said Mrs. Truebody firmly. 'Not in my kitchen. Not in my house! Can you imagine what the old mistress would have said about having boys kidnapped from her household? You tell me what you want, Miss Phryne, and I'll contrive it.'

'Stout fellow,' exclaimed Phryne, warmed by acquiring a reliable ally. 'Start by asking all of your staff when they last saw Tarquin. He can't have vanished into thin air! Last seen by me at about ten o'clock going out of the Templar tent. Ambushed, I suspect, by the third standard lamp post near the drinks tent.'

'I'll send in some more coffee,' said Mrs. Truebody, and bustled out.

Phryne drew her gown around herself and rubbed her eyes. Ground glass in the cold cream meant that she had not been able to clean her face, which felt gluey with old make-up. She got up and prowled around the housekeeper's room. She had two clocks, a tall one and a small cheap alarm clock. Neither contained any clue.

Phryne watched Mrs. Truebody go from person to person, from egg-sheller to bread-slicer to rasher-cutter and ask the questions, and each person shook their head. Damn. Perhaps he had been gathered up by a large eagle and flown to celestial regions. After all, he was Gerald's cup bearer and rather good at it, if you discounted the scowling.

A neat young woman brought in more coffee and another plate of biscuits. These ones had bits of candied orange peel in them and were just the thing for a hot sleepless night. Phryne said so. The girl smoothed her apron and smiled with unwearied bright brown eyes. She could not have been older than eighteen, an age at which 'midnight' is not a signal to go to bed, and sleep is considered optional.

'Oh yes, Miss. Mrs. Truebody made them herself. She's an angel with biscuits and sponges.'

'Are you an apprentice?' asked Phryne.

Minnie giggled, which was, Phryne discovered, her first response to any question. 'No, Miss, just a hired kitchen hand, but I'm learning a lot. I wish this party went on longer!'

Phryne didn't. But there was something she could ask this girl and she had better do it fast before Mrs. Truebody got back.

'Now, what about this ghost?' she asked. The girl looked frightened, giving only a token giggle.

'She's in the old scullery,' she whispered. 'Just a shape and a moaning and a terrible feeling of fear and despair. They say she was a kitchen maid and fell in love with a noble visitor. He ruined her and cast her away and she hanged herself there. But don't let Mrs. Truebody hear you ask about her! She doesn't believe in ghosts.'

'In any case there's no reason for that ghost to hurt you,' said Phryne consolingly. 'She'd be after men, surely, not girls like herself.'

'Oh,' said the girl, struck by this new idea. 'No, of course. You're right, Miss.'

'Last of all,' said Mrs. Truebody, coming into the room. 'Minnie, when did you last see that gold child, Tarquin?'

'When he came in about dinner, Mrs. Truebody. I haven't been out of the kitchen since.'

'And neither have you,' said Mrs. Truebody. 'Tell everyone, ten minutes more and then we all have a cup of tea and a sit-down. We have done very well. As soon as your eggs are all shelled, Minnie, you, Hannah, Betty and Annie can go and get some sleep. Tell Gabriel I said he was to walk you to your corridor.'

'Yes, Mrs. Truebody. Thank you, Mrs. Truebody,' gasped Minnie, and took her leave. Phryne saw one of the huge young footmen shamble up from his position at the knife sharpening table, grunting an agreement.

'The girls are worried about this ghost,' said Mrs. Truebody wryly. 'I, on the other hand, am now worried about abductors. Both will have to be tough to get past our Gabriel. Not a bright lad, but very strong and he likes the girls.'

Phryne and Mrs. Truebody contemplated Gabriel, twenty-two years old, half a ton of solid beef and several axe handles across the shoulders. Yes, it would be a bold ghost or abductor who took him on.

'So, what news?' asked Phryne, dragging her gaze away from the giant footman.

Mrs. Truebody tutted. 'Nothing useful. Most of them only saw the boy when he came here before dinner. We haven't really been out of the house all night. But Sam saw something that might be of use. I told him to come in when he's finished the carving knives.'

Sam could have been Gabriel's twin and in fact was his cousin. He hulked into the small room and stood clenching and unclenching his huge hands, as out of place as an elephant in a glass foundry.

'Tell the lady what you saw, Sam,' prompted Mrs. Truebody.

'More what I smelled,' said Sam in a roar, which he immediately modified to a hoarse whisper. 'At about eleven o'clock I was coming back from the drinks tent with a box which had the beer for us and the bottle of gin for—' He flinched under a blowlamp glare from the housekeeper. 'I mean to say, a bottle of gin. When I got under that third light I could smell gin real strong, so I stopped and took out the bottle in case it was leaking. It wasn't. There was glass on the ground, so I reckoned that someone had dropped a bottle. That's all,' he said, beginning to sidle out of the door. Sidling was not one of his skills but he managed a sort of sideways shuffle.

'Wait. Did you see a label on the lamp post?' asked Phryne.

The huge brow corrugated in thought. 'Yair, I reckon I did. I thought, must have been left over from the unpacking. That all?' he asked hopefully.

'Did you see anyone around?' Phryne asked.

'Lots of people,' said the huge young man, surprised. In retrospect Phryne thought it a foolish question, too. She nodded and Sam escaped, trying not to mow anyone down in his enthusiasm to leave.

'Anything else we can do for you, Miss?' asked Mrs. Truebody.

'Yes. Give me an escort with a torch and tell me how many clocks are in the house.'

Mrs. Truebody nodded intelligently. 'For your riddle, Miss? Quite so. Apart from these two, there are only three. The big grandfather in the hall, the Swiss one with the cuckoo in the study and the case clock on the mantelpiece in the library. Those rooms ought to be empty. I'll lend you little Billy, he's lighter on his feet than Sam.'

'Good. Then I shall leave you in peace and thank you very much for your kindness. And your coffee and biscuits, which were first rate.'

'Very kind of you to say so, Miss,' said Mrs. Truebody, bobbing a curtsy. She promptly dispatched Phryne into the darkened house with a gangling youth, all knees and elbows, who carried a bright electric torch.

Little Billy (who had clearly been named by that method which called redheads Blue and bald men Curly) asked no questions but led the way to the tall grandfather clock. Phryne opened the door with care, and Little Billy let the beams of his torch fall inside. Nothing, except what one ordinarily finds inside a grandfather clock, with the addition of several lost keys, a pen nib and a lot of dust.

The case clock in the library was likewise empty of any interesting clues. Little Billy still asked no questions, which marginally unsettled Phryne. This might have explained why her hand slipped when opening the little door in the cuckoo clock, and the cuckoo dashed out, shouting 'cuckoo!' at the top of its voice. In a noisy classroom during the day it would have attracted attention. In the hushed early hours of the dark house it sounded like the trump of doom. Even worse, something which had been sleeping unnoticed on the study couch stirred. It was shedding blankets as Little Billy and Phryne fled, halting just outside the door, trying not to breathe.

The pestilential bird cuckooed twice more. The sleeper thrashed a little, monotonously cursed the night, the mosquitoes, the beer, and even the canton in which the clock had been made as well as all cuckoos everywhere, and then fell asleep again. Little Billy and Phryne stayed still until their hearts had stopped trying to leap out of their respective breasts, and then crept back beyond the green baize door, where Little Billy carefully extinguished the torch and grinned.

'That was fun!' he said blissfully.

Phryne refrained from clipping him over the ear. Youth will be served, she thought, though sometimes with parsley and white sauce.

'Thank you for your help,' said Phryne, who was still panting slightly with reaction. 'Tell Mrs. Truebody I'll talk to her tomorrow. Goodnight, Billy.'

Phryne slipped away to her own room. It had not sprouted any new lethal traps in her absence. She washed her face in cool water, jammed a chair-back under the locked door handle, and fell asleep, wrapped in her mosquito nets, to await what the morning might bring.

Friday, 28th December

She woke earlier than was her wont, hungry. Outside it was light and almost cool. Phryne washed and put on a cotton dress and loose trousers, clapping a broad brimmed straw hat on her head. Breakfast, her guide to the party informed her, would be served in the breakfast tent, and the scent of bacon wafting towards her proved a sure indication.

There, laid out on trestles draped in the purest white linen, was a full country house breakfast such as Phryne never thought she would see again outside her father's establishment, where he insisted on it. If there were no porridge, kedgeree, kidneys, devilled bones, bloaters, kippers, various kinds of eggs, chops, ham, bacon, fish cakes, collops of venison, curry, toast, marmalade, coffee and tea in oceans and stacks and oodles he threw the nastiest of tantrums and remained beastly all day. Often the only edible meal in the household was breakfast, because most French chefs objected to making such barbaric dishes at such an hour.

And here it all was, with the addition of fruits and grilled tomatoes at the height of their succulence. And glasses of cold water ready for the sachets of hangover-alleviating fruit salts which were piled into little baskets down the length of the table.

Phryne had always found that food made her think better. She took a large plate and loaded it with scrambled eggs, toast, grilled bacon, mushrooms and tomatoes. Then she sat down at a trestle table to eat it. The first forkful decided her on Mrs. Truebody's remarkable skill. The bacon was crisp, the eggs moist, the tomatoes and mushrooms just right and the toast not cold. A feat, a palpable feat.

Minnie recognised Phryne and brought her a china cup and saucer and a pot of coffee. Phryne smiled at her.

'Have you had some breakfast, Minnie?'

'Hours ago,' said Minnie airily, adding her customary giggle. 'I never saw such a breakfast, never. You want to try the devilled bones, Miss, they're very good. And the kippers are real Scotch. So is the marmalade.'

'I'll try some presently. Minnie, what would you say if I said that I was looking for time?'

'Plenty in the garden, Miss,' said Minnie. 'I'd better go,' she added, and fled.

Phryne smiled, and took up another forkful of eggs. Thyme. What a nasty little mind it has, to be sure. But Phryne was not going to be separated from a good breakfast so easily. 'Foundation of the day!' her loathed pater used to announce, and in that he had been right. An empty stomach was no basis for a complicated problem.

After more toast with the Scotch marmalade and a small dish of fruit salad which emphasised the mango and pineapple, Phryne dabbed at her mouth and sauntered into the herb garden, which adjoined the house and was laid out like a knot garden, formal and beautiful. The rising heat was bringing up the volatile oils and the scent of rosemary was strong enough to sting the eyes. There was a whole bed of thymes: lemon thyme, apple thyme, Greek thyme. Phryne had no difficulty finding where someone had scrabbled a little hole. In it was a sealed jar which had once held jam. In the jar was a slip of paper. She unfolded it. There were only two lines in the same educated script as the first:

'Once I drank deep when I was a tree/Now all of you can drink from me.'

'Gnomic,' observed Phryne, replacing it in the jar and screwing on the top. She picked herself a small bouquet of sweet herbs, in case anyone had been wondering what she was doing in the garden, and then strolled into the grounds to find a tree to sit under. She did not want to talk to any Templars this early in the morning. She had a book, and she wanted to smoke a meditative gasper and reflect.

A wooden seat was almost hidden under a massive hornbeam. Phryne ensconced herself there with Miss Christie's latest and lit her cigarette with pleasure. The sun struck gold through the leaves, she was delightfully full, and the unknown riddler had not actually cheated. He had rules and was keeping to them. Phryne had none, which meant, she considered, that she would defeat him in the end.

She had read a chapter or so when something ploughed through the leaves and she saw it was her old friend, Mintie the goat. Drawn, perhaps, by Phryne's nosegay, which included mint.

'Look here, you can't keep shaking the place down for mint,' Phryne told the goat, handing over the herb a leaf at a time. 'Your mistress is going to think I'm a goat thief. You be off, do you hear, as soon as this mint is finished.'

'You got my goat again?' asked a cracked voice.

Phryne sighed. The hornbeam was a big tree but its shade was beginning to feel crowded.

'Yes, she's here,' she confessed.

'It's mint, you see,' explained the Goat Lady, in a good mood this morning, it seemed. This was soon explained. 'I come down early so me grandnephew's boy could gimme some of that toffy breakfast—I been eating for an hour,' she said proudly, patting a rounded belly. She disposed her dresses gracefully as she sank down on the wooden seat next to Phryne. Although the Goat Lady smelt, as one might expect, very strongly of goat, she was not otherwise offensive and Phryne did not move away.

'Some goats just have a real yen for some sort of tucker— I've known 'em to go for pineapple tops, for lacquered straw hats, for leather shoelaces, even for cigarette butts. And they'll do anything to get a mouthful of whatever it is. This one's got a yen for mint. She must have followed me up, remembering that she got some here last night. Goats are smart. They remember things.'

Phryne reached her last leaf and showed her empty hands to the goat.

'Sorry, that's all,' she said. The goat nudged her companionably and sat down at her knee like a large dog. Phryne scratched her behind the ears. This attention was well received. Phryne was beginning to warm to this goat.

'There now,' said the Goat Lady. 'She likes you. Can tell about people, too, goats can. Well, hoo-roo,' she said, getting up and summoning her goat with a gesture. 'See you round, maybe.'

'Maybe,' said Phryne. The small encounter had not been too wearying, so she returned to Miss Christie. That Hercule Poirot. Clues were always transparent to him. What would he make of this riddle game in which Phryne had got herself involved?

'Probably say "*Tiens!*" and whiffle his moustache,' muttered Phryne bitterly. 'That's what he usually does.'

And where was Tarquin? He was a pest, but he was still a small boy, and someone had to look out for him.

Fictional crime lost some of its charm. Phryne stared at the message in the little jar and tried to think.

Satan's Whiskers
1 part gin
1 part Grand Marnier
1 part dry vermouth
1 part sweet vermouth
1 part orange juice
dash orange bitters

Shake together and serve with a twist of orange peel.

Chapter Seven

It was somewhere up the country, in a land of rock and scrub,
That they formed an institution called the Geebung Polo Club.
They were long and wiry natives from the rugged mountain side,
and the horse was never saddled that the Geebungs couldn't ride;
But their style of playing polo was irregular and rash—
They had mighty little science, but a mighty lot of dash:
And they played on mountain ponies that were muscular
    and strong,
Though their coats were quite unpolished, and their manes
    and tails were long.
And they used to train those ponies wheeling cattle
    in the scrub;
They were demons, were the members of the Geebung Polo Club.

                —A.B. Paterson,
          'The Geebung Polo Club'

Presently a young man in a caftan came looking for Miss Fisher
and found her under her tree. It was Jonathan, the reciter of the
previous day. He looked hungover and was speaking care-fully,
as if a sudden move might jar his teeth loose.

    'Miss Fisher? Gerald wonders if you would favour him with
a few words.'

'More than a few, if he likes,' said Miss Fisher graciously.

'And the polo demonstration game begins in an hour,' added Jonathan, who was clearly not going to be out in the heat and dust looking at something so hearty and healthy. Phryne followed him to the Templar tent where Gerald was sitting at a small table with Mr. Ventura.

'You will just have to manage,' she heard Gerald say, and Mr. Ventura, evidently displeased, gathered up a portfolio of papers and barged past Phryne without a greeting.

'Trouble?' asked Phryne.

'Just a little man with no concept of magnificence,' said Gerald. 'Have you found Tarquin, Phryne?'

'Another clue,' said Phryne, and summarised the night's events. Gerald examined the paper in the little jar and professed bewilderment.

'Have you spoken to your sister yet, Gerald?'

'No!' He jumped. 'I mean, no, there hasn't been time, I…'

'Come along,' said Phryne, not unkindly. She took his hand and conducted him into the other half of the space behind the dais, which was divided in two by a rich purple curtain.

Isabella was discovered reclining in her bath, surrounded by acolytes who were washing her hands, paring her nails, combing her hair, and generally vibrating around her like a set of attendant bees. Phryne expected them to buzz, or at least, hum. They all looked up when Gerald and Phryne came in. Pam, Sabine, Marie-Louise, Minou and Even Sadder Alison. What on earth was wrong with the girl?

'I need to talk to you, Isabella,' said Gerald wretchedly.

Isabella waved a hand at the acolytes and they all fled.

'What is troubling you, brother?' she asked in her creamy voice. Isabella did not talk much, making the greater impression when she did. Gerald sat down by the bath and took one of the immaculate hands. Phryne took a chair.

'Someone has stolen Tarquin from me,' he said.

The perfect eyebrows arched. 'Oh?'

'And I wondered if you had him,' put in Phryne, who also wondered what it took to dent Isabella's ceramic serenity. More than this, it appeared. Phryne added, 'If you have got him, can we have him back, please?'

'It is unworthy of you,' said Isabella gently, speaking entirely to Gerald and ignoring Phryne completely, 'to allow such a thought to enter your head. Me, steal? And a child? A moment's thought will show you how ridiculous this is. What would I want with the child and where would I hide him, attended as I am every moment by my friends?'

'True, they would have to know about it too,' observed Phryne judiciously.

Isabella's beautiful face did not grimace, in fact she showed no expression, but her voice hardened. 'Did you help me to look for my little Marigold, brother? Did you care what happened to her?'

'What did happen to her?' asked Phryne, with such fervent sincerity that the sibling quarrel was temporarily derailed. Both sculptured faces turned to her and she put up a hand to fend off all that loveliness.

'We came here three days before the party began,' said Isabella.

Phryne interrupted. She had no time for stream of consciousness narratives.

'Begin with acquiring the child. Did you get her at the same time and from the same place as Tarquin?'

'Yes,' said Gerald. 'We went to the orphanage together. We each wanted a child with no living relatives. I found Tarquin immediately—he found me, rather, he was sitting outside the housemaster's room, being punished for trying to run away. He just threw himself at me and clung—it was very touching. But Isabella had to search through all the girls for her choice. They didn't have a very wide range and most of them were quite impossible, shrill and vulgar. But Isabella has excellent taste and she found the only pearl amongst the beads. Pretty little creature,' mused Gerald. 'Dark hair and eyes, like Tarquin. We both wanted a contrasting child.'

And you chose one as though you were picking out a puppy from a litter, thought Phryne. She remembered Ruth saying to her, 'You can't just take one of us and leave the other behind, as though we were kittens.' She had been right, which was why Phryne had two adoptive daughters. Cruel to select just one and leave the others. That was probably pretty rough on kittens, too. But one could not rescue every cat in the world and Phryne supposed that the children had been pleased with their change of fortunes—at least, she knew that the obnoxious Tarquin had been. And how pleased his orphanage must have been to see the departure of that little troublemaker.

Phryne dragged her attention back to Isabella.

'I knew she was the right one, even though she was dressed in that dreadful institution uniform—grey serge, in this weather!—and her hair was dragged back into a plait. She had dark, restless eyes. I asked her if she wanted to come with me and be my daughter, and she said yes. So we arranged it. The place is dreadfully overcrowded, and the smell!' Isabella looked around for an acolyte to fan her and, finding none, fanned herself. 'I think they were glad to see two of the children settled, even though Gerald and I are not…conventional.'

'Right, so you collected the children and brought them with you to this place?'

'We stayed one night in Melbourne to get them some clothes and things. Tarquin's gold suit,' said Gerald. 'Marigold's clothes.'

'She was dressed as a nymph,' said Isabella. 'A filmy layered dress in shades of apple blossom. She loved it. She paraded in front of the mirror like a little fairy.'

'So you came here with both children,' prompted Phryne.

'We were staying in the house while the marquees were set up and the organisation under way,' explained Gerald. 'One had to supervise to make sure that Tom Ventura didn't cut any corners. Which he is prone to do,' he added. 'The acolytes came down the next day in a charabanc. And vans with the rest of the delicacies. How poor old Syl complained about riding with the tinned crab!' Gerald laughed, a jovial rumble such as a god might have given, and Phryne's mouth curved even though she didn't think it funny. Gerald had that effect on everyone.

'We had a fuss, settling them all into their tents and so on,' said Isabella. 'And then I noticed that the child was missing. She didn't come to lunch. I sent people around, asking, and Gerald just said, "She's run away, you can't trust those gypsy eyes," and refused to take it seriously. Then someone came and told me they had seen the child at the Geelong road entrance, getting into a car.'

'So I was right,' said Gerald. 'She just used you to get out of the orphanage. She had somewhere to go and she went there.'

'Gerald, you are so unfeeling,' drawled Isabella.

Phryne agreed. 'Put a sock in it, Gerald dear. If you want me to find your Tarquin I need all the information I can get. Isabella,' she said, leaning forward and taking the pale hands in her own, 'who told you that they had seen Marigold on the road?'

The comely face looked up blankly, blinking away two tears which ran down the flawless cheeks. 'I don't remember,' she said.

'Try to recall,' urged Phryne. 'I'm going to do some prospecting,' she told the golden twins. 'You think about it and let me know as soon as you can,' she added, and left their company. She heard the quarrel begin again as she let the flaps fall.

The Hispano-Suiza was just drawing up in the forecourt when Phryne came out of the Templar tent. She felt a rush of gladness at seeing Mr. Butler and Dot again. They were so normal. Dot subjected Phryne to a hard stare and, finding her free of visible signs of disease, wounds or moral degeneration, smiled.

'I've got your things, Miss,' she said. 'Are you having a good time?'

'Intermittently,' said Phryne. 'Yes, Mr. Butler?' Mr. Butler had been waving a hand.

'I'd like to find my old friend Tom Ventura,' said Mr. Butler. 'If you wouldn't mind, Miss, I'll just take the car round the back and see how he's getting on.'

'By all means,' said Phryne, and the big car slid away, to general admiration. She led Dot into the denuded house and gained the Iris Room, where she shut both of them in.

'Here's your clean underthings,' said Dot, unpacking her bag. 'And the dress you asked for, and…this. The craft lady delivered it this morning, real early. I hope it's what you wanted, Miss. Horrible looking thing.'

'Yes, but beautiful in its way,' said Phryne, putting the box on the mantelpiece.

'I suppose so,' said Dot reluctantly, piling clean knickers into Phryne's drawer. 'Everything's all right at home, Miss. Mrs. Butler is making pies today and the girls have gone to visit their friend Rebecca. They're sorry for her because Jews don't have Christmas. Mr. Lin called and asked after you, Miss, and said that if you needed him you had only to call.'

'Nice of him,' said Phryne absently. 'Now listen, Dot, this is the situation. Two children have gone missing and some-one is threatening to kill Mr. Templar. These events may or may not be connected. I'm going to tell you all I know in case someone knocks me on the head and I forget it all—no, don't look like that, I was joking. So far the trickster hasn't managed to outwit me, though of course he may in future.'

Dot listened attentively as Phryne rehearsed all that she knew, had learned or suspected about the Templar ménage and its assailant. At the end of the recital Dot said, 'Well!' and then, 'I wonder if the little girl really did run away?'

'A question which I have been considering, Dot dear. Isabella seems to have assumed it on one person's evidence, and now she can't even remember who told her. She has, of course, got cotton wool between her ears. I think she was offended that the girl would run away from her magnificent condescension and decided to ignore her disappearance out of pique. I agree, not nice. But, as Hemingway would say, the rich are different.'

'Yes,' said Dot sourly. 'They're rich. Only difference I've ever seen.'

Phryne grinned. With Bert, Cec, Dot, Lady Alice and her sister Eliza, she was not going to be able to develop delusions about the plutocrats being superior to the working classes.

'Indeed. I don't want to call in the police yet, Dot, because that would spoil the Last Best Party and because I don't think they have a hope of finding anything out in this bizarre gathering. I, being one of it, might have a better chance. I'm in possession of a clue, though what it is pointing to is another matter.'

'Yes,' said Dot. 'Anything I can do?'

'Ask around in Werribee whether they've had gypsies through,' said Phryne. 'I know they travel with carnivals. If the child was actually a gypsy she might have run if she could rejoin her people—then we don't need to worry about her. But if not—well, we'll have to keep looking. The child is ten and ravishing, apparently. She would not be safe on her own.'

'Not with all these nasty people about,' said Dot. 'And I don't just mean your party,' she added, wise in the ways of criminal investigation. 'Well, I'll be going. Got your list for tomorrow? Good-oh. You be careful, Miss Phryne,' she added, giving Phryne a worried kiss, and took her leave to collect Mr. Butler from the kitchen and return to St. Kilda.

She found Mr. Butler finishing a cup of tea in company with the balding worried Mr. Ventura. 'One day down,' said Mr. Butler bracingly. 'Only four to go. You can manage it, Tom. You don't need to worry about the kitchen or the food, Mrs. Truebody's doing that and she works like a Trojan—and makes very good tea, too,' added Mr. Butler. Mrs. Truebody smiled a little and handed over a fresh supply of lemon and passionfruit biscuits. Mr. Butler took three and Dot took one, tasted, said, 'Delicious!' through the crumbs, and asked for another in a napkin to beguile the homeward journey.

Mrs. Truebody supplied a small cardboard box and filled it with assorted biscuits, and Minnie brought out a thermos flask, refilled with good strong tea with milk and sugar. Mrs. Truebody felt that driving in a car was a dangerous and exhausting occupation and the driver and passengers needed to recruit their strength frequently. And she thoroughly approved of Miss Phryne's attendants, who showed a suitable appreciation of her administrative skill and her food.

Tom Ventura bit moodily into a lemon curd tart, heedless of the cream on his moustache.

'Just because nothing's gone wrong yet,' he argued, 'don't mean that nothing will. It's the polo demonstration this afternoon, and anything might happen when those ponies get up speed. And the tennis players waving rackets all over the place. And the swimmers in that cold water…'

'Give it a rest,' said Mr. Butler affectionately. 'You dose him with a nice cup of valerian and chamomile tea, Mrs. Truebody. Always used to work in my mother's day. Then you get your head down and have a nice sleep, Tom. I'll see you tomorrow. You ready, Dot?'

'All ready,' said Dot.

Carrying the thermos and the laundry bag, Mr. Butler led Dot, bearing the box of refreshments, out to the car and settled his companion in the front seat. Dot had graduated to sitting next to the chauffeur and found it less exciting than the back seat. Dot did not like being excited.

'We've got to stop in Werribee,' she told Mr. Butler. 'Miss Phryne asked me to find out if the gypsies had been this way recently. Then we can rest under those pine trees and have a nice cuppa and the rest of those biscuits.'

'I don't want you to breathe a word of this to Mrs. B,' said Mr. Butler in a whisper, 'but those lemon and passionfruit biscuits are better than hers.'

'I won't say a word,' promised Dot, slipping a hand into the box and collecting two biscuits, one for Mr. Butler and one for herself. 'And I think so, too.'

◇◇◇

Phryne Fisher considered that she just had time, before the polo demonstration, to follow up the clue which had been buried in the thyme. 'Once I drank deep when I was a tree/ Now all of you can drink from me' clearly meant a barrel, and there couldn't be too many barrels around, even in a large establishment like Chirnside. She settled her hat and went to the door of the drinks tent.

'Not open until noon,' said a tall young man, barring her way with a brawny arm. Phryne gave him a ravishing smile.

'I'm on a treasure hunt,' she said in a thrilling whisper. 'If you let me examine your barrels I'm sure that Mr. Templar wouldn't take that as an infringement of the rules.'

'I don't know, Miss...' he hesitated, then took the coin she pressed into his large, wet hand. 'Come in then, before them other thirsty buggers notice,' he said, and Phryne slipped inside.

There were four barrels in store and one which had been broached, sitting in its cradle. Phryne tapped and examined all four, finding nothing except things which one expects to find in and on barrels. When she turned her attention to the barrel on the cradle, it had no telltale label.

'Are these all the barrels you have?' she asked.

'Yair, lady, don't you think there'll be enough?' exclaimed the barman jocularly.

'You never know,' said Phryne mysteriously, and slipped out into the sunshine again. Damn. Still, there was the house, which might well have barrels in the cellar. She would have to wait until after the polo now. People were already making their way to the huge ground, where goals had been set up, patrolled by men on horses. Two other men in white coats, evidently umpires, were cantering up and down a long rope, fixed to the earth with tent pegs, which apparently was some kind of boundary.

About now, Phryne knew, some likely young man who fancied his chances would arrive at her shoulder, offering to tell her all that she never wanted to know about the rules of polo. She found a shady spot and leaned confidently against a tree. And there he was. Tall. Well dressed. Scented with liniment.

'Hullo-ullo-ullo,' he said breezily. 'I'm Ralph Norton, Miss Fisher, we met at the gate. I was driving that little Austin.'

'To the public danger,' said Phryne severely. 'And you're hoping to catch my interest by telling me all about polo?'

'Er…' said the disconcerted young man. 'Er, well, yes, Miss Fisher.'

Always a mistake to be seen to be too intelligent, Phryne told herself. She relented. 'Very well, then,' she told Ralph, who really was rather ducky in his tight polo clothes and polished boots. 'Instruct me.'

There was a pause while Ralph tried to work out if this astounding young woman was somehow mocking him. Phryne actually saw the moment when he decided that she couldn't possibly be, fine fellow that he was. He straightened his shoulders. He took a deep breath.

'Polo is played by two teams of four, in eight chukkas, which last for seven minutes each. The aim is to get the ball through the goals at either end, there. You have to hit the ball with a polo mallet, those big bamboo-handled things.'

'Following you so far,' said Phryne gravely. 'Who are the two teams?'

'Well, there's us, the Grammar Boys, we all went to school together, except for Johnson and he's a good chap, you'd never know, and there's the up-country lads—they even have girls on their team, bad show altogether. Our captain complained but Templar said they could field werewolves as long as they played well. Girls can't possibly ride as well as men, so we will beat them easily—but it's not a good show, you know.'

'Indeed,' murmured Phryne. 'You're playing in the real game too?'

'Yes, Miss Fisher. Two o'clock on Monday. Will you be watching?'

'Oh, yes,' said Phryne. 'And would you care to wager a little on your inevitable victory? Say, five pounds on the Wonnangatta Tigers?'

'Done and done,' said Ralph promptly.

'And you will be,' said Phryne with a smile.

'Oh, good show,' said Ralph, as the first riders came prancing onto the ground. 'There are our chaps. And there's the others. You'd think they could clip their ponies, at least. They're as shaggy as old sheep.'

The Wonnangatta Tigers were not sartorially splendid, it was true. They were all wearing a uniform, more or less, blue shirt and scrubbed white moleskins. Thereafter they differed; the hat was of the rider's choice, and ranged from old leather through dainty white canvas to new straw. Their ponies matched the riders. They were shaggy, as Ralph had observed. But they were bright eyed and danced a little on their hoofs. Phryne thought them charmingly rustic.

The Grammar Boys, on the other hand, were gorgeous. Their jodhpurs were impeccable, their shirtfronts white as snow, their uniform of red and gold almost too bright to view without smoked glasses. Their ponies were polished to a fine gloss, their manes and tails bobbed or braided and their tack gleaming.

The first demonstration was put on by the Tigers. Eight of them lined up to watch an umpire fling out the ball, and then they were off in pursuit. They rode raggedly, all knees and elbows. Phryne saw Jill in the middle of the melee, shouting. But they bullied the ball down the length of the field and through the goals.

Phryne particularly noticed a small pony, apparently called Mongrel, ridden by a long-legged boy called Dougie. They looked absurd as a pair, but it was Mongrel who somehow crept through the pack and allowed Dougie to flick the ball out from under another pony's legs, and then shepherd it down the ground, running with a curious scurrying, sure footed gait which was neither a canter nor a gallop but something that Mongrel had clearly invented for himself. When the ball went through the wide goal Phryne distinctly heard the pony snigger.

'Odd-looking beast,' commented Ralph.

'It is undeniably effective,' Phryne pointed out.

'Mmm,' said Ralph. 'Here they come again. By Jove, some of them can ride, all right. Look at that chap on the grey!'

Phryne wondered whether she should tell Ralph that the chap on the grey was actually Jill, a palpable girl, and decided not to ruin his day quite yet. There would be time for good old Ralph. The Tigers belted the ball through the opposite goal to massed cheers.

'Oh, well done!' said Ralph. 'Must go, Miss Fisher. See you later, perhaps?'

Phryne decided she didn't dislike him as much as all that and watched while the Tigers came panting off the ground and the Grammar Boys came on.

My, but they were brilliant. They lined up, eight of them in red and gold like an Assyrian cohort, and saluted the flag. Then they trotted around in a tight circle, their ponies dancing and occasionally jerking their heads out of control, clearly keyed up and nervous with all these new sights and smells. Highly strung, thought Phryne from under her tree. I suppose they breed them for sensitivity. How are they going to cope with country matters, I wonder? Birds and beasts and heat? I bet they haven't been ridden more than once a week. Whereas those Tigers' ponies probably spent their colthood wheeling cattle in Gippsland scrub. Well, we shall see.

It was a polished, well-drilled display. The ponies' neat little hoofs flashed, drumming the hard ground. The riders barely moved in their seats. The ball sped up and down the ground, foiled neatly every time it appeared that someone was in a position to shoot for goal. After ten minutes, Ralph rose in his stirrups, gave the ball an almighty whack, and it flew through the goal. At this all of the Grammar Boys gathered round to congratulate him before they trotted off the field and surrendered their mounts to their stable boys.

It had been an interesting demonstration but now Phryne should resume her prowling, searching for barrels. Before she set off for the house she thought she ought to go and congratulate the girls on their performance. She went down the slight slope to the horse lines, where ponies were being unsaddled, rubbed, walked, and finally allowed to drink water with the chill taken off.

'I say, Miss Fisher, wasn't that a good show?' asked Ralph, grinning hugely.

'A very good show,' agreed Phryne cordially.

'Stay for a stirrup cup?' he asked, waving a bottle of iced champagne.

'Not today,' said Phryne. 'But thank you.' She walked on through the Grammar Boys' lines and into the huddle of animals and people which was the Wonnangatta Tigers' encampment.

'Well done, Jill,' she said to the young woman, who was rubbing down her coal black pony.

'Thanks,' said Jill. 'Stand over, Black Boy, damn you! Gosh, it's hot, isn't it?'

'Forfeit,' said Ann, who had not ridden and was standing by with a tray on which reposed a bottle of beer and two glasses.

'All right,' said Jill, leaning for a moment on the pony's side while she groped in her pocket. She tossed a penny onto the tray.

Phryne looked her question and Ann giggled. 'It only makes it worse when someone is forever saying "it's hot" when it's really hot,' she explained. 'Jill has already had her chance to say "it's hot" today.'

'It is, however,' said Phryne. 'You ride very well. What did you think of the Grammar Boys?'

'They're good,' said Ann. 'And they've got real purebred polo ponies and lots of remounts. But we're fast,' she added loyally.

'Well, my money's on you,' said Phryne. 'Now, I've got to find a barrel.'

'There's one over there,' said Jill, not asking why Phryne was looking for a barrel.

So there was. It was a large barrel full of water for the horses and there, stuck to its side, was the telltale luggage label with the clerkly script on it. Phryne peeled it off carefully and read it aloud: 'Your next will not inebriate/But causes you to cerebrate.'

'Oh, a riddle game,' observed Ann. 'But that's a hard one. What on earth does it mean?'

'I can't imagine,' said Phryne grimly.

The Joker was mildly distressed, which was his approximation of strong emotion. The acolytes were so pretty. The music was so sweet. He liked music. But a contract was a contract, and at least, provided he acted with skill, the corpse would be very beautiful.

Chapter Eight

Things are seldom what they seem
skim milk masquerades as cream
Highlows pass as patent leathers
jackdaws strut in peacock feathers.

W.S. Gilbert
H.M.S. Pinafore

Phryne collected her luncheon hamper in a bad mood. She stalked across the grounds in a worsening mood and then exclaimed in disgust. She saw that someone was already sitting under her hornbeam tree. Curses on them. She approached, ducking under the long hanging branches decked out in brightest green, ready to evict and possibly maim the trespasser.

The young man jumped to his feet. Phryne did not know him, but he was good looking and apparently civilised and he had come here, as she had, for refuge from the sun and a nice quiet read. Phryne picked up his book, which had fallen from his lap when he stood up. It was, she saw to her delight, *Whose Body?* by Miss Dorothy Sayers.

'Phryne Fisher.' She held out her hand. The young man shook it.

'Nicholas Booth. Pleased to meet you.'

'You came here for some peace and quiet, eh?' continued Phryne, briskly. 'So did I. So you can have that end of the wooden bench and table, and I'll have this end, and we needn't interrupt each other.'

'If you're sure you don't just want me to go away…' He had cornflower blue eyes and Phryne had a weakness for cornflower blue eyes.

'No, not at all. You being here will protect me from any other invaders. And I am a great admirer of Miss Sayers.'

'Golly, Miss Fisher, so am I. What are you reading?'

'*The Murder of Roger Ackroyd*, by Miss Christie,' said Phryne. 'Now, let's sit down and make ourselves comfortable before someone gazumps us.'

She arranged her hamper and thermos at one end of the wooden bench and seated herself a judicious distance away from the young man. The hamper contained a selection of very good sandwiches, a bunch of grapes and some of Mrs. Truebody's superlative biscuits in a small cardboard box. The thermos contained, by Phryne's especial direction, hot black coffee. She propped Roger Ackroyd against the hamper and began to read. After a moment's delay, the young man did the same and they dined amicably in complete silence, except for the rustle of greaseproof wrappings and the turning of pages.

The day grew hotter. Lunch had been filling and perfect for a hot day. Even liberal doses of coffee weren't going to keep Phryne awake. She had read the same line five times with-out the faintest idea of what it meant. She gave up and shut the book.

Nicholas Booth was already asleep, neatly and unobtrusively. Phryne knew that sleeping outdoors was utterly forbidden to any lady. She lay down on the grass, relying on her citronella to keep insects away, pillowed her head on her bag, and closed her eyes just for a moment.

When she awoke it was past three o'clock, the heat was appall-ing, and she knew the answer to her riddle. When she tried to sit up she remembered why taking naps on hot days was so unwise. It had the effect of a sweet sherry hangover.

She staggered to her feet, feeling as if she had been hit over the back of the skull with a blackjack. Fortunately, there was still coffee in her thermos and she gulped the life-giving fluid, concentrating on the answer, making sure that it didn't vanish like a dream. Nicholas Booth was still asleep, and she did not wake him as she gathered her things and left the shade of the hornbeam, heading for the kitchen.

The cup that cheers but does not inebriate, in the old Temperance parlance, was, of course, tea. The array of things which could contain a note which related to tea—pots, cups, urns, kettles, caddies—was huge, but the thing could be done by a determined woman who was getting rather tired of being pulled about as on a leash by someone with a twisted sense of humour. It was here, she thought, that a few accomplices would be useful, but she dared not share the secret more widely, especially with the kitchen maids so nervous already. She needed a pretext and went in search of Mrs. Truebody.

The housekeeper was taking a well-earned rest, sitting in her upholstered chair and drinking a refreshing cup of—well, tea, Phryne noticed.

'Someone has played a little prank on me, Mrs. Truebody,' Phryne said. 'They've borrowed a not very valuable ring and I will only get it back if I can solve the riddle. Now it occurs to me that your assistants handle most of the tea-making apparatus in the house. I'm happy to give a small reward to the one who finds either the ring or another label like this—with writing on it. By the way, do you know the fist?'

'No, Miss Phryne,' said the housekeeper. 'Young men will have their fancies, I suppose. Leave it with me, I'll see to it,' she said, and Phryne took her leave.

The day was wearing on. The cries of the tennis players were dying away. Just the moment for a nice swim, now that the sun was off the lake. She had time before collecting her costume for this evening's Japanese revel.

Ten minutes later Nicholas Booth, who had woken up as if hungover, stunned by heat and had also sought the haven of the lake, looked up from his watery cradle to see something flash across his gaze like a crimson bird. It was a woman in a red bathing cap and a red costume, who had entered the water in a flat, expert dive. She came up spouting, turned over and floated.

'I'll wager that feels better,' he said to her.

'It certainly does,' she agreed. 'Ah. Mr. Booth. What's that strange little island in the middle of this lake?'

'It's artificial,' he said. 'It's supposed to have a shell grotto in the middle but it's all locked up.'

'I can live without a shell grotto,' Phryne told him, 'but I'll race you to the island.'

She was off in a flash. Nicholas turned over in the water and launched himself into a powerful crawl. Phryne did not have a recognised stroke. She swam, he saw, like a seal, diving just under the water and coming up periodically for air. And she was fast. Her hand slapped the shore of the little island before his and she turned a laughing face to him. He was enchanted.

'Well done!' he said. 'You must have been a mermaid in a previous life.'

She smiled at him and he had the odd feeling that he had just passed some sort of test. Phryne anchored herself by one toe and relaxed back into the water.

'I think we ought to consider that an introduction,' she said. 'My name is Phryne, Mr. Booth.'

'And mine is Nicholas.'

They shook wet hands. Nicholas joined Phryne, mooring himself alongside her. She noticed that he was tall, young and prettily made. Not marble-perfect like Gerald—someone had broken his nose for him at some past date, and his mouth was too wide for beauty—but pleasantly male.

'So what brings you to the Last Best Party, Phryne?' he asked.

'I knew the Templars in Paris. I thought it would be interesting to see them in such a new and rustic setting. You?'

'Oh, I'm just a boring public servant. The Templars bring a lot of glamour into my humdrum existence.'

Phryne had prudently obtained a supply of gin slings and had borrowed a couple of glasses from the drinks tent. Her expensive English thermos flask kept things ice cold as well as piping hot, just as the advertisement had said. Nicholas laid down his bag of letters and poured drinks as requested. He wasn't used to strong cocktails and sipped carefully.

'What have we here,' said Phryne as she spread out the letters, ordered them according to the numbers written in the top left hand corners and read them. They were not informative. 'Not the same hand as my labels,' she said after comparing the two. The riddles were written in a scholarly hand in blue ink. The letters were scrawled in black ink on Woolworth's paper. The letters were short and all repeated the same phrase: 'Die, you fraud'. Some added, 'I will kill you', or 'Watch every shadow'. They were not signed or even set out like letters.

'Not very informative at all.'

'I see what you mean,' said Nicholas Booth ruefully. 'Hardly worth pinching, really. Someone thinks Gerald is a fraud, and is intending to kill him. Odd, you know, you could call Gerald many things, but fraud isn't one of them. He genuinely believes in what he does—or so it seems to me,' he added, deferring to Phryne's opinion in the most charming manner.

'Oh, I agree.' Phryne sipped her drink thoughtfully. 'Cheap paper, post office ink. Might have fingerprints but they'd be Gerald's and yours and mine and Isabella's by now. Nothing helpful on the envelopes. Bundle them up and put them back, will you? No need to upset the Lady more than necessary. I'll wait here for you.'

She sat quite still, looking like the expensive Japanese dolls that doting sailors bought for their little daughters in Tokyo, which are immediately put on a shelf as too fragile to play with. Nicholas took the vision of her with him as he walked too briskly for his garments back to the Templar tent.

There was a tap on the door which stirred Phryne out of her trance.

'Yes?' she asked as Minnie bobbed a curtsy to her.

'Oh, Miss, you do look beautiful! Mrs. Truebody's compliments, Miss, and can she see you for a moment when convenient?'

Minnie had evidently learned this piece of antique courtesy by heart and was anxious not to forget any of it. Phryne picked up her fan, secreted a number of items in her sleeves, and accompanied the young woman to the green baize door.

Mrs. Truebody was flushed and beaming. 'I've found your label, Miss Phryne,' she said. 'After the whole staff went through every teapot and cup and kettle we own. You'll never guess where it was.'

'No, where?' asked Phryne, intrigued.

'In the Toby jug! You see, your clue said that you had to cerebrate, and that means brains, and so I thought it might be a head, and there it was. Not that it helps, perhaps,' said Mrs. Truebody, handing over the blue bordered label.

'Wonderful,' said Phryne. 'Here's the reward, and a couple of bob for the staff—I take their efforts very kindly, Mrs. Truebody. Thank you all very much.'

The door had swung open and the whole kitchen was staring at Phryne in her butterfly silks. She blew them a kiss and went back to her room, where Nicholas Booth was waiting.

'You left the door open, anyone could have got in,' he exclaimed.

Phryne shrugged, a very un-Japanese movement.

'At the moment, dear boy, they seem to be able to get in whether I lock the door or not. Did you get the doings back to Isabella without being noticed?'

'Yes,' he said.

'And I've got another clue. Same hand, same ink. "I am the kindest, deepest, first. Sinless and wicked and needed and cursed".'

'What does that mean?' asked Nicholas, his brow crinkling.

'Not the faintest at the moment,' said Phryne. 'But I am carrying all my clues on my person for the present. So it can go in my nice little card case with the others,' she told Nicholas. He had caught sight of other objects in her sleeve.

'Phryne, a pistol?'

'My very own little pearl-handled Beretta for which I have a licence. Don't fret,' she said, leading the way out of the Iris Room. 'I won't shoot you unless I have a reason.'

'Oh, good,' said Nicholas Booth gloomily, following in her magnificent wake.

Dinner was to be appropriately Japanese. Phryne wondered how her joints would stand up to sitting on the ground for an extended time and decided that others would crack before she did. The area in front of the Templar tent was decorated with paper lanterns and silken banners. What sounded like a real Japanese orchestra was playing music on stringed instruments which set Phryne's teeth on edge.

'The RSPCA will hunt them down for what they are doing to that cat,' murmured Nicholas Booth, wincing. A young man with a sensitive ear, it seemed.

'What sort of music do you like?'

'Bach,' said Nicholas. 'And Beethoven. And I'm very partial to a bit of jazz. Have you heard that woman singing with the Three T's? Rip your heart out of your…er…well, chest. You?'

'Jazz,' said Phryne. 'Gilbert and Sullivan. Vaughan Williams. Bach when he isn't being too mechanical. Sometimes he sounds just like clockwork.'

Nicholas' mouth opened to defend his beloved composer but Phryne was going on. He had noticed this conversational habit of hers and there seemed nothing to be done about it.

'Mozart. And jazz,' she concluded. 'Play your cards right and I'll introduce you to Nerine, your jazz singer. She's an old friend of mine.'

'Gosh, Phryne, really?' Nicholas' eyes shone with heroine-worship. Nerine had that effect on all susceptible—that is, functioning—males.

Phryne nudged him. 'Remember what you promised to do. Watch for the reaction. Let's lurk under this tree for a moment. I want everyone to be there and sitting down before I make my entrance.'

'You're good at grand entrances?' asked Nicholas with studied innocence.

'Yes,' said Phryne honestly. 'I'm already twenty-eight. I might be able to make two or three more great entrances, the ones which, when one wakes at three in the morning from a nightmare, one drags up to warm the bones.'

'I didn't mean…' Nicholas began, obscurely feeling that he had insulted her.

'Vanity, vanity, all is vanity, that's what you were thinking, eh? You'd be right. Nothing wrong with a little vanity. If we cannot love ourselves we can certainly not love anyone else.'

'I think you're on shaky theological ground there,' Nicholas told her.

She looked entrancing in the fading light, her whitened face and red lips mask-like and mysterious and unbearably exotic. He wondered what her mouth would taste like if he kissed her now.

'Possibly. Anyway, who died and made you Pope? Come along, my presbyter. And keep your eyes peeled.'

She folded her hands in her sleeves, leaving the bracelet to gleam brown and red and cream against the vermilion outer robe. Nicholas followed as Phryne, an almost perfect geisha, walked with tiny steps to the edge of the gathering, now all sitting on the ground. The musicians saw her and worked their way toward a crescendo. Drums beat. Strings wailed.

Phryne made a slow bow to Gerald and another to Isabella, and someone in the gathering gasped aloud. Nicholas located the noise. And noted another person whose jaw had dropped and whose eyes were like saucers. Then he seated himself next to Phryne. The experiment had been a success. Around her sleeve Phryne wore a papier-mâché bracelet which depicted, in very realistic colours, a coral snake curled and ready to strike.

◇◇◇

'Today is Holy Innocents' Day,' said Dot.

'Who were they?' asked Ruth.

'Don't they teach you any religion at that school of yours?' demanded Dot. 'When Herod heard that the child Jesus had been born, he sent his men out to find him, but they failed. And the Magi, who had promised to come back and tell him where the baby was, they were warned by an angel and went away. So, to make sure that he killed the baby Jesus, the cruel King Herod—'

'Oh, yes. Ordered the soldiers to kill all the children,' said Ruth. 'I forgot it because it's so awful. What sort of king makes his soldiers kill children?'

'Almost any sort,' said Jane. She was a student of history.

'Well, they shouldn't,' declared Ruth. 'It's unfair.'

Dot shrugged and went on with the story. '"Take the mother and child and flee into Egypt," said the angel.'

'Why did they have to take a flea?' asked Ruth.

Jane giggled, and therefore got no chocolate once the misunderstanding was sorted out.

Chapter Nine

All thoughts, all passions, all delights, what-
ever stirs this mortal frame,
all are but ministers of Love,
and feed his sacred flame.

S.T. Coleridge
'Love'

It did not take long before conversation broke out again, but
Phryne had elicited that moment of silence which was her acco-
lade. She accepted a tiny cup of green tea and asked Nicholas,
'Did you hear?'

'Yes,' he said. 'I say, Phryne, this tea hasn't got milk or
sugar.'

'No, it's green tea, just drink up,' she advised kindly. 'Think
of it as flavoured hot water. This meal may prove to be a revelation to you, my meat and three veg man.'

'Nothing wrong with meat and three veg,' said Nicholas.

Phryne flipped open her fan and smothered a high-tension
giggle. She used the fan to cover both their mouths as she leaned
close to him and asked, 'Who gasped?'

'Sylvanus,' said Nicholas. 'But the one with the face like a
goldfish was Jonathan.'

'I do hope the trickster isn't Syl,' she said, sotto voce. 'I've always liked him and I thought he liked me, and that coral snake was a murder attempt. If my cat hadn't had very fast reflexes and hadn't woken up cross I might have been fatally punctured. Still, one can never tell with people. Do you know anything about Jonathan?'

'A bit. Your cat killed it?'

'Yes. I should imagine that he is presently being overfed with smoked salmon by my sister, who never saw the reason for cats as house pets before. Of course, they aren't often called upon to kill snakes in Christmas packages. Go on.'

'He's twenty-five,' said Nicholas. 'He joined up with the Templars in Paris, where he has family, a sister and a younger brother. His father is a wine importer, based in Lyons and London. Got a house in both cities. Fairly rich family. Jonathan went to Oxford University but was sent down without taking a degree. Read history and classics. Nothing known against him,' he said.

'I wonder why he was sent down without a degree?'

'Don't know. You could ask him,' said Nicholas.

'So I could. Oh, how very nice, we have miso soup.'

'What's that when it's at home?' asked Nicholas, glaring down into the cloudy depths of the bowl. Phryne tapped his wrist with her folded fan.

'Bean paste, perfectly pleasant. Just pick up the bowl in both hands, like this,' said Phryne, shaking back her sleeves to demonstrate. 'And sip.'

Reluctantly, Nicholas allowed that the miso soup was not actively poisonous. Phryne eyed him with amusement.

'The last bastion of conservatism,' she commented, 'is food.'

'Oh, I do agree,' said Guillaume, who was sitting on Phryne's left side and sipping with enthusiasm. 'This is very good miso soup. I was in Tokyo for a couple of years,' he added. 'It was as much as my poor cook's life was worth to try Japanese dishes on the European visitors. I came upon him almost in tears once, saying that all he was asked to cook were large lumps of dead beast, and it was too much, and he was going home to Hansi province where he was appreciated.'

'Poor man! What did you do to comfort him?' asked Phryne.

'I ordered a huge banquet with all his specialities and invited the local warlord. I owed him a favour, anyway. He arranged that my goods didn't go missing off the docks.'

'For a small fee?' asked Nicholas.

'For teaching his sons English and French,' replied Guillaume. 'He was a forward looking man. They assassinated him just after I left to go to Paris. It was sad. He was a real loss. But in Paris I met the Templars, so it was a fortunate journey.'

'Indeed. Where on earth did the Templars get this Japanese feast? And the musicians?'

'They know a lot of people. I believe that they are all off a Japanese ship. Cooks as well, and the supplies. I have to import my miso paste directly from Japan, and my wasabi powder. No one keeps it here.'

'Are you likely to return to Japan?'

'Not soon,' said Guillaume. 'The situation is a bit…well, fluid. Politically. Nationalism, you know. Not comfortable for foreigners. Friend of mine had a crowd of about eight hundred outside his compound, screaming for his head on a pole. He just got onto a ship with his skin and his ceramics intact. He valued his ceramics much more highly than his skin, of course. Collectors are all the same.'

Phryne agreed and they discussed collectors and their strange ways—Nicholas knew of a collector of steam engines, and Phryne of a man whose life was devoted to stuffed fish— as the next course, a fine tempura of vegetables and seafood with a delicate soy dipping sauce was carried around. This introduced Nicholas to his next challenge: chopsticks.

'It's simple. You keep the bottom stick stable and move the top stick like a pair of pincers,' said Guillaume, demonstrating. Nicholas tried. After being briefly convinced that he had the wrong number of fingers for this skill, all of them thumbs, he managed to make the points meet and beamed with pleasure.

'Brilliant,' said Phryne. 'Not for us the humiliation of asking for a spoon. Take up a piece of fish, thus—' she did so— 'and dip it in your little plate of sauce, thus—' she held a napkin underneath to fend off the sauce from her kimono— 'and you eat it. Thus. Oh, very nice,' she added.

Nicholas managed to lift a piece of fish to his mouth and found the batter so evanescent as to melt on the tongue. He liked it. He said so. Phryne applauded and fed him a morsel from her own chopsticks. Guillaume smiled. He knew what that meant. So did Phryne.

Sitting across from Phryne were Alison, the sad English girl, her friend Amelia, Pam and Sabine. Sabine was urging Alison to try the battered fish.

'It's just like fish and chips, without the chips, my lamb,' she coaxed. 'And at least it's Christian food. Tomorrow it's Arabian and Gerald is such a madman about it all being authentic, we'll probably have to eat sheep's eyes. There, now, doesn't that taste good?'

Alison admitted that it did and ate some more. The servers carried around wide wooden dishes of beautifully displayed raw fish, seafood and vegetables carved into flowers. There was a dish of pale green paste with every platter. Nicholas sniffed it, said, 'Oh, horseradish,' and took a large mouthful before Phryne could prevent him.

Nicholas barely had time to notice that what he had bitten into was not, in fact, horseradish, when he was conscious only of the inside of his mouth bursting into flame and buried his face in the large napkin Miss Fisher handed him as his eyes spurted tears, his ears rang, probably with melting wax, and his nose spouted.

'Oh, my poor bairn, that's wasabi,' exclaimed Sabine in her soft Scots voice. 'Ten times hotter than the hottest vindaloo, but a rare thing to clear out the sinuses.'

Nicholas, who previously had not known that he had sinuses, nodded. They were clean and he had probably lost a portion of his brain cells, too. He reached for the iced water decanter and drank it, then grabbed for another and emptied it in turn. Gradually the burn died into a pain, and he stopped crying. He became aware that Phryne was apologising.

'I'm so sorry, dear boy, I didn't manage to stop you in time,' she said.

Nicholas felt a strange elation, as though the top of his head had blown off.

'Think nothing of it,' he said generously. 'What's this stuff?'

'That,' said Phryne, 'is a radish rose. That is raw fish, and so is that. That is sea urchin which tastes like spoiled egg yolk.'

'Say not so,' objected Guillaume. 'But I'll eat yours, if you like.'

'Feel free,' said Phryne. 'This,' she said, as a steaming platter of rice was carried to the diners, 'is steamed rice and to go with it is *toki teriyaki*, which is chicken. You will like it. Have some.'

Light headed with wasabi, Nicholas eschewed the raw fish and took a spoonful of the chicken. It was, indeed, good, almost as salty as vegemite. Sad Alison, Amelia, Pam and Sabine ate raw fish as though they had been suckled in Tokyo, and gossiped. Phryne and Nicholas listened idly.

'You haven't heard from your sister, then?' Sabine asked Alison.

'No, but I'm sure she'll be all right now that…now that we have all left. Mama has found her a nice place in a nursing home in Brighton.'

'That's good. And she still won't tell you?'

'Oh, she told me.' Alison's voice was leaden. 'Is this drink any good?' she asked, lifting a little pot of warm sake from its heater.

'It's a bit strong,' said Phryne, mindful of her failure to preserve Nicholas from the wasabi. 'I think you might like the plum wine better. Nicholas, pour the lady a drink, will you?

Traditionally served cold,' she said, dropping some pieces of ice into the glass from the covered ice bucket in front of her. She briefly wished she could crawl into the bucket, and reflected that Japanese food was at least appropriate for a hot climate. So were the clothes. Phryne was wearing three layers of silk and hardly felt them. It was like being dressed in strikingly coloured air.

Alison gulped down the plum wine and held out her glass for more.

'Nice,' she said, as Nicholas refilled her glass. 'Is there pudding?'

'Not in a Japanese meal,' said Guillaume. 'They don't do dessert, it's a Western invention. My cook used to say that sweets were only for children. Try some of the sea urchin,' he said generously. 'It really is delicious.'

The rest of the diners declined, so Guillaume settled down to a sea urchin feast with small cries of delight. Phryne was full. Holding back her sleeve with one hand, she poured Nicholas a cup of sake and had one herself, even though she was convinced that the faint, oily overtaste was actually turpentine. The musicians were going wild. A velvet curtain was being drawn between two trees. A heavily made-up person in remark-able robes leapt into the space.

'Oh,' said Sabine, delighted. 'We are going to have a Noh drama! How wonderful!'

'Hmm,' said Phryne ambiguously. She had already sat through the only Noh drama which she intended to endure in one lifetime. She pressed the fingers of her hand meaningfully on Nicholas' shoulder, pushing him a little away. He patted her hand in understanding.

'Well, before it begins, we must visit the amenities,' she told her fellow diners, rising stiffly from her knees. 'Back in due course.'

Nicholas stood up to escort her. As they crept away, Phryne heard Sabine tell Guillaume, 'I know this one. It's *The Ground Spider*!'

'Fabulous,' he responded.

Sad Alison did not speak. Phryne wondered about that bit of conversation she had overheard. Alison's sister had every reason to be sad, it appeared. Was it the usual, Phryne wondered, or something more arcane? And what did Alison mean when she said, she will be all right now that we have gone? Curious. Phryne was almost out of the circle of light when someone caught at her hem.

'Agape tonight,' said Jonathan from the ground. 'Are you coming?'

'Perhaps,' said Phryne, and removed her dress from his clasp.

'What is this agape thing?' asked Nicholas, when they had retreated to the refuge of the house. 'They've invited me several times but it sounded a bit iffy so I haven't gone.'

'It's not at all iffy, if by that you mean that your honour might be compromised,' said Phryne, leading the way to the WC near her own chamber. 'Just wait for me, I won't be long.'

Nicholas waited, and then replaced her. It had been a long dinner. When he came out she took him by the sleeve and led him into the empty dining room, where she sank down on a brutally hard bench by the window.

'Well, what is it?' he asked.

'*Agape* is Greek for "love",' she said slowly. 'Agape is also an ecclesiastical term in the Church of England for a love-feast. The Templar agape is a love-feast, with the added thrill of a method of avoiding a climax called karez. Have you heard of it?'

'No,' he said, a bit worried by the term 'climax'. Was it what he thought it was? Did women have them? He asked. Phryne laughed.

'Yes, it is what you think it is, and of course women have them,' she said. 'You haven't got a lady friend, then, Nicholas?'

'No,' he said. 'Well, yes, I have been walking out with a young lady, but I'm sure that she doesn't know anything about…'

'Then it is up to you to teach her. Recipe for a happy marriage, just ask Marie Stopes. Where was I? Ah, yes, agape. This sort of communion was thought to have been invented by the agapemonites. *Agapemone* means "abode of love". Other-wise known as the Community of the Son of Man. They believed in the spiritualisation of the matrimonial state, which was otherwise positively soggy with sin. They put all their possessions into the common stock expecting the end of the world soon, as instructed by their priest, one Henry Prince. They broke up in scandal because one of the sisters became pregnant. They aimed for purely spiritual unions, you see. Love-feasts supplied the human need for closeness.'

'What happened to the agapemonites, then?' asked Nicholas, his head spinning. No lady he had ever met had talked this way before.

'Despite the Holy Ghost having taken residence in his body, the immortal messiah died in 1899 and ruined his chances of ascension. He is supposed to have been buried standing up. So that he would be ready for the resurrection, you see.'

Nicholas laughed uncertainly.

'It was a dotty idea, I agree. But the love-feasts were adopted by the Templars, and the karez is the reason why they were not rubbed out by the Parisian police. Because nothing untoward happens in them. I'm going tonight, why don't you come with me? It's like fairyland. Just remember the rules. Don't smoke anything. Don't eat anything. If nothing else, a Templar karez agape is an experience.'

'You still haven't explained about karez,' complained Nicholas, as Phryne led him to her room and he watched her begin to remove the Japanese costume. She unaffectedly shed the headdress and all but the innermost of the kimonos.

'I'd just upset your modesty,' she said. 'Here. There's an exposition in the purple book. You read it, and I'll have a quick wash.'

She vanished, wrapped in her towel, and Nicholas took off his Japanese cap and started to read the essay on karez which had been provided for the partygoers. He was only a few lines into it before he was very glad that Phryne wasn't there. He was blushing as red as a sunset and Mrs. Truebody could have boiled a kettle on his head.

He rummaged for the vacuum flask, poured himself a cold drink, and managed to regain his calm. That a lady should have read such things! It was appalling. But somehow it was very hard to disapprove of Phryne, partly because he sensed that she wouldn't care a scrap if he did. And in any case, when she said that karez would not damage his honour, she spoke the truth. A virgin could indulge in agape all her life and still be classified as a virgin. He supposed.

His confusion was not much relieved when Phryne came back.

'All clear, then?' she asked him, nodding at the pamphlet, and he nodded back, not willing to enter into a discussion about it. 'Good. I've had an idea about that riddle. Go along and have your wash—what are you wearing under that robe?'

'Running shorts and a singlet,' he confessed.

'Very decent,' Phryne approved. 'I'll just sit here and write.'

Nicholas went. It seemed the simplest solution. His last glimpse of Phryne was her concentrated profile as she seized a pencil and a notebook and sat scribbling very quickly.

When Nicholas came back she was dressed in a simple cotton shift dress which left her arms and legs bare. She approved of his running clothes and picked up the bundle of their Japanese costumes, which she had carefully folded and rolled.

'The Noh play ought to be over by now,' she told him. 'Even Noh plays come to an end eventually. They must. Ah, yes, I hear the howling and the crescendo of drums which must mark...'

'A climax?' suggested Nicholas, who had learned a new word.

Phryne gave him a considering look. All she said, however, was, 'Indeed.'

They lurked on the outskirts of the gathering as the actors and musicians were applauded and left. The night was hot and still. Gerald Templar led the way into the purple tent, holding his sister by the hand. An antechamber had been set up where the initiates shed their costumes and put on tight calico drawers and a loose white caftan. Nicholas managed to find one to fit him and Phryne took his hand.

'Come along,' she said, and he followed her into the gloom.

The floor of the tent had been laid out with soft mattresses, covered in cotton sheeting. The company gave at the knees as they came in. Nicholas stayed close to Phryne's side as she found a suitable mattress and sat down on it, pulling the young man down onto his own mattress beside her.

Hubble-bubble pipes were lit. Smoke wreathed the still air. Nicholas began to feel light headed. It was a pleasant sensation. He lay down on his mattress. Caftan clad people moved slowly through the tent, offering trays of dark chocolatey fudge. Phryne waved them past, but took a bottle which seemed to contain water. She took a sip and passed it to Nicholas. It was cold water, tasting of roses.

Music began to play, sweet choral voices singing a chant which sounded rather religious. Then Gerald and Isabella came down and joined the congregation, and the love-feast began.

'Agape,' said Phryne to Nicholas, curling herself around so that she was lying beside him. 'Now you say "agape" to me.'

'Agape,' said Nicholas, and Phryne kissed him very gently.

Her underlip was like satin and she tasted of roses. He gasped and she smothered his gasp with her mouth. All around him he heard the acolytes murmuring like birds settling down to rest, as the pipe smoke rose to the roof in sweet clouds. He stroked Phryne's back under the white caftan, and she wriggled with pleasure. Someone was caressing his feet, soft hands like clouds. He had never been so aware of having skin. All of it seemed to be alive.

Phryne slid both hands down his back, relishing the feeling of orderly muscles, then cupped his buttocks, squeezing hard. He was now as aroused as he had ever been in his life. Still the sweet music went on, the delicate voices, the murmuring of the initiates. Lifting himself on one elbow he saw Gerald lying passive under the loving attentions of four people. They were stroking his face, kissing his mouth, touching his chest, sliding their hands down his thighs.

When he looked back the woman Sabine was kissing Phryne's feet, gradually working her way up her body, and Nicholas was almost shocked, except he seemed to have lost the knack of it. He surrendered. He forgot to think. He buried his face in Phryne's belly, mouthing and sucking, noticing that her skin was quivering under the thin fabric, which was becoming transparent as she perspired in the heat. The sharp points of her nipples invited suckling, and he suckled. She jerked, her hands closing into fists. Then she sighed and smiled like an angel.

'Lie back,' she said to him, and he lay down while Sabine transferred her kisses to his ankles and Phryne kissed slowly down his neck to his chest, chest to belly, belly to those parts covered by the calico chastity knickers. And they were no bar to her clever fingers, which wormed their way under the caftan and past the tight waist band to touch, to stroke, and then to perform one movement which would have made Nicholas groan with pleasure if Sabine had not covered his mouth with her own.

'Naughty,' she said to Phryne. '*Mechant.*'

Phryne agreed. '*Mechant* it is,' she said, and slipped down, supine, for Nicholas to fondle her again. He lost all sense of time. He would not have taken any bets on who he actually was. He did not know how often he had elicited that sharp sigh from Phryne. But he was weary and greasy with sweat and not all that steady on his feet when Phryne dragged him out of the throng. Most of them seemed to be sleeping. Phryne led the way into the antechamber and told him to reclaim his clothes.

'Just drop the others in that pile,' she said, shaking back her hair. 'I am so hot! Race you to the lake.'

She was off and he managed to struggle into his shorts and follow the sound of her flying feet. He sighted her as she reached the lake and pulled the shift over her head. Underneath she was as naked as the day she had arrived to grace the planet with her ineffable presence. She dived in and Nicholas tore off his clothes and splashed after her.

The water was cold and dark and sobering. It washed the sweat and juices of desire off his body. It felt good and he dived, feeling the heat leach out of his body into the water. Phryne surfaced beside him, spouting water like a nymph.

'I will never again go to an agape in this weather,' she declared. 'I nearly melted.'

'But it felt good?' he asked, suddenly unsure of the significance of all those little sighs. Did they mean what the book told him they meant? Phryne threw wet arms around his neck and kissed him.

'Lovely,' she said. 'You will make someone a very good husband. Useful lessons have been learned tonight. But nevertheless, Australian summers are too hot for karez. They're too hot for making love, as well. In my boudoir I have a basin of ice and an electric fan, which renders the nights tolerable. And tonight I have to sleep in that little room, stifled by the heat. Oh well, it's all in the interests of justice. And if I say Jack Robinson to you, my dear, what would you reply?'

'I don't know,' said Nicholas, sounding puzzled. 'What would you like me to reply?'

'You're very good,' Phryne told him. 'But I will find out, you know.'

'Find out?'

'Don't overdo it,' she advised him. 'Now, I'm going to float in this divinely chill water until I turn as blue as possible on such a night, then I'm going to bed. Thank you for a most enjoyable evening,' she added, kissing him again.

She released him and lay back in the embrace of the water, relishing the cold of the spring-fed lake. Nicholas grunted and did the same and they lay amicably side by side.

After about an hour the hearties woke and came leaping and shouting, and Phryne and Nicholas removed themselves discreetly, redressed and headed for the house. The Templar tent was silent. The lovers were all asleep.

The house appeared asleep, too, as they crept inside. Nicholas bade Phryne a decorous good night and was about to leave when Big Sam from the kitchen arrived and begged for Miss Fisher's assistance. One of the kitchen maids, it seemed, had gone suddenly mad.

'Noblesse oblige,' said Phryne.

'Perhaps I can help,' said Nicholas, and Big Sam preceded them to the green baize door.

They were so elegant and deadly, his ladies. Eleanora, Elissa, Madeleine, Mirielle and Belle. He gazed at them lovingly. Ever true. Ever beautiful. Ever faithful.

Chapter Ten

Helper and healer, I cheer—
Small waifs in the woodland wet—
Strats I find in it, wounds I bind in it—
Bidding them all forget!

Kenneth Grahame
The Wind in the Willows

The kitchen maid was Minnie and she had evidently been struck down with something. She was sitting on the floor in a dishevelled state. She had pulled off her cap and let down her hair, which was long and fine. She was muttering to herself.

'Oh, Miss Phryne, can you help?' asked Mrs. Truebody, as disturbed as she would have been with breakfast to cook and the bacon still undelivered. 'She's not drunk. I can't smell spirits on her.'

'Minnie?' asked Phryne. She knelt down next to the girl, took both her hands and pulled her around so that her face was in a bright light. Minnie winced and covered her eyes.

'Ah,' said Phryne. 'Don't worry, Mrs. Truebody, it's not serious. And it's not her fault, either. Did she by any chance clean out the fudge bowl? Or perhaps eat a burned corner?'

'Probably,' said Mrs. Truebody. 'No one is rationed in my kitchen.'

'Even though Miss Isabella would have told you not to allow anyone else to eat the fudge?' asked Phryne gently. Mrs. Truebody bristled.

'She had the brass-bound nerve to tell me who could eat what in my own kitchen!' she exclaimed.

'Quite. Do not, however, eat any of it in future. The people with the Templars are used to it—it's strong medicine,' said Phryne. 'We'll just take her to her bed and she'll be fine in the morning, though hungry.'

'I'll carry her,' offered Big Sam.

'Thank you,' murmured Phryne, who was very tired. 'You can go to bed, Nicholas. I'll see you in the morning.'

Nicholas, finding himself surplus to requirements, said goodnight and left.

Big Sam hoisted Minnie without apparent effort. She giggled. She kept on giggling all the way through the back kitchen and into the yard, then through the corridors to the servants' wing.

'The names are on the doors,' grunted Big Sam. Minnie was trying to curl his ear around her finger and the giggling was beginning to get on his nerves.

'Betty, Amy, yes, here we are.' Phryne surveyed the neat little room. 'Put her down on the bed, Sam. I'll just take off her shoes and maybe her dress, and tell her to go to sleep.'

'And she'll sleep?' asked Big Sam, rubbing his insulted ear and turning his back.

'Oh yes, they're very suggestible, the hash eaters.' There were rustling noises. Then Phryne said very firmly, 'Go to sleep, Minnie. Go to sleep right now,' and Sam turned back to see the maid's eyes closed.

'My word,' said Sam.

'Now, get me out of here and back to my own room by the fastest way,' ordered Phryne, 'or you might have to carry me, too.'

'I could do that, Miss, if you like,' said Sam admiringly. He liked women who took charge.

'I'll let you know,' said Phryne.

Big Sam had a long stride and Phryne had to trot to keep up with him.

'Fastest way's past the old boarded-up scullery,' he told her. 'Where the girls reckon they hear the ghost.'

'No ghost is going to get between me and my lawful bed,' swore Phryne. 'Lead on.'

Big Sam did as he was told. There was little lighting in the yard now that the house was asleep, and the shadows near the boarded-up scullery were as black as pitch. Phryne was suddenly assailed with a terrible feeling of loneliness and despair— not her own emotions, someone else's. She stopped dead to listen and Big Sam came lumbering back.

'Quiet,' she said, holding up a hand. 'Do you hear that?'

'Must be the wind,' said Sam uneasily.

'There isn't any wind. Listen. Like a child sobbing.'

'I don't hear nothing,' said Sam stoutly and untruthfully. He could hear it and it was giving him the willies.

'Do you keep any tools in any of these sheds?' Phryne demanded abruptly.

'What sort of tools?'

'Case opener, jemmy, anything to get those boards off?'

'There's a case opener in the back kitchen for crates,' he said.

'You'll go and get it,' she told him, 'then you'll come back here with a torch and we'll have those boards off. Come along, Sam,' she said. 'Great big bully like you afraid of a little ghost?'

'No fear,' he said, and obeyed.

Left alone, Phryne did not try to see, because it was too dark. She laid an ear against the boards and listened. The feeling of despair was overwhelming and she could taste brass in her mouth. If this wasn't what she thought it was, then it might well be a ghost. The sobbing continued.

Big Sam came back before she had time to get too frightened. He brought with him a case opener, a sledgehammer, a torch, and reinforcements in the form of Gabriel. They stood shoulder to shoulder, waiting for orders. Between them, Phryne considered, they'd have no trouble bringing down a good solid stone building, much less a mere assemblage of badly nailed planks.

'I want all those boards off as soon as you can,' she told them. 'But quietly, too. No need to wake the whole house.'

Big Sam grinned at Gabriel. They flexed a few muscles. Then they each took hold of an end of one of the boards and peeled it off the wall by main force. As a spectacle, it was impressive. Phryne held the torch and dodged flying splinters. In not much more than the average trice, the boards were all removed and a door stood revealed. Behind it Phryne could hear something wailing.

'Open that door, Sam,' she said urgently. 'Right now!'

Sam shoved his huge comrade aside and inspected the door. Then he crooked two sets of fingers in the gaps above and below it and hauled. Once, twice he hauled, stamping as the door cracked and protested. No door could have stood it. Immovable object became movable with Sam's irresistible force and broke in half. He dropped the bits and dusted his hands, grinning as Gabriel slapped him on the back.

Through the cloud of dust and broken door something wailed and slumped into the yard, and Sam caught it by reflex. It was a child.

Phryne took charge before they could react. 'Gabriel, go get Mrs. Truebody right away, but don't tell anyone else what has happened. Sam, you hold her up. I'm going to look into this prison.'

Phryne took the torch and inspected the ghost's lair. It was a small stone building with a flagged floor and roof. There was an old sink with a tap which dripped. There was a drain in the floor. There was nothing else. No crumb of food. No coverings. No bed. Not even a cup.

Phryne felt the sense of despair ebb and fade away. 'Alas, poor ghost,' she told the air. 'I'll take her away, and you can rest in peace. And when I find out who has done this, they will be sorry. I promise.'

By the time Phryne had left the old scullery, Mrs. Truebody arrived. She listened carefully as Phryne outlined her problem. The child had stopped wailing and was snuggled into Sam's embrace.

'She's been—oh, four days without food? There's a tap in the sink or she would have been dead. Someone in that ménage out there tried to kill her. I need to hide her in a safe place until I catch the assassin and she recovers. At least enough to tell me what happened to her.'

'Poor little mite!' Mrs. Truebody was affected. 'She can be… my sister's youngest child, here to recover from a…'

'Bout of pneumonia,' suggested Phryne. 'That's not infectious.'

'And needs feeding up,' agreed Mrs. Truebody. 'She can have the little room next to mine. We'll get her cleaned up and into bed before you can say Jack Robinson, with a nice bowl of my chicken broth inside her.'

'Do you understand?' Phryne asked the wild, ragged figure in the remains of a pink dress. 'These nice people will look after you until I can give you back. Will you stay with them?'

The child nodded. Then she whispered something. Phryne leaned close to hear.

'I want him to stay,' she said, touching a thin hand to Big Sam's chest.

'You'll feel safe if he's with you?' Phryne guessed. The child nodded again.

Mrs. Truebody blew her nose. Sam was affected, too. His eyes moistened and the end of his broken nose wiggled eloquently. Of course, this rescued scrap might have been the first child who hadn't taken one look at him and run screaming for its mother.

'He can stay,' said the housekeeper. 'Now, my girl, it's into the bath with you, and then we'll see about some food. You'll talk to me tomorrow, Miss Phryne?'

'Tomorrow,' yawned Phryne. She was exhausted.

As she walked away, Mrs. Truebody called, 'What's her name?'

'Marigold,' said Phryne.

She stumbled through the green baize door into the main house, found her own room, and neglected even to put a chair-back under the door handle as she tumbled into bed and was asleep before her head hit the pillow.

Saturday, 29th December

Usually Phryne woke all of a piece, knowing who she was and where she was (though not, on some occasions, the actual name of the person reposing beside her). Many of her bedfellows had informed her that this was one of her most irritating qualities. She had lost the devotion of a French poet, for instance, who had departed yelling, 'Can't you at least find some existential angst?' and she had been laughing too much to properly bid him farewell. Phryne knew who she was and what she was and she liked all of her.

This morning, however, found her lightly dazed, possibly from lack of sleep, and terribly, terribly hungry. Though she knew where to search for the next annoying little luggage label, she threw on some clothes, conducted a scandalously sketchy toilette and headed straight for the breakfast which was laid out, in all its splendour, under its awning.

With entirely undisguised greed, she grabbed the largest available plate and piled it high with eggs, bacon, kedgeree, grilled tomatoes, mushrooms, and something she couldn't quite identify but which might have been Swedish hash. It had corned beef in it, anyway. She carried the plate back to a table and demolished it so quickly that her silverware made a small tattoo all of its own. Then she went back for kippers, devilled kidneys, bubble-and-squeak and cold ham. This took her slightly longer, as the kidneys had been devilled with the kind of English mustard which comes in a powder and can only be eaten unaffected by old India hands who took their vindaloo at volcanic heat. Phryne fanned herself, dabbed her eyes and drank some water.

She was still hungry, however, and accompanied her pot of coffee with a lot of buttered toast thickly spread with Scotch marmalade. A white peach and, on mature consideration, another white peach, completed her meal and she sat back and sighed with repletion.

'Only three goes at the buffet?' asked a voice. Nicholas sat down beside her. His cornflower blue eyes were just as azure in the morning. 'I ate my way through five, and the waitress was dead lucky I was occupied when she came asking about tea or I might have devoured her as well.'

'I know. That's what breathing hash smoke does for you,' said Phryne, lighting her first cigarette of the day with pleasure. 'As my father used to say, "I could eat a cow; milkmaid, stool, bucket and all." And apart from starving, how do you find yourself this morning, Nicholas?'

'I just looked under the blankets and there I was,' he said, grinning. 'I feel fine. Not that yesterday wasn't strenuous. And lovely,' he added quickly, in case Phryne thought he had forgotten her most welcome erotic attentions, which he hadn't. And never would. He had a feeling that Phryne was branded on his mind. The day that had contained Phryne and wasabi had to be unforgettable.

'Well, there have been developments,' she said, and told him all about Marigold and what Phryne had done with the child.

'Why hide her?' asked Nicholas.

'Use your loaf,' said Phryne. 'Someone kidnapped her once, no reason to think they wouldn't do it again. She's staying with the admirable Big Sam between her and harm until I've worked out what is going on. Any kidnapper trying his luck with Big Sam is going to be seeking all around the grounds for his strewn limbs. Now, have you eaten enough? I have to go and follow another clue.'

'I'm with you,' declared Nicholas, taking an apple from the bowl on the table. Phryne decided that she really couldn't eat another peach, which seemed a shame. They were perfect peaches.

'What are we doing in the billiard room?' asked Nicholas, a little later. He was looking around for somewhere to discard his apple core. 'Feel like a game?'

Phryne gave him a look—the one that worked on traffic wardens—and he recoiled a little.

'The riddle said "I am the kindest, deepest, first". Now there is only one thing which could apply to all of those things, and that is "cut". The first cut is the deepest. The unkindest cut of all. Agreed?'

'I would point out that it says kindest, not unkindest, but all right,' said Nicholas, still holding the apple core.

'Throw that core out the window,' said Phryne crossly, 'and pay attention.' Nicholas opened the window, threw out his apple core, said, 'Oh, sorry,' and shut it again. Phryne continued: 'The next line says, "Sinless and wicked and needed and cursed". That sounds like a knife. A surgeon uses a knife for good, a bandit for evil. Both wicked and sinless, see? And when we add "needed and cursed" I think we have a military blade of some sort.'

'Why do you say that?'

'Partly because it would be hard to make a label stick to a knife in the very clean Mrs. Truebody's kitchen, where every knife is scoured. And partly because I can see the blue and white corner of a label on that sabre there, on the wall.'

'Simple,' said Nicholas.

'Even Sherlock Holmes said it was a mistake to explain,' said Phryne, rolling her eyes. 'Can you get it down for me, please?'

Nicholas reached and lifted and laid the sabre on the billiard table. He found an envelope glued lightly to the wall behind the weapon and brought that down too.

'Another riddle on the blade,' said Phryne. 'What's in the envelope?'

'A ransom demand,' said Nicholas slowly. 'But a strange one.'

'Well, of course it is strange,' Phryne told him. 'Everything related to the Templars is strange. Something normal would be the strange thing in this milieu. What does it say?'

'It says, "Buy ten thousand shares in Triceratops Holdings Pty Ltd before tomorrow closing. Otherwise Tarquin dies". No signature. That's all.'

Phryne examined the note. 'Plain paper, blue scholar's script. Same as the labels. Buy shares? That's an odd demand.'

'What about the riddle?' asked Nicholas.

'Luggage label as before: "Quarried, carried, carved and holed/Doomed to perpetual wet and cold". Nasty. His scansion is getting worse, have you noticed?'

'What are we going to do with the note?' demanded Nicholas, not offering any opinion on the poetic merits of the riddle.

'To whom is it addressed?'

'To Gerald Templar,' Nicholas replied.

'Then to Gerald Templar it must go. Why don't you take it to him, and I'll go and talk to Marigold.'

'Shouldn't we call the police?'

'No,' said Phryne, and he watched her departing back, straight and determined, and sighed. Then he went in search of Gerald Templar. Phryne went in search of a telephone. She needed information and Dot would get it for her.

Mrs. Truebody was resting after the exhaustions of breakfast and gathering her strength for an attack on lunch, which was again to be packed into hampers, after which preparations for dinner would begin. Who'd be a cook, thought Phryne. She remembered a shearers' joke about their cook: the boss demanded, 'Who called the cook a bastard?' to which the chorus replied, 'Who called the bastard a cook?' And the shearers' nickname for any cook was 'the poisoner'.

Phryne sat down next to the dozing Mrs. Truebody and closed her eyes. The kitchen noises were very soothing. She was neatly asleep in a moment and the maids smiled to see the two of them, the slim fashionable lady and the stout housekeeper, slumbering peacefully side by side.

After half an hour Mrs. Truebody awoke and her snort of consciousness woke Phryne, too. She blinked and yawned like a cat.

'We were both up late,' said the cook, signalling to Minnie for coffee.

'We certainly were. How is the child?'

'Well, Miss, I reckon a few days' feeding and she'll be all set to rights. In body. In mind, I don't know. She hasn't hardly let Big Sam out of her sight since you found her and if she tries to sleep she screams something awful. And the ends of her poor little fingers are all torn from trying to dig a way out through the stones. Should we get a doctor to her, do you think?'

'No, he would want to give her sedatives and that does not help in this sort of thing. Unless she's been injured—interfered with?'

'Not that I could see,' said the housekeeper, without turning a hair. Ruling a large establishment for forty years didn't leave a lot of human sinfulness unaddressed. 'I bathed her and put arnica on her bruises and iodine on her scratches and Elsie lent her a nightgown. She's been sleeping in snatches. Do you want to speak to her, Miss Phryne?'

'If I could,' said Phryne.

'Minnie will escort you,' said Mrs. Truebody. She raised her voice a little. 'Everyone else will return to their duties or all those guests will go hungry at lunch, and we will be shamed.'

This produced a flurry of activity. Gabriel, who had been sharpening knives, began to use them on paring legs of lamb and ham and a roast of beef into thin slices. Elsewhere, bread was being cut, tomatoes, cheese and onion portioned and lettuce shredded. An array of the most delicious cakes were today's desserts. Mrs. Truebody passed a large plate of chocolate cake to Phryne.

'This might persuade the child that you mean well,' she said, and smiled a very weary smile.

This brouhaha had been hard on poor Mrs. Truebody, thought Phryne as she allowed Minnie to conduct her to the servants' quarters. Another crime to add to the riddler's list of criminal charges.

'How are you feeling today, Minnie?' she asked. Minnie blushed.

'I woke up real hungry,' she said. 'But it's all my own fault, I did eat just a corner of the fudge, where it had caught and scorched. After they told us not to eat it. I won't do that again,' said Minnie. 'Here we are, Miss. Do you want me to wait?'

'No, I can find my own way back. You go and make up hampers—I don't want to miss out on another excellent lunch.'

Minnie bobbed an almost curtsy and vanished. Phryne knocked gently on the plain deal door. Big Sam opened it with the care needed from someone who could just as easily have wrenched it off its hinges. He grinned when he saw her.

'Come in, Miss,' he said.

'Hello, Sam,' said Phryne. 'How is your charge?'

'Hungry,' said Sam. 'Appetite like a wharfie. Marigold,' he addressed a figure sitting up in the maid's iron bed. 'Here's a lady with cake.'

Marigold, cleaned and combed and dressed in a flannel nightgown, was a different creature to the haunted wreck that Sam had carried out of the old scullery. Only her eyes were restless, never staying focused on one thing. Phryne handed over the cake, napkin and fork, and watched the child eat. Big Sam took his chair and put a bookmark in a small volume.

'What are you reading?'

'*The Wind in the Willows*,' he said, a little abashed. 'Marigold reads real good. It's about Mole and Rat,' he said.

'And Riverbank,' said Marigold. Her voice was uncertain. After all, she had done nothing for the last four days but scream. 'And picnics. Who are you?'

'This is the lady who found you,' said Sam, a little severely. 'She told me, break the door, and I broke it, and there you were.'

'That was you?' asked Marigold. She had dark hair and eyes. She reached out bandaged hands to Phryne. 'Thank you. I never thought I'd get out. I thought I'd die in there. In the dark. In the orphanage they used to lock us in the cellar when we'd been naughty. I always used to scream.'

Phryne took the injured hands in both of her own and sat down on the bed.

'I heard you,' she said. 'And I felt you. A terrible despair. The maids thought you were the ghost of a girl who killed herself.'

'Oh, her,' said Marigold. 'She was sad. She didn't mean me any harm. She was someone to talk to. In the dark. I think she's gone now. I think I felt her go when Sam broke the door.'

Phryne let this astonishing statement whizz through to the keeper.

'You're safe now,' she told the girl. 'Sam will make sure that nothing happens to you.'

'Yair,' said Sam, flexing a few muscles. Marigold gazed at him with adoration.

'He once picked up a bull,' she told Phryne. Phryne could credit it. Sam looked down modestly.

'Did you see the person who put you into that prison?' asked Phryne. 'I need to find them.'

'Yair,' said Sam again. 'Me too.'

He extended both hands. They were as big as hams. Then he clenched both fists. Tendons sprang up on his massive forearms. Muscles moved out of the way of other muscles. Marigold giggled.

'I didn't really see,' she said to Phryne. 'I was looking at the milking cows. I like animals.'

'House cows just behind the old scullery, in the yard,' said Sam.

'Then someone put a bag over my head and marched me to the scullery and threw me in and the door shut and then there was hammering.'

'I wonder why no one heard it?' asked Phryne, seeing the girl begin to tremble and knowing she didn't have a lot of time.

'It was dinner time. Everyone was doing something,' said Marigold.

'And the noise in that kitchen's real loud,' said Sam. 'No one would have heard. Now don't you take on,' he said to Marigold, engulfing her in a huge embrace. 'Here's Elsie. She's brought your morning tea. She'll sit with you while I go for mine. I won't be more than half an hour,' he said, replacing the child in her sitting position. 'And maybe the lady will read to you.'

'Of course,' said Phryne. 'If you remember anything at all about the person, you tell Sam and he'll tell me. This is our secret for the moment,' she added.

Marigold's face lit with the light of revenge. 'Yes,' she said.

Sam went out, Elsie came in, and Marigold was provided with chicken broth, a selection of sandwiches and another big slice of chocolate cake. She had milk to drink and Elsie had brought her own tea.

Marigold spooned soup. Elsie sipped tea. Phryne opened the book at the marked page.

'The Open Road,' she began to read. 'The Rat was sitting on the riverbank, singing a little song. He had just composed it himself, so he was very taken up with it, and would not pay proper attention to the Mole or anything else…'

Sherry Cobbler

Mix a cup of sugar with slices of lemon, orange and crushed pineapple. Add a cup of sherry, two cups of lemonade and a cup of shaved ice. Mix well.

Chapter Eleven

D'ye ken that bitch whose tongue is death?
D'ye ken her sons of peerless faith?
D'ye ken that a fox with his last breath
cursed them all as he died in the morning?

John Woodcock Graves
'John Peel'

Saturday, 29th December

Phryne found Dot staring incredulously at a man who was dressed as a woman. Several of the Lady's men liked to wear the clothing of the opposite sex. The man in the fetching lilac petticoat and chemise was joined by a young woman with cropped hair who was wearing flannel bags and a singlet. They kissed passionately.

That was too much for Dot, who averted her eyes. When Phryne reached her, she might have been praying.

'Come along, Dot dear, is that your basket? Good. This way.'

She took Dot's hand and conducted her to the Iris Room. Dot faltered.

'Miss, that man…and that lady…'

'Yes, and it just shows you what you've missed by being such a good girl, eh? How are things at home?'

'All well, Miss, the girls are behaving. Luckily they like Miss Eliza. And if they annoy her she threatens to read Marx to them. Oh, and that bad black cat stole the whole knuckle end of the ham. Just whipped it off the kitchen table neat as neat and was out of the door like a shot. Miss Eliza told Mrs. B not to worry because he had saved your life and deserved a few treats.'

'I can see that by the time I get home Ember will have to be greased to fit sideways through the door. No mail?'

'Here's your letters, Miss.'

Dot handed over a bundle and Phryne leafed through it. Bills, bills, flyers from fashion houses and invitations to various parties. Nothing interesting. No letter in neat scholarly blue. But what was this? A slim envelope addressed to the Silver Lady in Lin Chung's own hand. Phryne put it in her bosom for later perusal.

She gave the remainder of the mail back to her companion, who was teetering on the verge of telling Phryne something she didn't like to tell. Phryne prompted her.

'Well, Dorothy?'

'Someone has been ringing up, Miss, and when we answer the telephone they just hang up. It's very annoying and Mr. Butler roared at them last time. They haven't called since. He's complained to the telephone company and they say they can't do anything about it. Could it have something to do with your investigation, Miss?'

'Possibly. Blow a whistle down the phone next time. That ought to crack the malefactor's eardrum for him. Or her, of course. What news about that company—what was it? Sauropods Inc?'

'No, Miss, Triceratops Pty Ltd. I rang Mr. Jamieson the stockbroker,' said Dot, proud of her mastery of the frightful technology of the telephone. 'He doesn't know a lot. It's a mining company, prospecting in the Pilbara for silver, lead and zinc. I've written it all down,' Dot added. 'He said that there's been a lot of interest in it lately. It's been selling far better than expected.'

'Not surprising, if people are being blackmailed into buying the shares.'

'But, Miss, the market's closed for the holiday. It won't open again until the second of January. After New Year, you know,' said Dot. 'What's the point of buying shares now?'

Phryne thought about it.

'The investor's money is in the hand, Dot dear, and the company doesn't have to prove itself until the market opens again. Classic in its simplicity, and explains why the ransom note only arrived today. I couldn't have gone any faster finding the clues—well, I admit I have been a trifle interrupted, perhaps. Led astray, even. But this pretty scheme relies on the market being closed. I shouldn't imagine there's so much as a penny's worth of silver, lead or zinc in the Pilbara. So as soon as the market opens again the shares will crash and voila, the blackmailer keeps the money. Legally. Did Jamie tell you any-thing about the directors?'

'He was a bit cross, Miss, he's on holiday himself. But he said he'd ask around. The Companies Office is closed, of course.'

'For the holiday,' Phryne nodded. 'All right, Dot, well done. We shall make a telephonist of you yet. Mrs. Truebody, who is the housekeeper here, has agreed to take messages for me on the house phone. Here's the number. Call me if you find out anything that might help. Now, have you got some clean knickers for me?'

'Yes, Miss, of course, and all the other things you asked for,' said Dot, shocked that Phryne would think she would forget anything. She collected the laundry bag, gave Phryne a fresh one, and laid out the underwear and sundries in the small room's chest of drawers. If Dot wondered how Phryne had managed to get, simultaneously, grass stains, water stains and wine stains on her simple cotton shifts, she didn't comment aloud. 'I'll bring the folly dress tomorrow,' she told her employer. 'What's your fancy dress tonight?'

'Arab, I gather,' said Phryne. 'Son of *The Son of the Sheik*. Well, that's that. Where's Mr. Butler?'

'Talking to that Mr. Ventura. Mr. B's sorry for him, I think.'

'And he deserves it,' said Phryne. 'Gerald and Isabella must be hell to work for. Sorry, Dot, shouldn't have said hell.'

''That's all right, Miss Phryne,' said Dot equably. From what she had overheard, that was an understatement.

'Come and we'll have a chat with Mrs. Truebody,' said Phryne. 'And we can collect Mr. B as well, before his poor abused ears fall off.'

After waving bye-bye to Dot, Phryne found herself at something of a loose end. It was still early. The polo match wasn't until Monday. She didn't feel like swimming.

She opened Lin Chung's letter. In his exquisite hand it said simply: 'If you need me, call, and I will come. Yours in every possible way, Lin.' That was agreeably lacking in preconditions. Phryne kissed the letter. She did not need Lin at this moment, in fact she had a point to prove about how well she could manage on her own, but she might need him in the end and it was nice to know that he would come if she called.

The weather, which had approximated the genial atmosphere at the heart of Mt. Hekla, had cooled with the coming of a south-west wind, but this was accompanied by an annoying amount of blown dust. Phryne had just decided that under a hornbeam was the place to be when she heard the drumming of hoofs and threw herself aside. She had not been in any danger. Ralph Norton brought his pony to a halt as though all four feet were on a sixpence, and grinned at her.

'No need to fling yourself around like that, Miss Fisher, my Caroline can stop on a penny and jump like a cat. Isn't she just the most beautiful girl you've ever seen?'

Caroline was mouse-coloured, with red and gold ribbons braided into her mane and tail. Phryne stroked the soft nose and the pony whickered, breathing hay scented breath down her neck. She had deep, gentle eyes. The fact that Ralph Norton doted on her improved Phryne's opinion of him. Horses had a tendency to bite large holes out of hypocrisy or cruelty.

'She is,' said Phryne. 'And she's as glossy as silk. How do you get her hoofs to shine like that? It can't be just ordinary boot polish.'

'It isn't,' said Ralph, dismounting and feeling in his pocket for a carrot, which he gave to the pony. 'It's blacking mixed with champagne. A little expensive, but brings the hoofs up like nothing else can. Has to be French champagne, mind, not that awful Australian stuff.'

To use the words 'extravagant' and 'outrageous' to this young man would have been using language he did not speak, Phryne reflected. Caroline shifted on her burning bright hoofs and nudged Ralph for some more carrots. He obliged. She munched.

'Coming along on the hunt?' asked Ralph. 'I can borrow a mount for you, if you feel like coming out for a day's sport. Gerald Templar is riding, and so is Miss Isabella. They say she rides like Diana herself.'

'I've seen her in the Bois de Boulogne,' said Phryne. 'A very good seat, I admit. No, I am not coming along on any hunt— what are you hunting? Surely not a fox?'

'No,' said Ralph. 'They're bringing it in now—see? Here come the hunters. I say, just look at Miss Isabella.'

Phryne looked. Hair clubbed severely, male riding clothes immaculate, Diana's own self, Miss Templar, trotted past on a tall bad-tempered chestnut gelding. It ramped, almost bucked, and kept snatching mouthfuls of leaves off passing trees.

'I'll buy that horse at your funeral, Isabella,' called Gerald.

He was also immaculate, from polished boots (champagne blacking again? Phryne wondered) to snowy stock with pearl pin. His roan mount was more docile, or perhaps Gerald was controlling it with more skill.

'Don't say rude things about Tonnerre,' said Isabella. 'He doesn't like it.'

'I couldn't say enough rude things about Tonnerre,' said Gerald frankly.

'Just because you are riding that sluggard Acorn,' observed Isabella, as Tonnerre backed, flinched and conceived himself threatened by a blown piece of paper. She coaxed his wild head around, explaining that it was just a piece of paper and not the horse-eating monster he seemed to have identified in it.

'She's good,' said Ralph, breathing heavily through his nose. 'That brute is a…well, brute. Her brother shouldn't let her ride it.'

Gerald seemed to share his opinion. 'I wish you'd ride Nuthatch. He won't actually try to kill you.'

'Hush,' chided Isabella.

Phryne saw that both polo teams and a reasonable number of the hearties, who had beguiled the previous days playing sport and emptying barrels, were gathered in a rough line, waiting for the Templars. Phryne saw Jill on Black Boy and Ann on George, and Dougie on Mongrel. And Nicholas on a rangy grey which was idling away this tedious waiting time by chewing its bit.

Gerald and Isabella rode to the centre of the line. Standing beside Phryne was Sylvanus, who had a large pocket watch in his hand.

'Now,' said Gerald.

Two men had hauled up a large cage and, at this signal, opened the door. Nothing happened until the beast within turned around and saw a gateway to freedom. Then it took off like a medium range shell.

Phryne had time to see that it was a fallow deer. Sylvanus began counting, checking off the seconds by reference to the watch. The deer flew towards a distant patch of grey green which marked the beginning of the forest. There it would be very hard to find. Dogs whined. Horses shifted restlessly. Sylvanus counted.

'Twenty-eight, twenty-nine, thirty,' he said.

'Tally-ho!' cried Isabella, and she and Tonnerre sprang into the chase. The hunt was up. Ralph whooped and followed. In a minute the drumming of hoofs had faded, and the two work-men began to pack up the cage.

Phryne sat down on a lawn chair where she could see the hunt, and Sylvanus slumped down beside her.

'The unspeakable in pursuit of the inedible,' he observed. 'As the divine Oscar said.'

'Yes,' said Phryne, who disliked hunting. She had been dragged along a few times by a rather charming MFH, and she had found the spectacle beautiful and the blood-lust distaste-ful. Red-faced squires watched happily as the fox was killed and dismembered by belling hounds. Men who had never had to depend on their hunting skills for their next meal watched and cheered.

Phryne ate meat and if pushed could have killed her own dinner. If it was her or the chicken it wasn't going to be her. But she rather liked foxes and could not see why, if they raided farms, they should not be decently and quickly disposed of, rather than tormented until they died. It was no use hunters saying they did it for the sport. If so, they might as well hunt an aniseed drag. No, they needed that blood reward. It was disgusting.

''scuse me, Miss,' said one of the workmen, touching a finger to his forehead in what Phryne thought to be an exaggerated, if not actually sarcastic, show of deference. 'Can we have a word with you about this cage?'

Phryne was on the point of saying something like, 'Go away, there's a good chap, and don't get involved in blood sports again,' when she caught the shadow of a wink in a very bright eye and got up.

'Forgive me, Syl, I'll be back in a jiff.' She moved out of earshot.

The taller workman was dressed in a blue singlet and mole-skins; the other wore a shabby farm overall. He actually had some hay in his hair.

'You're overacting,' she told them quietly.

'Fooled everyone up to now,' the taller man told her. 'Bert and Cec say hello. We got in on the delivery of that poor animal for them capitalists to massacre for sport, doing the hungry man's family out of a meal as usual. Snatching the food from his starving children's mouths.'

Phryne doubted whether the children of the poor ate much venison but she agreed with the sentiment.

'Come and let's show Syl that we are looking at the cage,' she said, walking around it. 'It collapses, doesn't it?'

'Yair, just held by these rings at each corner. Easy as pie. Bert reckons you got a bad man here, Miss. Dunno why he thinks that 'cos he never told me. But he sent me, I'm Ted, and Rob Yates to look after you. And since if we don't he'll have our—' he hastily censored what he had been about to say and interposed another metaphor '—guts for garters, here we are.'

'That Bert is a man of his word,' said Phryne.

'Too right,' said Rob Yates, which was something Cec was fond of saying. It must have been a family trait. There were an extraordinary number of Yates. They were polyphilo-progenitive to a remarkable degree.

Phryne looked at them both. They would blend in to the domestic staff without any difficulty. They must have been men of gallantry and resource or Bert would not have sent them. Too proud to accept any help? Not Phryne. Not when it came in such useful packages. Rob and Ted could be very useful.

'Wonderful. Collapse the cage and go along to the kitchen. Tell Mrs. Truebody that I sent you to do some of the rough work now that one of her footmen has become a child minder. You'll like her. She's a wonderful cook.'

'Yair, we asked around and they said the work was hard and the hours were long but the grub was tops,' said Ted hungrily.

'Did Bert tell you anything about his bad man?'

'Nah,' said Rob, unconvincingly. 'Not what he looks like. Only that someone has hired him.'

Phryne waited. Ted looked at Rob. Rob looked at Ted. Ted shrugged. Rob spoke.

'He's a gunman, Miss.'

They all heard a distant crack of a rifle in the forest. Phryne thought of William Rufus. Even being King of England didn't protect you from an arrow in the thorax if someone really wanted to kill you…

'Oh well, not much to be done at the moment,' she said. 'Keep your ears open and we shall try to prevent disaster. Here's the situation at present.'

Phryne told them about Tarquin, the riddles and the child Marigold. They nodded.

'Not so good,' observed Rob. 'Well, hoo-roo, Miss.'

They collapsed the cage in a tinkle of bars and carried it away and Phryne returned to the lawn chair.

'I heard firing,' she observed.

'The young idiots are trigger-happy, I expect,' said Sylvanus. 'Here, take my opera glasses.'

As was to be expected, Sylvanus' opera glasses were elaborately decorated with panels of mother of pearl. They were lightly etched with classically nude young men. But they had German precision-made lenses and were obviously very expensive. Phryne watched the forest spring into sharp focus. Yes, there were the hunters—and there was the deer, too, cowering out of sight of the foremost riders. She saw the Wonnangatta Tigers in a skilled onrush, threading their way through the trees with effortless ease. She saw Gerald on Acorn and Isabella on Tonnerre. She also saw something else, but she did not jump to her feet. She took a moment to suppress any quiver in her voice.

'Interesting. But I've never liked blood sports. See you at lunch, Syl.'

She handed back the glasses and sauntered away towards the horse lines. Only when she was out of sight did she run.

Phryne skidded into the Grammar Boys' camp and grabbed the nearest lackey.

'Mr. Norton's stableman—where?'

The man pointed. Phryne went on. The man was English, sensible and middle aged, which was good. He could not be

daunted but he could be persuaded. And he was used to obeying orders.

'Mr. Norton offered me one of his remounts to join the
hunt,' she told him.

He put down the hoof he was examining and turned his
attention to Phryne. He knew her. This was the woman his
master had spent such a lot of time cultivating. She was unlikely
to be a horse thief.

'You'll need a fast one to catch 'em,' he said. 'You'll need this
one. Can you ride, Miss? Like that?'

He was surveying Phryne's loose cotton shift and sandals.

'I can ride a bit,' said Phryne. 'Find me an overall, will you?
And I can get on with saddling. What's your name, pretty?' she
asked, as the pony's intelligent face came around.

'She's Buttercup,' said the stableman. 'Her gear and tack's
just there.'

He went off to borrow a pair of overalls from a stableboy
while Phryne heaved the saddle onto the patient back and
swiftly trussed the pony into her everyday rig. By the time the
attendant came back with a bundle of denims she was shortening the stirrup leathers.

'Overalls and boots, Miss,' said the man. She dragged them
on with scant regard for decency. The boots were a size too big
but better than trying to ride in sandals.

'Give you a boost?' asked the man, but Phryne had leapt to
horseback and was away like the wind. Ralph Norton's stableman watched her go until he was satisfied that she would not
fall off. In fact she made quite a nice little rider—a bit rough,
like these Australians always were, but quite secure in her seat
and going like the clappers.

Buttercup, Phryne discovered, was a neat little pony with
a very respectable turn of speed. She had clearly felt left out
when the other horses went hunting and wanted to join them.
The ground was flat and well watered, the forest approaching
more rapidly every moment, and Phryne laughed and loosed

the reins, letting the beast have her head, as she obviously knew what she was doing.

It had been too long since she'd been riding. The only riding schools available to her within easy reach of St. Kilda were either entirely stocked with elderly, bitter, superannuated screws that hated humans and tried their best to, for instance, rub them off against a convenient tree, or expensive haunts of the rich. These made Phryne uncomfortable. The horses were well bred but the patrons were not, and the female private school accents that squeaked and chirped around her, always talking about money, made the experience wearing. Perhaps she could buy her own beast and find a suitable stable for it.

Buttercup jinked around a wombat hole and Phryne sat up straight and gripped with her knees. Better pay attention. Where was the hunt? She heard the dogs yowling just ahead and to one side, near the river. Phryne did not appreciate the music of the hounds. It reminded her of a wolf pack demanding that the passengers fling another serf out of the droshky. She urged Buttercup on and the pony flicked her ears in agreement.

They came to the bank. Phryne recalled the map. This was the Werribee River, and here it was a slow and lazy creature, sprawled out like a bather in sunlight. Deep, perhaps, in the middle, but muddy at the edges. Phryne, knowing that hunted animals often sought water, rode along the riverbank, hoping that Mole and Ratty were not at home to witness this senseless carnage.

The noise of the hunt burst suddenly out of cover, the deer a brown flash ahead of the foremost hound. Just as Phryne managed to insert Buttercup between the hunter and the hunted, the deer took to water and bucked and plunged through the mud until it gained the middle. It swam strongly. A fusillade of shots followed it. Phryne drew Buttercup back before she kicked one of those irritating dogs. They were leaping and bounding, baying at the tops of their voices, expressing the outrage that a decent dog felt about being cheated, I say, sir, cheated, by their lawful prey.

Phryne slid out of the melee and tried to triangulate what she had seen through the opera glasses with the trees on the ground.

It was very difficult. The hunt had poured down to the riverbank. Gerald was there on Acorn, Isabella on Tonnerre. Phryne was trying to avoid Ralph Norton in case he objected to her choice of horse, but she allowed Buttercup to manoeuvre herself through the scrub and into a reasonable clearing. It looked familiar. That was the tree she had seen. It had a heavy right-angled branch on one side and one with two forks on the other. The man with the gun was still there. He sat easily in a high crotch of the old gum, rifle lined up along the branch. Ready for action. Ready to assassinate someone.

Phryne was unarmed. It would not be wise to draw attention to the man, who had taken such pains to avoid notice. But she had boots and an overall and had spent her childhood climbing trees. She dismounted, tethering Buttercup loosely to a bush. Then she started to scale the other side of the gnarled tree, moving like a shadow. The man stirred, perhaps detecting her presence by a change in the air, for she was sure that she had not made a sound.

He turned his head. It was Nicholas.

'Today is the feast of Thomas of Canterbury,' said Dot, opening the book. The picture showed three knights stabbing an unarmed monk to death. 'He was a famous bishop who offended the king. Annoyed, the king said, "Will no one rid me of this troublesome priest?" and three of his men heard, and travelled to Canterbury, and killed Thomas.'

'Poor king,' said Jane.

'Poor king?' demanded Dot. 'What about poor Thomas?'

'But he went straight to heaven, as you've explained,' said Jane reasonably. 'I bet the king didn't mean his knights to actually go and kill Thomas. He just lost his temper. But they went ahead and did it. So the king has to pay for the sins of the men and for his own.'

'Hmm,' said Dot. This struck her as very dubious theology indeed.

Chapter Twelve

What thing is it that never was nor never shall be? —
Never mouse made her nest in a cat's ear.

John Wardroper
The Demaundes Joyous of Wynkyn de Worde

Phryne paused with one hand round a branch and one foot grop-
ing for a hold, like the slow loris she had once seen at London
Zoo. Nicholas! What was that estimable young man doing in a
tree with such a very efficient looking rifle?

She hung there for a moment, thinking. There were two rea-
sons for being in a tree with a rifle. Well, three, she told herself,
slightly numb with surprise, if you included complete raving
lunacy, but he had shown no signs of it so far. The other two
were, to shoot someone on the ground and accomplish a murder,
and to shoot a fellow sniper and prevent a murder. Of the two
Phryne thought prevention more likely, but she was not sure and
approached her climb with a slightly less carefree attitude.

It was a simple climb. A goat could have easily managed it.
So, possibly, could Buttercup, who was watching Phryne with
interest. Foot by foot Phryne ascended. Nicholas did not react,
even when her boot slipped on a loose piece of bark. He might
have taken her for an unusually heavy footed pigeon. His whole

attention was concentrated on someone—in the next tree, perhaps?

Phryne examined the tree. It contained, as far as she could see, seven quarrelling cockies, sulphur crests rampant, two harassed magpies, a juvenile magpie making hoarse, wheezing 'I'm only a baby and you haven't fed me!' noises and a fast asleep koala. The marsupial was curled in an upper quadrant, and surely Nicholas wasn't going to shoot a koala? It was, for a start, illegal to shoot koalas. Not to say unsporting, to kill a beast who only woke up from a little twenty hour nap to munch dreamily on gum leaves. And this one had a baby on her back. It was also out like a light in the manner of baby koalas, who retained a fierce grip on their mother's fur even during the deepest slumber.

Phryne managed to creep up behind Nicholas and lay a finger on the gun before he noticed her. He gave a huge start and only kept his perch by grabbing with both hands. This gave Phryne the rifle. She held it securely.

'How about "Dr. Livingston, I presume?"?' she said affably.

'What are you doing here?' he gasped.

'I might ask the same of you. Someone in the hunt needs killing?'

'I…I can't tell you,' he said miserably. 'I wish I could. But I'm not doing anything wrong, Phryne, I swear.'

'All right,' she said, giving him back the gun and watching him reassume his place. 'Who is the intended target?'

'I don't know,' he said distractedly.

'I mean, who is the assassin trying to kill?' Phryne persisted.

'How the devil did you know about that?' Nicholas was astounded enough to swear in front of a lady.

'I have my sources,' said Phryne with a regrettable hint of smugness.

'And they said that someone was going to be killed today?'

'No, they said that a gunman had been hired to kill someone here. No time was specified. But during the hunt seems a sound notion. Lots of ordnance flying about. What are those idiots hunting? The deer got away.'

'Did it? Good.' Another fusillade wounded the day. 'They're shooting low. Rabbits, perhaps.'

'That noise will have scared every scut from here to Warburton into a nice safe hole.'

'I didn't say they were good hunters,' said Nicholas shortly. This was true.

'Well, unless I can help you up here, I'll reclaim my pony and follow the guns. A nice country house thing to do. I shall squeal at every shot and exhibit feminine weakness,' she said, turning round and feeling for a foothold.

'That ought to slay 'em,' grinned Nicholas. Not the grin of a cold blooded murderer, Phryne felt. On the other hand, she reflected as she climbed down and remounted Buttercup, she hadn't met many murderers. Maybe they all had cornflower blue eyes.

The situation on the ground was confused. Horses and ponies shuffled and backed, foiled by the dense scrub. Phryne allowed Buttercup to find her own way through and several times had to duck aside as guns exploded far too near her. The pony twitched her ears unhappily. This, one could see her thinking, was not what she had signed up for. She was a polo pony, and this was not polo. And she was right. Unarmed, there was not a lot Phryne could do while mixed into this melee. Contrariwise, she could do some nice surreptitious searching if she went back to the house now. Everyone seemed to be at the hunt, either watching or riding or beating the bushes. Phryne leant down low over Buttercup's neck until they reached a wide gravel drive, where the pony picked up her pace, hearing or scenting her stablemates ahead.

'Tally-ho!' yelled a cultivated voice. Phryne saw over the flat the fast loping form of a hare. The hunt streamed out of the belt of forest, leaving the koalas to their well merited slumbers. Phryne on Buttercup lagged behind, watching the riders emerge, the Tigers in a screaming mob, the Grammar Boys in close formation, the rest of the guests distributed in between them. Shots were still being fired. Phryne could not see by whom.

The hunt belted off after the hare. This struck Phryne as plain silly. She waited until the closest rider was out of rifle reach and turned the pony's head towards the mansion. Just then she heard three thumps in the bush and Buttercup reared, front hoofs beating the air. Phryne kept her seat as if glued to her mount. She could not see what had scared the beast so badly. A snake? A piece of paper? Existential angst? The more highly strung the horse, the more likely it was to see monsters.

Then the monster hopped meekly across the ride. Grey-brown, paws folded like a maidservant clutching her shawl around her shoulders, eyes averted like a nun. The most in-offensive of creatures, anxious only to escape notice and get her baby home unperforated.

'Down,' said Phryne to Buttercup, doing things with heels and reins. 'It's a wallaby. They seldom, if ever, eat horses. There, now, it's gone. Calm, Buttercup, calm. You really haven't seen one of them before, have you? It's gone now, and we'd better go too, before more wildlife hops along to frighten the wits out of you.'

She rode at a sedate pace back to the horse lines and surrendered Buttercup, her borrowed boots and the overall.

'They lost the deer,' she told the stableman. 'Now they're hunting hare.'

'That ought to keep 'em busy,' he commented. 'Ol' Miss Puss' a lot harder to catch than Ol' Marse' Reynard. They'll be hours and come back blown, I'll warrant,' he said, running a diagnostic hand down the pony's heaving flank. His severe expression hardened into very severe. 'You been riding her hard, Miss?'

'No, she panicked when she saw a wallaby.'

'Ah,' said the stableman, examining the pony's mouth. 'In the old days the Chirnsides used to leave the fillies and colts three months in the paddock next to the old house, so that they'd get used to kangas and wombats and such. Just like we used to leave them in a field next to a train line, so they could get used to the fact that the train never left its track. That was when I used to work for the Duke of Northumberland, that was. We had patience in the old days, not to shock or ruin a young horse.

Now it's all rush, rush, rush. These young men all want instant results without putting in the time or the training.'

'True,' said Phryne, wishing only to find some privacy in which to treat her partly skinned inner thighs. The stableman gave her a smile.

'You get some liniment on them limbs, now,' he told her, 'or you'll be stiff as a plank in the morning.'

'Thank you,' said Phryne, and limped back towards the house. The guns were still rattling. If someone was going to be shot, Phryne felt that it served them right. She liked hares, too.

Phryne washed her honourable wounds and put on suit-able snooping gear. But she was foiled. In every tent, one piker or another was reclining or drinking or playing cards. It was not going to be a lucky day for sleuthing.

Phryne blew out a frustrated breath and decided that what she needed was to cool down, though the day was only pleasantly warm. It was still too early for lunch and she wanted to think about her riddle, preferably without sounds reminiscent of the gunfight at the OK Corral. She was floating in the middle of the cold lake water when a splashing alerted her to company. It was Nicholas.

'Hello,' said Phryne with some reserve. She disliked people wantonly keeping secrets from her.

'No one got shot,' he told her.

'Oh, good.'

'Are you cross with me?' he asked.

'Yes,' she said, floating quite still, an elegant red accent in the grey lake.

'Well, can we swap information? That's not the same as telling secrets.'

'Isn't it?'

'No,' said Nicholas, forcing his conscience back into its box and jamming on the lid. He could hear it squeaking, but it was possible to ignore it. Phryne decided to cooperate.

'Two old friends of mine, wharfies, sent word that someone had hired a gunman to assassinate someone here. No more than that, and I admit it isn't all that helpful.'

'I got the same information. Just that there was a killer and he had a gun. Murder for hire isn't something we want to see introduced into Australia.'

'Quite,' said Phryne, smothering a private smile at the 'we'. 'Well, that explains why you were up a tree. Did you see anyone acting suspiciously?'

'No,' admitted Nicholas.

'Neither did I. Although I don't call chasing off after an innocent hare sane behaviour.'

'They'll have another chance after lunch. Then there's trap shooting.'

'Using pigeons? I shall alert the RSPCA.'

'No need, not unless they're interested in the clay sort. And then, targets. All good chances of making a terrible error: gun went off when I dropped it—misadventure, your Honour,' said Nicholas with a touch of bitterness.

'Yes. It's going to be a busy day. Let us therefore lie here quietly and contemplate the riddle. Quarried, carried, carved and holed/Doomed to perpetual wet and cold. Stone, perhaps? But why would it be always cold? I haven't been riding for a while and I am sore in several private places.'

Nicholas found his mind contemplating how those private places might be made more comfortable and blushed bright red. Phryne smiled and let her mind wander to Lin Chung, and silk sheets, and icy air blown by a fan.

Then she sat up, sank, coughed, and hauled herself ashore on the little island.

'I think I've got an idea,' she said.

The house was quiet. A large stack of luncheon boxes reposed on the verandah, ready for collection. Clothed again in another of her bright cotton shifts, Phryne was waiting for Nicholas to return from his tent in the usual habiliments of a gentleman on holiday: his customary flannels and loose shirt. She contemplated the luncheon boxes. They were very pretty, Phryne noticed, well made of light wood and painted inside and out. Each one had a different identifying picture on its lid: horses for the polo persons, sports motifs for the hearties, flowers for the Lady's Own, a cheerful bunch of vegetables for the vegetarians, three classical Greek gods for the Templars, little deco pictures for the others, in case they had forgotten how to read…

Phryne could smell egg and bacon pie. Her stomach growled. Nicholas arrived suitably dried and dressed. His stomach answered hers. He looked at her imploringly.

'Can't we just find our lunches?'

'No, because we will want them later. But,' she said consolingly, 'we are going to the kitchen. I'm sure Mrs. Truebody will organise a smallish banquet or two for a boy with beautiful eyes.'

'Yes, that's all right for him, but what about me?' grumbled Nicholas, revealing to Phryne another man who did not know he was attractive.

'Just come along with me,' she said firmly.

Mrs. Truebody was pleased to see them and offered tea, coffee, biscuits, sandwiches and perhaps 'a sip of my special punch'. Nicholas settled down with a happy sigh and Mrs. True-body looked at him fondly.

'So nice to see a young man who can eat,' she commented. 'Some of those out there wouldn't touch a ham sandwich if they were starving. One of them gave me a lecture on how wicked I was to serve meat and how long meat—' she lowered her voice '—remained in the lower intestine! Was that a thing to say to a decent woman, I ask you? In her own kitchen?'

'Certainly not,' said Phryne, taking a sandwich which had been lovingly built on a base of ham, to which had been added French mustard, thinly cut gruyère cheese and shredded lettuce. The next one she selected was a voluptuous concoction of cream, chives, perfectly almost-hard boiled egg on paper-thin brown bread. 'Probably inaccurate, too. I mean, how do they know? And if they do know, the experiments must have been too, too indelicate. It's a religion, Mrs. Truebody, and religions are not sensible. How is your patient this morning?'

'Slept for three hours last night, Minnie says. She's eating like a pig, poor little thing. I started her off on soft food, you know, soup and so on, but now she just eats everything.'

'Let her do so,' said Phryne, 'if she's hungry. I can't think of a better diet than this for someone who was so long starving in the dark.'

'Worse things happen at sea,' said Mrs. Truebody. 'I reckon she'll come round soonish. She's still got Sam. Never thought he had the makings of a sick nurse but he's been really good with her. Not coddling her temper, but very comfortable to be with.'

'Like a father gorilla,' said Phryne, taking another egg sandwich. 'Might personally be a bit grumpy with the little gorillas but they live in the confident knowledge that anyone who attacks them will be thoroughly dismembered. It reminds me of a quote from *The Water Babies* by Charles Kingsley. We might read that to her next. Now, am I mistaken in thinking that you have an American refrigerating machine?'

'No, Miss Phryne, we do have one. Mr. Ventura insisted. It's in the back kitchen. I don't go near the thing. Gabriel looks after it. Not that it isn't very serviceable. Keeps everything ice cold. I've made my sherbets and ice cream for the Arab feast tonight and they are already firm. But I don't know if I like these new inventions.'

'I will leave my friend here to refresh the inner man,' said Phryne, 'and just go and have a look. I've got one in my own house, and my housekeeper says that it is a great convenience.'

Phryne collected Gabriel, in case the machine should prove inimical to human inspection, and saw that it was, indeed, a larger version of her own ice-maker. It squatted, puffing, its blue pilot light casting an eerie glow in the dark back kitchen, which contained nothing else but an abandoned tea-trolley, a scarred butcher's block and an array of very old and rusty pots.

'Open the left hand door for me, will you?' she requested, and Gabriel hauled against the seal. The interior was stacked with shallow trays full of different coloured fruit derivatives. No sign of the luggage label. 'Now the right,' instructed Phryne, and the heavy door came open, revealing a miscellany of articles. Gabriel grabbed a frozen orange, which he pocketed with a wink. Frozen oranges were new to the huge man's diet and he wanted to become used to them.

'The little girl likes that stuff,' Gabriel informed Phryne, pointing out best milky ice flavoured with chocolate.

'Good, well, get me a spoon and a dish and we shall take some to her,' said Phryne, and Gabriel left her alone with the machine. It puffed. She rummaged.

Just as Gabriel returned with a dish and a spoon in a pot of hot water, Phryne found the luggage label. Small, white with blue edges. And the writing on it was dripping away, readable only as 'the smear'. Phryne smiled a self-satisfied smile. The riddler had made a mistake at last.

'Good, Gabriel. Now, I'll hold the bowl and you scoop. That ought to be enough,' she said as a small mountain of chocolate ice cream grew under his energetic and wristy spoon action. 'Don't forget to replace your frozen orange with an unfrozen one. I'll just go and say hello to the child.'

'All right, Miss,' agreed Gabriel. As she left she saw him rip the frozen fruit apart with his bare hands and suck eagerly at the icy juice. They built them strong in Werribee, she reflected. Must be all that fresh country air and healthy exercise. And, of course, Chirnside butter, cream, eggs, cheese, home killed meat and home smoked bacon, home baked bread made from home ground flour and fresh fruit from the orchards.

Marigold had left her bed and was sitting in the small courtyard. She still wore the flannel nightgown and her feet were bare. Sam was sitting at her side, deck of cards in hand, teaching her to play…

'Five card stud?' asked Phryne. 'You're teaching her poker?'

'And she's a real shark,' grinned Sam. 'She's won almost all me matches.'

'I've brought some ice cream,' said Phryne to the girl. 'Is there anything you want to tell me?'

Marigold was flushed with the triumph of beating Sam at his own game. She accepted the ice cream. Sam rose and lumbered away, saying that he would return in a jiff or two.

'I've remembered something,' said Marigold, spooning busily. 'I never had ice cream before I came here. It's bonzer.'

'Mrs. Truebody is an artist,' agreed Phryne, taking Sam's chair and picking up his cards. The deck, she felt as she handled it, had been adroitly stacked. Sam was playing to lose, which is quite as hard as playing to win.

'What is all that noise outside? It sounded like guns,' said Marigold nervously.

'Nothing to be concerned about,' Phryne told her. 'They're hunting. So far all they have caught is a cold. All they are likely to catch, too. What have you remembered?'

'A smell,' said Marigold. She began to tremble. Phryne took away the empty bowl and put her arms around the girl. Marigold shuddered strongly but she had control of her mind, and her voice as well. This was a child with stainless steel courage. But all the colour had left her face.

'Sweet,' said Marigold. 'A sweet smell, like flowers. That's all. I don't feel as well as I thought I was,' she said to Phryne. 'I'd like to go back to bed, please.'

Phryne conducted her back to the narrow iron bed and tucked her in.

'You've been very brave and you don't have to think about it anymore,' she said. 'Now, settle back and listen.'

Phryne found the bookmark and announced, ' "He is indeed the best of animals," observed the Rat. "So simple, so good natured and so affectionate."' By the time Sam came back, Phryne had read almost a chapter and Marigold was asleep.

Phryne borrowed some things from Minnie, collected Nicholas, obtained writing materials and some glue, and affixed the illegible label to the verandah, above the lunch boxes, in the manner made notorious by the martyrdom of Bill Posters. On her own sheet of paper she had printed WHAT NOW? in capitals.

'Where did you find it?' asked Nicholas.

'In the ice-maker. The answer was ice.'

'Oh,' replied the young man. Phryne patted her own notice.

'That ought to produce something,' she said. 'Now, we are going to make sure that the remaining people stay in their tent, and then I am going to search this house from top to bottom. I'm tired of being led around by the luggage label. It was diverting for a while but if that child's in durance vile it is time he was released.'

'Agreed,' said Nicholas. 'How do we make sure that they stay put?'

'Paper games,' said Phryne promptly. 'I am providing all the makings of a game of consequences, and I am about to make sure that Sylvanus takes control of it. If ever a man had a guilty secret, it is him.'

'Probably whole loads of them,' said Nicholas. 'Though my… er…friend in the police said that none of them had criminal records in Australia.'

'They have scarcely had time,' chided Phryne. 'They haven't been here very long. Hello, Syl,' she said affectionately, stooping to kiss the fat man's cheek. 'I want you to do me a favour.'

'Anything, princess,' he replied. 'Including my worthless life and my even more worthless fortune.'

Phryne explained, Sylvanus accepted the paper and pencils. He did not ask for any further instructions.

Phryne let him go, then led Nicholas back into the Iris Room, where she shed the shift and put on Minnie's oldest black dress and her cleanest spare apron and cap. Outside the door, someone had left the old tea-trolley, now laden with towels. This would assist Phryne's disguise. Nicholas, who found that he had quite forgotten to breathe as Phryne was flinging off her clothes, breathed.

'I've got the pass key,' she told him, adjusting her cap and tying back the wings of her black hair. 'You're my cockatoo. I'll search, you watch. Deal?'

'Deal,' he said.

An hour later Phryne and Nicholas had finished with the top floor. They had opened cupboards and wardrobes and chests.

They had penetrated the roof space, disturbed a colony of tiny insectivorous bats, encountered a fair number of rats and one very cross hunting cat, but found no trace of the missing boy. Phryne, who was thorough when she felt like it, had tapped every panel and followed every echo. It would be like the Chirnside brothers to have made a romantic secret room in their mansion, but one had not been found.

The guests had brought some odd things into the house, it was true. Phryne wondered why anyone would import a huge backgammon board, a large empty fish bowl, a coffee set in white bone china, a Tiffany lamp or a dog collar and a set of chains, though she could make a shrewd guess about the last. She did not do so out loud in case she offended Nicholas' sensibilities. Clothes ranged from very good to very basic, and underwear from ragged (Sylvanus) to embroidered peach, apricot and black satin (several people, none of them female). Phryne was dusty and Nicholas had spiderwebs in his hair.

'Down to the ground floor,' said Phryne, and he followed, trying to remove dust from his flannels by brushing them with a sweaty hand. This had the effect of making him look as though he had tried to tunnel out of the Château d'If in his pyjamas.

The ground floor contained the public rooms, which were unlikely but had to be searched anyway, and the kitchen and usual offices, which had already been searched. Phryne whizzed through the billiard room and the parlours, tapping and testing and rolling back carpet to check on interestingly soft spots. Nothing.

As she began to tackle the tenanted rooms, Nicholas leaned in the open front door and saw that the purple tent was closed and gusts of laughter were coming from it. He had never thought that the Templar ménage was much given to laughter. It sounded vaguely sinister. But at least Syl was keeping them amused and inside.

The rattle of a trolley announced that Phryne was returning.

'Come with me,' she ordered. She showed him the room called Rose. It was very small and hung with red roses in glazed chintz. There were roses on the table in a silver vase and a rosy spread on each of the two single beds.

On the dressing table was a stack of cheap paper, and beside it a ragged pen, a pen knife, and a well of cheap black ink.

'Whose room?' he asked.

'Amelia and Sad Alison,' said Phryne.

The Joker drank one small glass of cognac to compose his nerves. His time was near. Soon the perfect moment would be utterly perfected by death. He held out his hands. The tremor had subsided. They were as steady as a rock.

Chapter Thirteen

Wink is often good as nod;
Spoils the child who spares the rod;
Thirsty lambs run foxy dangers;
Dogs are found in many mangers.

W.S. Gilbert
H.M.S. Pinafore

'No sign of the luggage labeller?' asked Nicholas.

'No. But here is the writer of death threats. Hmm. They ought to have gone through a round of consequences by now. I want you to go into the tent and collect the waste paper.'

'Do what?' asked Nicholas. It had been a long day and it was getting longer.

'Just do as I say,' said Phryne sweetly, and sat down on Sad Alison's bed.

As soon as Nicholas had gone she felt under the mattresses, looked through every bag and pocket in both the hanging and folded clothes, and even emptied out the water in the dressing table jug. She gathered a few hints as to the backgrounds of both girls. Amelia's father was writing her furious letters from Lyons, offering to send the passage money if she would come home and promise '*pas de betises*' in future. Sad Alison had a photograph of

Gerald on the washstand and a bundle of letters from someone signing herself 'your loving mother' reporting on the condition of 'your disgraced sister'.

Amelia had a bottle of cognac under her bed, and Sad Alison a box of powders marked 'to be taken when the pain is severe' with a doctor's name and a dispenser's address in London. Phryne judged them to be morphine by the taste. Chronic pain could explain Sad Alison's sadness, perhaps. The only other fact she elicited from her search was that someone had broken a glass in the room; a scatter of prismatic dust coated a section of floor.

Nicholas returned with a bundle of papers, all folded. 'I don't know why you wanted these,' he said.

'Don't you?' asked Phryne, carefully unfolding and stacking them. 'Did you notice the order in which the players were sitting?'

'Yes, I did,' he said.

'Where was Alison?'

'Sixth in line,' he said promptly. Phryne made another tick on her mental checklist. Someone had trained his observation and memory. 'Amelia was seventh, next to her.'

'Good. Have you ever played consequences?'

'No,' he said, sitting down on the other bed.

'You take a piece of paper, and you write a name on the top. Here's an example. "Lily Langtry." With me so far?'

'Yes,' he said. Phryne hoped he was not going to sulk.

'Then you fold over what you have written and give the paper to the person next to you. They write "Met..." and the name of another person—in this case, "Saint Dominique" —and fold it over again. Then they pass it along and the third player writes a place. "In a lift." The fourth writes what was said, folds the paper, the fifth writes a reply, folds the paper and passes it to the sixth, who writes the result of the exchange. In this case: "He said, fine weather we are having." The reply is "She said, I love you passionately," and the consequence is "And the result was a breach in the League of Nations".'

'What a waste of time,' said Nicholas. Something was definitely bothering the young man with the cornflower blue eyes. Phryne did not care.

'Not if you want a handwriting sample,' Phryne told him. She laid out the threatening letters and the consequences and pored over them for quite three minutes before she invited Nicholas' scrutiny.

'Pretty clear, isn't it?' she asked.

'Yes, they're the same,' he said.

'Then I'll just go and cut Sad Alison out from the mob,' said Phryne. 'I'll bring her back here. Don't fall asleep,' she said airily. Nicholas snorted.

Sad Alison yielded to Phryne's tug on her hand and followed her in lamb-like docility. They crept out as Sylvanus announced that the next game out be Book Rhymes. He had a huge fund of poetry to draw from and some of the acolytes were alert enough to play word games now. The difficulty of Book Rhymes was to get the metre and scansion right. The sense took care of itself and thus was frequently absent.

'The year is dying like the night,' he announced as Phryne and Sad Alison reached the door. A female voice capped it with, 'But certainly it serves him right!' and there was applause. On the noise of clapping Phryne and Sad Alison departed.

'Where are you taking me?' asked Alison.

'To a place where you will find some answers,' said Phryne.

Nicholas looked up as they came into the small rose-decked room.

'Why is he here?' asked Alison, shrinking into Phryne's side. Phryne had no patience with shrinking females. Her own view was that what Sad Alison needed to do was to eat carrots to clear her skin, wash her stringy, greasy hair in a lemon vinegar rinse, and pull herself together. To this end she uncorked Amelia's bottle of cognac and poured a solid tot.

'Drink this and listen. I will a tale unfold. And when I get it wrong you will correct me, right?' Phryne administered the brandy. Sad Alison sipped and choked. 'You encountered the

Templars in Paris,' said Phryne. 'You and your sister. No need to spit out good brandy, I know you have a sister and that she is now sitting disgraced in a Brighton nursing home. Am I right?'

Alison nodded. Her eyes brimmed. Nicholas produced his handkerchief. Alison took it and wiped at her tears.

'I say, Phryne, you're a bit rough,' he protested. She awarded him the Look again and he subsided.

'Elaine,' said Alison. 'Her name is Elaine.'

'Good. Elaine told you and your mother that the father of her child was Gerald Templar.' Nicholas stared. Phryne pressed on relentlessly. 'Right?'

'Yes,' sobbed Alison.

'No one else would have called Gerald a fraud. You and Elaine had been in karez. You thought that the Templars were, if not actually asexual, at least not...'

'Cheats,' snarled Alison suddenly. 'I believed him, we believed him, when he said we were in no moral danger, and then...'

'So you stayed with the Templars in order to revenge your sister's lost honour,' said Phryne tonelessly. 'You wrote death threats in black ink on Woolworth's paper. You repeatedly tried to poison him. What else did you do, eh? Did you send me a snake? Did you put ground glass in my cold cream?'

'No, that was—' Alison bit her tongue.

'Amelia,' said Phryne. 'The remains of the grinding are still on the floor over there. I noticed them when I was searching the room. And Amelia wants to hurt me because...?'

'She hates you because Pam thinks you're beautiful. Pam said so. Lots of times. So Amelia thought she'd make you less beautiful.'

Phryne accepted this explanation.

'So Amelia did the ground glass. What about the other things?'

'No,' said Sad Alison sadly. 'I don't know anything about any other things.'

'And Tarquin?' asked Phryne, taking the girl's hands and compelling her attention.

'I don't know where he is!' said Alison. 'I just wanted to kill Templar, because my sister Elaine—'

'Lied to you,' said Phryne flatly.

'What?' asked Nicholas.

'It's well known that Gerald Templar is incapable of increase. He's sterile. Not impotent. Just sterile. Why else would he be adopting boys when a sensible man would breed his own sons?'

'She...lied?' gasped Alison, wringing Nicholas' handkerchief.

'Oh, have some more brandy, Alison, and try to pay attention. This is a serious matter,' said Phryne crossly. 'We need to find that child. He may be in danger. I tell you, and it can be confirmed if you wish, that Gerald Templar could be many things to your sister Elaine but the one thing he could not be is the father of her child. Do you believe me?'

'Yes,' said Sad Alison.

'Was there someone in the ménage that Elaine liked?'

'Not really,' said Alison. 'I am thinking of Franklin, the boy she wanted to marry but my father wouldn't let her. Then he was killed in a motor accident. At around the same time as she said...Oh, I have been so wicked.' She burst into tears.

'Ah, Amelia,' said Phryne, as the young woman came puzzled into the small room. 'Can you comfort your friend? She's had a shock. You're French, you should be taking better care of her. Get her a proper hair rinse and some skin cream. And if you ever attack me again, Pamela or no Pamela, I'll make you regret it. Do you know where Tarquin is?'

'No,' said Amelia, grabbing for the cognac bottle. 'I don't know. I'm sorry. I was jealous. Alison? What shock is this?'

'She can tell you all about it if she likes,' said Phryne, conscious that she was still wearing a maid's costume. 'I will see you both at dinner. Goodbye,' she said, and the two girls stared at the door, which shut quite hard behind Phryne and Nicholas as they went out.

Alison and Amelia drank more brandy and wept, Alison for her own wickedness, Amelia for her jealous nature.

'You're a genius,' said Nicholas, as Phryne divested herself of servitude and reassumed her own clothes. He had almost got used to her changing her costume in front of him. Almost.

'Thank you, but we have only solved a little bit of the mystery. The scholarly blue ink of the luggage label writer is not in those handwriting samples. So, who is the riddler? Who sent me that coral snake and all those warnings, who's ordered a murderer to be sent from Melbourne, and where is poor little Tarquin?'

'I did ask around,' said Nicholas diffidently. 'Yesterday I went back to Melbourne. About that snake, you see, they can't be all that easy to come by. I mean, you can't just walk into a pet shop with those bunnies and kittens and puppies and ask for a deadly reptile from the Caribbean and can they gift-wrap it for Christmas, please.'

'No, I suppose not,' said Phryne, interested. 'What did you find out?'

'The shops were all shut,' said Nicholas. 'But I found a collector and asked him. Queer coots, those collectors. This bloke answered the door with, I swear, about ten foot of carpet snake wrapped around his chest. Beastly thing poked its tongue out at me.'

'It was just tasting the air, dear boy. I can tell that you are not going to become a bosom friend of our reptilian brothers and sisters.'

'Fair turned my stomach,' confessed Nicholas. 'I say, you haven't got a bottle of anything here, have you?'

'Sorry, we drank all the cocktails and I haven't got around to having my flask refilled, such has been the pace of events lately. I'll get you something directly the bar opens. Go on. You fascinate me.'

Nicholas, recalling the horror of that nose to scaly nose encounter, decided that it had been worth it if he could fascinate Miss Fisher.

'Well, he went on about how beautiful they were, showed me all sorts of nasty creepy-crawlies and made me say they were very pretty, and finally told me that a Mr. Forest had bought his last coral snake. Paid cash. Description: average height, average build, hair sort of brown, eyes didn't notice.'

'If Mr. Forest had been a snake he would have looked more carefully,' commented Phryne. 'Mr. Forest, eh? I wonder who that could be. I don't think we've got any Forests amongst the throng, but we can find out. Now, it must be just about lunch time.' She consulted her watch. 'And the hunt should be returning soon. My intuition tells me that the bar will be open to supply stirrup cups, and I owe you a drink. This afternoon, furthermore,' she lured Nicholas into the corridor, 'Nerine will be singing for your special delectation, and Nerine's art never goes stale.'

'But, Phryne, what about the gunman, and the luggage labeller?' he protested.

'I am waiting on developments,' Phryne replied. 'And there is no rule in the detectives handbook that says I can't enjoy myself while I am waiting. And if there is,' she added, 'it's silly and I don't propose to take any notice of it.'

'Right,' said Nicholas.

'And after that, we shall set Syl to conduct more parlour games, and by their charades we shall know them.'

Nicholas surrendered.

They collected their luncheon boxes from the pile on the verandah and took refuge under the hornbeam tree. The weather was almost cool. Phryne had put on a loose, sky-blue cardigan. Suddenly she seemed struck by an idea and left with a brief promise to return soon and a warning that the person who ate her passionfruit biscuits would regret it.

She was back before he'd had time to do more than eye the biscuits lustfully.

'What have you been doing?' he asked, as she threw herself down on the grass and grabbed for the thermos.

'Just took a dress or two and some cosmetics and things to poor Sad Alison,' she said. 'I was rather harsh with her, you were right. And it's cruel to criticise someone's appearance if they don't have the means to change it. I borrowed some white vinegar from

Mrs. Truebody and Amelia promised to help Alison with her hair. That ought to stop both of them from crying anymore.'

'Interesting,' observed Nicholas, grinning.

'What?' asked Phryne through a gulp of coffee.

'I didn't know you had a conscience,' he said.

Phryne sniffed. 'Then you really haven't been paying attention to what Jack Robinson told you about me.'

'You keep saying that name,' said Nicholas.

'So I do. What sort of biscuits did you get?'

'Orange. Want to swap me for a passionfruit one?'

'If you like,' said Phryne, looking at him thoughtfully.

There was a fusillade of guns and a baying of hounds.

'Ah,' said Nicholas. 'The hunt has returned.'

Bert had accepted an invitation to lunch at Phryne's house with Jack Robinson only because he adored Mrs. Butler's food and he was worried about Phryne. Otherwise he would never have been seen at the same table as a cop, even though this one was quite a decent one as cops go. And neither would Cec, his best mate. They had shared many experiences, including that of a Turkish beach which was the last word in discomfort, and both of them valued luxury. Lunch with Mrs. B was always to be defined as a luxury. He settled his lapels and reached for his beer, avoiding Jack Robinson's policemanly regard.

'This gunman, he's bad. The brothers from the Longshoremen's gave us the office. He's a stone cold killer. Cec and me met him once so we couldn't go ourselves, and I sent men I can trust, but still...'

He took a long draught. Mr. Butler always kept his beer just at the prime, cold, pub temperature. Just the thing on a hot day—or, indeed, any day.

'But surely this is exaggerated,' protested Miss Eliza. 'This Joker sounds like something out of Sexton Blake.'

'Stands to reason there must have been someone to copy all those villains from,' said Dot reasonably.

'And he's the original assassin,' said Jack Robinson heavily. 'We got word from London. Never had a picture taken since he was twelve. French mother and American father. Speaks a lot of languages fluently. In fact, they said he could have been anything he wanted, but he wanted to be a murderer.'

'Some blokes are real strange,' commented Bert, passing his glass to Mr. Butler for a refill. 'Where are the girls today?'

'I sent them to buy some cakes at the other end of Acland Street. Only the Jewish shops are open. Isn't there something we can do to warn Miss Phryne?' asked Dot.

Mr. Butler served a small cup of perfectly made beef bouillon. The company sipped reverently. Lady Alice disposed of hers by picking up the bowl and drinking from it.

'So we don't have a photo. Do we have a description?'

Jack Robinson sighed. 'Not really. Moderate height and weight, possibly brown eyes, brown hair.'

'Looks pretty much like everyone,' said Cec. 'Useful, in his profession.'

'Well, so we know his name?'

'Last time anyone almost caught him, he was going by the name of Linda. John Linda, travelling in chocolate. That wasn't his name, of course. But he got into the strongest prison in France and assassinated a prisoner who was going to give evidence which would have locked up a whole drug smuggling ring. And he strolled out again as cool as you please and vanished.'

'The Yanks say that he killed a union man when he was sitting up in his own chair with a shotgun on his lap,' said Bert disconsolately.

'How was he killed?' asked Robinson, professionally interested.

'Fine blade to the heart. Stiletto, maybe a hatpin. No one saw a thing. It's like he really can disappear. Is that fish and chips, Mr. B?'

'Fish and *pommes frites* it is, Mr. Bert,' replied the butler. 'And a dish of green peas, and some *salade verte vinaigrette*.'

Cec, who despite having worked a six month stint on a trawler really loved fresh fish, decided to squeeze in his bit of information so as to give his appetite free range.

'The bloke I was talking to said that this Joker had been seen wearing a vicar's clothes—you know, with a collar on back to front. Flathead, eh? You beaut.'

'That's why he's so hard to describe,' said Robinson. 'He can look like anyone and sound like anyone. And sometimes he wears ladies' clothes.'

'So who's to say that he isn't a woman?' asked Dot.

Jack Robinson dropped his fork. Mr. Butler gave him another without comment. The detective inspector opened his mouth to refute Dot's comment, then closed it again, and then employed it for eating green peas. Maybe she was right. Who was, indeed, to say that the Joker wasn't a woman?

'He was convincing enough in female disguise to…er… distract a prison guard,' he admitted. 'He's a small bloke with small hands and feet and—yes, all right, Dot, he might be a female. Though I hope not.'

'Why?' asked Miss Eliza, set to bristle on behalf of her sex.

'Because I'd hate to think that a woman could be capable of Joker crimes.'

'Bad enough that anyone is,' agreed Dot. 'Mr. Bert, Mr. Cec, you say you met this Joker? Why can't you remember what he looked like?'

'Just can't,' said Cec, who had engulfed several fish and was now picking bones out of his palate. 'I usually got a good memory and since I heard about him hunting Miss Phryne I been trying real hard to remember. Was it brown eyes or blue eyes? What shape of face? And I can't recall a thing, not a blo— blessed thing. He must be like that bloke on the radio, the Shadow, that has the power to cloud men's minds.'

'Not a lot of power needed there,' snorted Miss Eliza.

'Now, Miss, don't go crook at us,' begged Bert. 'We're all friends here.'

'So we are,' said Lady Alice.

Miss Eliza muttered an apology.

'What sort of men have you sent out to help her?' asked Dot. She had hardly touched her meal. Mr. Butler knew that this would displease Mrs. Butler and frowned. Dot noticed this and picked up a token chip and bit into it. It tasted wonderful so she ate another and then started on the toothsome fish in its delicate batter.

'I sent my old mate Ted. Cec and me was in the army with him. Good bloke, cool under fire. Good hand to hand fighter, too.'

'And I sent my cousin Rob,' said Cec. 'He's a champion rifle shot and he and Ted are used to working together. They were the best we could find, since we didn't dare go ourselves and run the risk of giving the show away. This Joker bloke, he gets real indiscriminate when he feels threatened. The Longshoremen brothers said that when he was trapped at the waterfront once he shot five cops and a timekeeper just in order to cover which way he had gone. Shot them dead.'

'We can't have the scum of America coming here,' protested Jack Robinson.

'You might be a bit late,' said Bert, sardonically. 'By about a hundred years. Mind you, we started with the scum of Britain, so we might as well vary the mix.'

'Oh, very witty, Bert,' said Robinson.

'I mean it,' said Bert. 'Reason why I never believe the commos when they talk about conspiracies by the state is that the state isn't any better at conspiracies than the rest of us. Worse, even. The state couldn't find its backside with both hands—sorry, ladies. There's always someone who'll blow the secret, to feel important or because they're half pi—I mean, full of ink.'

'The only secret never known is kept by one who's all alone,' quoted Dot.

'That's right,' said Cec. 'Two, if one of 'em's dead.'

'Apple pie and cream,' said Mr. Butler.

'Do we know who the intended victim is?' asked Phryne.

They had finished their lunch and were idling under the tree preparatory to a field expedition to the bar, which was presently full of hearties and horsemen (and at least one horse).

'We guess that it must be the Templars,' said Nicholas. 'That makes it easier to guard them.'

'Which we are not doing at present,' she pointed out.

'This Joker, he's got a twist. He likes to kill people in their proper setting. He waited ages to kill a famous painter in the Louvre. The French police said that he had hidden in a niche for at least two days, all to get the perfect shot at the perfect place.'

'So he isn't likely to kill the Templars while they are hunting,' said Phryne. 'Certainly not characteristic, I agree. What would constitute characteristic?'

'Karez,' said Nicholas, blushing. 'Or maybe the Arab party beforehand.'

'Likely,' said Phryne.

'Of course, he may be after you,' said Nicholas.

'Me? Why?'

'Upset some husbands? Annoyed some wives?'

'No,' said Phryne. 'I made a policy decision a long time ago, no married men. It has served me well in the enemy reducing department.'

'I see,' said Nicholas, and was about to add something when, from the bar tent, came a long, loud shriek of dismay and horror.

They were on their feet instantly, and running.

Bosom Caresser

1 part brandy
1 part orange curaçao
yolk of one egg
teaspoon grenadine
Shake together with ice.

Chapter Fourteen

A little kindness—and putting her hair in
papers—would do wonders with her.

Lewis Carroll
Through the Looking-Glass

The person who was screaming was Sabine, which was unlike
her. The reason for her screaming was immediately apparent.
Laid out and nailed to the only timber structure in the tent,
the actual frame itself, was a dead fox. Very dead. Dead and
mutilated and crucified.

Phryne and Nicholas pushed to the front. Phryne bundled
Sabine into Pam English's arms.

'Take her away and make her some valerian tea,' she ordered.
'Everyone get back, please, we shall have this cleared away in a
moment.'

Ted and Rob, summoned by the screams, had materialised at
her side. 'Take this poor creature down,' she said to them. 'Keep
it carefully. And the piece of paper it is holding in its teeth. Do
this fast or we shall have hysterics and tears before bedtime.'

Ted, who was carrying a hammer and a canvas sack, agreed.

'We were just on the way to fix one of the horse pavilions,'
he said. 'So we've got all the tools we need. You keep the mob
back a bit and let the dog see the rabbit.'

Phryne and Nicholas, now assisted by the bar staff and some of the hearties, pressed the shocked aesthetes back.

'Lots of drinks in just a moment,' said Phryne soothingly.

'What? Never seen a dead fox before?' demanded the hunters. 'It's just a dead animal, nothing to get all worked up about.'

'You saw the paper in its teeth?' asked Nicholas in an undertone.

'Yes, but I didn't want to draw attention to it. Ted and Rob will smuggle it to me. In fact,' she said, conscious of a discreet tug at her sleeve and opening her hand to receive a folded note, 'even now it may be winging its way towards me. Good work, chaps,' she said to the workers as they carried the shrouded corpse out of the tent. 'Now, what shall we drink?'

'I'll have a mint julep,' purred a Southern voice, and Phryne was delighted to introduce Nicholas to Nerine. She snuggled very close to him in order to see his face. This was fine with Nicholas.

'You coming to hear me later, honey?' she asked, and he agreed with unspoiled enthusiasm.

Phryne drifted away, paper in hand. The display of the dead fox meant 'I am a better hunter than you'. And the note in its mouth said 'Make your will'. Vicious, flashy and cryptic. She was beginning to really dislike this assailant.

She remembered that she and Nicholas had left their lunch-eon boxes under the tree, went to fetch them, and passed Sylvanus, also carrying two.

'You did a lovely job with the consequences, Syl,' Phryne told him. 'How about a nice drink? Then perhaps we shall have charades while the hearties blast the landscape. It really isn't safe outside with all these guns about.'

Sylvanus gave an affected shiver. 'All too masculine for me, dear. Charades it is. What have you done with your young man? The one with the beautiful eyes?'

'I left him with Nerine, the jazz singer,' said Phryne. 'She'll take care of him.'

'Half his luck,' murmured Sylvanus, unexpectedly.

They deposited the boxes on the verandah. Phryne noticed something, and sent Sylvanus to the tent ahead of her.

Someone had replied to her message, 'WHAT NOW?'. On a wearyingly familiar luggage label in the same old blue clerkly writing was another riddle: 'No gold was ever wrought so fair/Yet no fair lady wears them in her hair'.

'Damn,' swore Phryne, and detached the label. Then she stuck up one of her own. It was on a piece of pink gummed paper: 'If, by midnight, Tarquin isn't in his place/Resign your membership of the human race'. Not perfect, perhaps, but it made Phryne's point.

She went to find Nicholas and located him in the middle of a Nerine mint julep. He had the look of a codfish which, in the midst of an interesting thought, had been hit over the head with an anchor. Proximity to Nerine often had that effect. Not only was she gorgeous, but she was the acknowledged mistress of the non sequitur. For the susceptible, Nerine's conversation was bad for the mind.

'And make one for Lady Phryne,' added Nerine, after instructing the barman again about crushing the mint into the sugar 'real good'. The bar was loud with congratulatory hunting cries, although they did not even seem to have run down their hare. Several hearties in hunting pinks were roaring reminiscences of successful hunts into their fellows' receptive ears. Phryne caught the word 'Chink' and stopped dead.

'Not the same as the day we threw that Chink into the Thames, though,' said one red-faced young man. Phryne marked him down.

'No Chinks here,' said another, with regret. 'And there was that wog in Paris. "Let go of me, you cads!" he howled and then— upsadaisy! Splash!'

The others roared with laughter. Three of them. Phryne made careful mental notes. Tall and thin, smaller and thin, red-faced and embonpoint.

'What are the names of those gentlemen?' she asked a Grammar Boy, who looked embarrassed.

'They're not altogether the thing,' he confessed. 'British, of course, not some of us. Beldham, Belcher and Travis, I believe. Saw you riding Buttercup, Miss Fisher, good show! Ralph is boasting about how well you managed her. She's a touchy beast.'

'Yes, but very nice otherwise, lovely gait,' said Phryne absently. Belcher, Beldham and Travis. They were in for a very wet surprise as soon as she could arrange it. And Ralph Norton would not be looking for her with blood in his eye, ranging for revenge for her high-handed assumption of his pony. That was good. 'So, how did the hunt go? Did you kill?' she asked in the correct form.

'No,' said the Grammar Boy. 'But it was a glorious run. Everyone says that it's much harder to catch a hare than a fox.'

'Ol' Miss Puss will give a run to Ol' Marse Reynard, as a hunting friend of mine used to say,' quoted Phryne.

'Oh, absolutely, Miss Fisher.'

Phryne moved on before the young man could offer her a drink. She was not in the mood for huntsmen today.

On one of the larger tables a shaggy pony was standing confidently, balancing beautifully on its small hoofs, drinking something out of a bucket. Phryne hoped it wasn't champagne. She recognised the Wonnangatta girls and long-legged Dougie. The pony was his mount, Mongrel.

'I can't imagine how you got him onto the table,' said Phryne to Jill. 'And how on earth are you going to get him down without breaking several legs—the table's and his?'

'Easy,' yelled Dougie, and chirruped. It was a small sweet noise but Mongrel pricked up his ears, minced to the end of the table, and dropped neatly down onto the floor.

'Amazing!' called Phryne.

'Always been a nippy sort of neddy,' said Dougie, scratching Mongrel between his hairy ears. 'I better get him out. That fizzy wine always goes to his head.'

'They're putting the polo match on tomorrow instead of Monday,' Jill told Phryne. 'You'll be there?'

'I certainly shall,' she promised.

Jill and Ann went back to join the chorus of 'More beer, more beer, more beer, more beer' to the tune of 'Auld Lang Syne' which the Tigers were singing almost tunefully. The advantage of that sort of drinking song was that even the most profoundly sozzled could not forget the words. By the time Phryne fought her way to her own peer group, Nicholas had secured the mint juleps and they were on their way out of the tent.

Outside it was almost quiet. Nerine met her band, the Three T's, and they all went to the jazz pavilion, where there were empty seats. Phryne saw that Nicholas had divined Nerine's state of eyesight and was steering her efficiently.

The band had beer. Several large jugs of it. Phryne tasted her julep. It was the essence of mint, icy on the tongue. The Three T's were constructing a song list.

'"St. James' Infirmary",' said Tabitha. 'Then "Kitchen Man", and perhaps, Nerine, do you want to sing "St. Louis Blues"?'

'Oh, please,' said Phryne. 'I love the way you sing "St. Louis Blues". And Nicholas hasn't heard you sing it.'

'Then he surely shall,' said Nerine, leaning a warm breast on the young man's arm. Nicholas blushed.

'Then we'll do "Tiger Rag",' continued Tabitha.

Phryne sipped her drink.

The jazz concert was all that a jazz concert could be. Phryne knew that the hunters were trap shooting by the noise and whooping, and presumed that charades were preparing in the Templar tent whence she must shortly go, but in the meantime the day was drowsily warm, the mint julep was reposing on top of her lunch with perfect amity, and the music was wonderful.

'St. Louis woman, love her diamond ring,' sang Nerine with aching perfection. 'Drag my man round, by her apron string. If it weren't for her powder and her store bought hair,…' Nerine clawed at her own glossy black locks '…that man of mine won't go nowhere.'

Nicholas was as fascinated as a bird before a snake, with the added advantage that Nerine would not eat him. Well, probably not. At least, not all at once.

'I never loved but three men in my life,' Nerine told the enthralled audience. 'T'was my father and my brother and the man who wrecked my life…Well I walked that floor and I wrung my hands and cried. Got the Saint Louis Blues and I can't be satisfied.'

The last word was a whisper, but everyone in the pavilion heard it, even over the small war happening beyond. There was a silence before the applause began. Nerine bowed, clasping her hands. One of the French girls near Phryne exclaimed in either envy or admiration, '*Quelle poitrine!*' What breasts!

Nicholas stiffened. Aha, thought Phryne, he speaks French. Better make sure. She leaned over to him.

'But they are beautiful, don't you think?'

'Of course,' he replied, clapping. 'More! More!'

Nerine tottered on the edge of the dais and Tommy drew her gently back.

'Gotta give the others their turn,' she said, and was led away to thunderous applause.

'I'm going to play charades,' said Phryne to Nicholas. 'Do you want to stay here? I'll see you later.'

'Mmm,' he said, and Phryne slipped away.

The tent was full. Most of the acolytes did not favour strenuous or violent activity. Which meant they didn't throw people into rivers, thought Phryne approvingly. She sat down near the door to watch the charade which was taking place on the stage in front of her.

Phryne had always liked parlour games. They had been the only harmless amusement of her childhood. Even her ne'er-do-well father had sometimes joined in. While not as exciting as robbing the pig bins outside the Victoria market, challenged by street boys and stray dogs, they had provided, for a little while, a factitious but cosy sense that the Fishers were actually a family, rather than the collection of bloody-minded self-absorbed individualists that they were…

A young acolyte was draped in a cowskin rug—where on earth had he got that?—and was making rushing, ramping movements, stamping on the stage and goring at the audience with two crooked fingers at his forehead as horns. Cow, or bull. First part of the word. The audience yelled, 'Bull,' and were affirmed. Second part. The bovine personage departed. Two people strolled onto the stage, one a very haughty young lady with a parasol and one a young man in a white suit and boater. He sat down on a seat. She strolled past him. As she did, he took off his hat and gave a massive grimace. The audience looked puzzled. The young lady— who was actually, Phryne realised, a young man, and wasn't that Sabine in the flannels and straw hat?—gave an atrocious wink. Phryne had the word but didn't want to upset the play.

'Whole word,' signalled the players. Now a man, stripped to the waist and wearing someone's green theatrical tights, came on stage with a longbow made of a curtain rod. He raised an imaginary arrow—Phryne's favourite kind—and aimed and fired into the wings. Someone there said, 'Well done, archer! You win the cup!' Then the players all came back to the stage and bowed.

'Bull's eye,' announced Phryne. Sylvanus stood up from Gerald's throne and caught sight of the speaker.

'Oh, well done, most sagacious Miss Fisher. Will you favour us with a charade?'

'I'll just go and find some props,' said Phryne, and went out as three people began to pull imaginary vertical ropes in what was probably the first part of a word beginning with 'ring'. Phryne had a wonderful charade word. She had stumped her family circle with it. All she needed was the small carpet from her room, a comb, and something to approximate a gown and coronet.

When she came back, laden with her props and a borrowed theatrical costume (Iolanthe, if she was any judge), the second part of the word was being acted. A smiling gentleman was opening a door and ushering a lady into a house, perhaps, and accepting a large envelope with RENT written on it in big crayoned capitals. It was as Phryne had thought, but it was someone else's turn to guess.

'Ringlet,' pronounced Jonathan. Sylvanus congratulated him and sent him off to assemble his own little play.

There followed a hilarious skit which involved a lissom Amelia, in sola topee, attempting to catch a butterfly with an invisible net. She danced very well, Phryne thought. The collector danced off to be replaced by Sad Alison in the sola topee as the Great White Hunter, scowling at a blacked-up boy who seemed to be reading out a list to him. As the audience remained entirely blank, the hunter stalked off to be replaced by a person who mimed, with accompanying noises, a cat being released from—a bag, of course. Phryne was not sure if sound was canonical.

The second part of the word involved the Great White Hunter relaxing after a long day's shikar. He dispatched the blacked-up servant for a drink, sending it back repeatedly until the *trink-wallah* finally staggered in under the weight of a bucket, then packed and lit a soothing and well-deserved pipe. Whole word, and all the participants marched onto the stage, skirling and hooting in mime. Bagpipe, and Phryne had hopes of Sad Alison, who had unexpected thespian abilities. Her Great White Hunter had just the right blend of parody and acute observation which made him really comic.

An American voice near Phryne said very quietly through the laughter, 'Well, will you look at that! The girl's a natural.'

Someone else murmured, 'Yes, sir, a natural.'

A man near Phryne nodded. Who were these people? Phryne didn't remember seeing them before. However, the charades continued.

Jonathan had assembled a choir of four. They were all dressed alike in hastily gathered white garments and boaters. They signalled first syllable, and then began to make some sort of inaudible music. Not singing. Their lips did not move. But they were clearly making a musical noise.

'Hum,' suggested a bright spark amongst the women. This was correct. The hummers went off. On stage came a person dressed in an approximation of a soldier's uniform (Iolanthe again?). He beat frantically with invisible sticks on an invisible drum. Whole word. Three people leaned back in chairs. A book dropped from one slack hand. Sewing lay untouched in a woman's lap. The third player yawned behind her fan. The tedium was practically crystallising on the air.

'Humdrum,' said Sabine. There was general applause.

'They're good,' said the American voice again.

'That they are,' said the second voice.

The third man just nodded.

Phryne went to the stage with her impedimenta. That might make a good charade word, too, she thought, as she faced the audience and signalled first syllable, squeezing her thumb and forefinger together.

'First syllable, very small,' said the audience. 'In? An? On?'

Phryne signalled that 'on' was correct. Then she made the finger and thumb again.

'Small? Smaller?' as she squeezed them together. 'A?'

Phryne nodded. Then she took out her comb and tried to comb her hair. She swore under her breath. Her hair really could have done with a good combing, and possibly a rosemary and egg rinse. Or beer, of course, there was a ready supply of beer. From the stage she could see the three Americans. One very well dressed, rather corpulent man with a watchchain, two followers in neat grey suits. They stood out like three black dogs on a white counterpane. The audience called out suggestions: 'Tangle? Snarl? Mat?'

'Mat' it was and Phryne did the little word gesture.

'A?'

'A' was accepted and Phryne enveloped herself in a rich red robe and stuck the fairy queen's crown on her head. Then she adopted a look of lordly condescension and waved a hand at the peasants. They went though all the variations of queen and lord before someone finally happened upon 'peer'.

And now it was time for the whole word. Phryne took off her robes, laid out her carpet, sat down cross-legged upon it in imitation of a yogi, and folded her arms. There was a dumb-founded silence.

Then Gilbert, the young man with the scented bath fetish, began to laugh helplessly.

'What?' demanded several voices.

'Can't you see it, you dolts? It's the cleverest today,' he giggled. 'Onomatopoeia. On-a-mat-appear. Oh, well done, Miss Fisher!'

Phryne bowed and went back to her place.

The last charade of the afternoon was Sylvanus'. He came on stage with a tall young man who was holding a branch above his head. The young man swayed and bent. 'Wind?' the watchers guessed. 'Breeze?' Sylvanus unshipped something from his shoulder and began to chop. The young man shrieked silently. Phryne was unsettled. This was far too cruel for an afternoon's amusement. This was charades, not grand guignol.

'Tree,' she called. Sylvanus grinned at her.

Then the stage was set for a family dinner. Several people were sitting on the floor on cushions (probably for tonight). Sylvanus was draped in a long rich garment and had a blue kefiyah on his head. He looked surprisingly authentic as a sheik of the desert. His concubines offered him tea and he drank it, sighing and putting a hand to his head theatrically. If it had had a caption the scene would have been entitled 'Oh, woe!'

Then running, stumbling, came a half-naked man, clothed only in a sheepskin. His hair was long and disarrayed, his body striped with mud, his feet filthy. Husks still clung to his skin. An unprepossessing sight but Sylvanus leapt to his feet, cast his robe around the boy, and started shouting orders. One of the men objected, but was sent off immediately. The prodigal had returned to his father.

'For this my son is come home…' said Phryne.

'Son!' called Marie-Louise.

Whole word. Sylvanus, wrapped in a black cloak, lurked in a corner. Another person, equally wrapped, approached him. Sylvanus handed over an envelope marked 'CASH' and received in return a roll of paper marked 'SECRETS'.

'Treason!' exclaimed Sabine.

Everyone applauded, then began to stand. Five o'clock and the hearties and horsemen would be out of the bar by now. Everyone felt they had done well and deserved the drink of their choice. They needed a wash and brush-up before they dressed for the Arab feast, and someone was going to have to charm some butter from the housekeeper to get the burned cork off Minou.

'Remarkable,' said the American.

'Yes, sir,' said the second man.

The third man nodded.

Phryne decided on a swim. The water was cold, her hair needed a wash, and there was something about lying in water, supported and buoyant, staring idly at the sky, that assisted her thought processes. She lathered and rinsed her hair before she went into the water. Definitely an egg shampoo when she got home. That fierce combing had pulled out what felt like handfuls of hair. Meanwhile she had a riddle to solve and an assassin to foil.

Phryne rocked in the cradle of the deep, half asleep, not consciously thinking…

When she swam ashore she had no clue as to the identity of the assassin, but she thought she might know where Tarquin was. And who had kidnapped him.

Her bath was scented with roses, for innocence. As usual, Gilbert was waiting for her, and slipped inside saying, 'Oh, divine! Heaven must smell like this.'

'If it doesn't, I'm not going,' replied Phryne. 'But then, I might not have the option.'

She liked her Arab clothes. Fortunately the weather had cooled a little, or they might have been too heavy to endure. She had a loose white shift, ankle length, a loose dark red robe, a lot of tin jewellery and several filmy black veils. Presumably these were to be disposed as the wearer thought fit. Phryne let them drift down over her head and pinned them where they fell. It made a fluid and elegant effect. She left a long edge so that she could cover her face. She remembered being mistaken for a man in Egypt, when she had been dressed in drill trousers suitable for investigating dusty tombs. Women washing at a well, unveiled, had thrown the skirts of their gowns over their heads, revealing their salient attributes but covering their faces. Strange place, Egypt. Phryne had not liked it much. The antiquuities were fine but the weather was atrocious and the veiled women made her uncomfortable. What was seething behind those blank exteriors?

Nicholas joined her, looking like an extra from *The Son of the Sheik*, though his butter-coloured hair and fine blue eyes rather ruined the illusion. He looked, in fact, just like one of the romantic heroes in railway novels. Phryne said so.

'Thanks,' he murmured. 'I think. Tell me how to comport myself at an Arab feast, Phryne.'

'Simple. Eat with your hands, but only your right hand. Easy way to remember is to sit on your left hand. Your left hand is unclean. The food will be very tasty and easy to eat with the fingers. You will like it,' instructed Phryne.

And she was right, thought Nicholas, scooping in another mouthful of saffron rice and roast lamb. No one had asked him to eat a sheep's eye, though he was willing to do anything once. The mood of the gathering was affable. The flat bread was odd but tasty, and so were the beans in oil, and those little red peppers that packed such a punch. Forewarned by his wasabi experience, he had tasted them very gingerly and had escaped with merely a second degree burn to the soft palate. Gerald Templar, looking very fit after his day in the saddle, had announced that there would be no karez that night, so Nicholas could afford to relax a little.

Phryne, reclining next to him, was remarkably attractive, though she was just a bundle of garments, sketchily hinting that there might be a womanly shape under them. The hash scent of the hubble-bubbles was almost subsumed by very strong incense, smelling of sandalwood.

The poetry recitation was beginning, and since they knew what poem Nicholas would recite, he had not been asked. Phryne had a poem prepared. The theme was 'regret'. Gilbert stood up to recite, draping his robe gracefully. What he recited was unbearably sad, but he showed no sign of being affected, speaking as clearly and unemotionally as a child.

'So we'll go no more a-roving
'So late into the night.
'Though the heart be still as loving
'And the moon be still as bright
'For the sword outwears the sheath
'As the soul wears out the breast
'And the heart must pause to breathe
'And love itself have rest.
'Though the night was made for loving
'And the day returns too soon
'Yet we'll go no more a-roving
'By the light of the moon.'

Gilbert sat down. The whole company was on the verge of tears. He smiled a faint, amused smile.

Sylvanus leapt to his feet. 'Oh the harems of Egypt were fair to behold…' he began.

Oh, good old 'Abdul the Bul-Bul Amir', thought Phryne, blinking back tears. Crass, crude, and very biological, and it utterly destroyed the air of complete despair that Gilbert had generated.

Phryne had no time for despair. She had solved her riddle, and seated across from her, triumphantly unveiled, sat Alison, sad no longer, occasionally stroking the glossy tresses of her beautiful chestnut hair.

The Joker had gone for a little swim in the lake, avoiding the hearties. It was a pity that the hunt had not killed, but he could wait for his taste of blood.

Chapter Fifteen

For they waddied one another till the plain
was strewn with dead,
While the score was kept so even
that they neither got ahead.

A.B. Paterson
'The Geebung Polo Club'

After Abdul had come to his well-deserved conclusion, Phryne stood up to speak her deceptively artless Verlaine. Written about what he could see from his prison window, it had always moved her by its simplicity, speaking of the blue sky and the branch shaking above the roof, the bell ringing, the peaceful murmur from the village, and the prisoner's cry, 'My God! This is what life is!'

'Le ciel est, par-dessus le toit
'Si bleu, si calme!
'Un arbre, par-dessus le toit,
'Berce sa palme.

'…Mon Dieu, mon Dieu, la vie est l^.
'Simple et tranquille.
'Cette paisible rumeur-l^
'Vient de la ville.

'Qu'as-tu fait, ô toi que voil^
'Pleurant sans cesse
'Dis, qu'as-tu fait, toi que voil^,
'De ta jeunesse?'

For a change, Sylvanus did not sneer, possibly because of
what Phryne could have said about 'Abdul the Bul-Bul Amir' as
a poem for decent company. Or even Templar company. There
were murmurs of appreciation.

Then the Lady rose, supported by her acolytes.

'She doesn't often recite,' said Nicholas. 'That was very pretty,
Phryne. All I know about Verlaine is scandal.'

'There is more to know,' Phryne informed him, as Isabella
began her poem. Her voice was beautiful, sweet and clear. Her
choice was 'The Nymph Complaining for the Death of Her
Fawn', by Andrew Marvell.

'The wanton Troopers riding by
'Have shot my Fawn, and it will dye.
'Ungentle men! they cannot thrive
'Who killed thee. Thou ne'er didst alive
'Them any harm: alas! nor cou'd
'Thy Death yet do them any Good...'

One of the three American gentlemen sitting behind Phryne—
she really must find out who they were when she had a moment—
said, 'Wonderful.' The second said, 'Wonderful.' And there was
a pause while the third, presumably, nodded.

'Upon the Roses it would feed
'Until its lips ev'n seemed to Bleed
'And then to me 'twould boldly trip
'And print those Roses on my lip...'

Strong, sensuous images flooded through the company: the fawn
kissing the nymph on her reddened mouth, the nymph with

the snow white skin and flaxen hair of the Lady, her cool hands caressing it in death, blood on her white gauzy gown.

Phryne shook herself free of the spell. Wonder of wonders, now Gerald was going to recite. He stood up from his throne after the applause for his sister's recitation had died away and said conversationally:

'It was many and many a year ago,
'In a kingdom by the sea
'That a maiden there lived whom you may know
'By the name of Annabel Lee;
'And this maiden she lived with no other thought
'Than to love and be loved by me.

'I was a child and she was a child
'In this kingdom by the sea
'But we loved with a love that was more than love
'I and my Annabel Lee;
'With a love that the winged seraphs of heaven
'Coveted her and me.'

Phryne saw his hand stretch out to his sister. They stood together, pale and paler, fair and fairer, while the golden voice continued the dreadful tale which had made Poe's readers shudder and throw the paper into the fire. For a while Phryne lost the thread of the poem, contemplating the Templars: so beautiful, so strange, as alien as if they had come from another time or another planet in one of Mr. Wells' machines.

'But our love it was stronger by far than the love
'Of those who were older than we;
'Of many far wiser than we;
'And neither the angels in heaven above
'Nor the demons down under the sea
'Can ever dissever my soul from the soul of the beautiful
      Annabel Lee.

'For the moon never beams without bringing me dreams
'Of the beautiful Annabel Lee;
'And the stars never rise but I feel the bright eyes
'Of the beautiful Annabel Lee;
'So all the night tide I lie down by the side
'Of my darling—my darling—my life and my bride,
'In her sepulchre there by the sea,
'In her tomb by the sounding sea.'

After that, there was no more poetry. There seemed, as Phryne remarked, nothing more to be said.

'Was I right or was I right?' asked the American gentleman, sounding very pleased, even smug.

'You're right,' said his second.

'Yes,' said the third, speaking for the first time. Then he nodded, just in case.

Arabic music broke out from a hidden corner (where there was probably a gramophone). Platters of sweets were carried in, and little bowls of sherbet and ice cream. Mrs. Truebody's ice cream was good, though not as good as Mrs. Butler's. Phryne leaned back and enjoyed it, and the strong aniseed tasting liqueurs which accompanied the dessert.

'Arak,' she told Nicholas.

'Tastes like licorice. I've got someone to meet,' he said, getting up. 'Will you excuse me?'

'Nerine?' asked Phryne.

'Nerine,' said Nicholas, and went, relieving Phryne of a difficult decision but leaving her a little disgruntled. She ate more ice cream. Ice cream was reliable. Young men were not.

Belly dancers romped in, all jingly bracelets and skin shining with sweat. The drums pounded. The dancers twirled and gyrated. Phryne was not in the mood. She slipped out of the tent and, after a phone call to Dot, put herself to bed relatively early. Saturday was ending in virtuous isolation, which might not have been what she'd had in mind but appeared to be all that was on offer. She closed her eyes resolutely. And slept.

Sunday, 30th December

Phryne rose betimes, ate a solid breakfast, and sat down on the verandah to await the coming of the Hispano-Suiza and the heartening presence of her familiar friends. She was becoming keyed up: a hunting alertness was refining her eyesight and interfering with her digestion. Tonight, the Feast of Fools, would produce the assassin. He or she must be caught. Ted came and leaned in the doorway beside her. He was carrying a yard broom.

'No news?' he asked, speaking like a prisoner, not moving his lips. This also allowed him to retain his hand rolled cigarette in his mouth.

'None,' sighed Phryne. 'But the attack must be tonight. This Joker is peculiar about killing people in the midst of their favourite activity, apparently. Tonight the Templars will be doing their favourite thing, at about eleven, and that is when he will strike. And we have to stop him.'

'We have to stop him,' repeated Ted.

'That's right.'

'When no one else has ever laid a glove on him?'

'Yes.'

'Jeez,' said Ted.

'Indeed.'

They said nothing for a while, looking out at the rolling green parkland and the men setting out the goals and the boundary rope on the polo ground.

'Reckon we've got our work cut out for us,' said Ted.

'We have,' said Phryne.

Silence fell again.

'I better get a move on,' said Ted, and went away.

The next visitor was Nicholas. He looked haggard. A night with Nerine really took it out of a man, Phryne knew. She had seen the pallid specimens on the morning after, gulping restorative coffee and whimpering at sudden noises. Some of this had to do with her consumption of Kentucky sour mash bourbon, which an Eastern Market wine merchant imported especially for her. The rest was all down to Nerine herself.

'Any coffee in your thermos?' he asked, sitting down suddenly. 'The stuff at breakfast tasted like dishwater.'

'Here,' Phryne supplied him. 'Keep out of the sun. Would you like some aspirin?'

'Yes,' he said weakly. 'About ten will do to start with.'

'There's a paper or two in my bag.'

He picked up the decorated Pierrot bag but seemed unable to work the catch. Phryne took it from him out of pure Christian pity and handed over the drug. He washed the powders down with more coffee.

'I feel awful,' he confessed.

'You look like the "before" picture in a Beecham's Pills advertisement.'

'That woman can drink,' he said. 'We drank a lot of drinks. And she sang a lot of songs. It's all a bit of a blur, actually.'

'I can imagine. Sit quietly here in the shade and you'll feel better in half an hour. Not in mid season form,' she said, patting his hand, 'but better than you do at present.'

'Couldn't feel worse,' he groaned.

'Is this your very first hangover?' asked Phryne. 'What a sweet, sheltered life you have been leading, to be sure. Why not go and lie on my bed? It's nice and quiet there, better than your tent. Here's the key. I'll come and wake you presently.'

Nicholas had never been so grateful for any favour. Clutching the thermos and his head he staggered into the house to find the Iris Room where, with any luck, there might be blessed darkness and coolness and all the other things of which he stood in need.

Phryne did not chuckle until he was safely gone. First hangover. Poor boy. When had she first experienced a hangover? Ah, yes. At a schoolgirl festival of some sort. She and Bunji Ross had got into the sweet sherry. The next day she had been expelled again, but she would have welcomed being executed, she had felt so sick…and apart from an unfortunate encounter with some methylated raki in Paris, that was the last hangover she had had. Phryne didn't like pain. It hurt. She avoided it whenever she could. And if that meant not drinking that fifth cocktail, then there it was. It was an imperfect universe.

But a very pretty one, this morning. A little wind had picked up, just enough to take the edge off the heat. The grass was green. The sky was blue, just like Verlaine's sad little poem. At least Phryne had no intention of weeping without cease over her misspent youth. She had not so much misspent it as invested it wisely, and she only regretted the bare minimum of it.

She sat basking in the early morning sun. Presently the big red car swished to a halt beside her. A young woman in a terracotta hat and jacket, carrying a suitcase, alighted.

'Hello, Dot,' said Phryne sleepily. 'Isn't it a lovely day?'

'Yes, it is,' said Dot, who was now enjoying her post breakfast drives with Mr. Butler. 'I've been to early mass and that's why we're a little late. Here's your stuff, Miss,' she said, offering the suitcase.

Phryne stood up to go into the house and then remembered Nicholas.

'Oh dear, I just recalled that there is a young man in my bed, sleeping off a hangover. No, don't look shocked, he debauched himself in other company than mine. I just offered him a bed, not one with me in it. Never mind. We can tiptoe. Any more information about the man we are thinking about, Dot?'

'No, Miss, just what I told you last night. Mr. Bert and Mr. Cec are real worried about you. And Mr. Robinson.'

'I'll be careful. And I'm armed. And forewarned, as well. Did you bring the extra ammunition?'

'Yes, Miss, it's in the case. You think this might come to shooting?'

'It might, then again, it might not,' temporised Phryne, not wanting to worry Dot unduly. 'I'm going to brief my accomplices this morning, before the polo match.'

'Well, I knew this was a Godless gathering, Miss, but that is too much!' exclaimed Dot, really offended.

'What?' asked Phryne. 'Keep your voice down, remember the afflicted.'

'The polo match!' said Dot.

'What about it? You consider polo anti-Christian? You might be right, at that. All those ball games strike me as having originated in some barbarian army, where the Mongol hordes played catch with enemy heads.'

Dot dismissed the Mongol hordes with a gesture. 'Miss, it's Sunday!'

'Oh,' said Phryne, who had not given the Sunday Observance Statutes a thought. 'So it is. One rather loses track of the days. Never mind, Dot dear. You can pray for the heathens and I'll try to keep the Templars alive, what about that? Now let's just put the case inside and collect the laundry really quietly. You have never had a hangover, so you will not know the tortures that Nicholas is suffering.'

Dot subsided. Phryne put the case in the room, picked up the laundry bag, collected her empty thermos and closed the door. The young reprobate was snoring like an orchestra. Another reason not to sleep with him, thought Phryne.

'Did you bring the money? I might have to pay my army,' said Phryne.

Dot gave her a purse. It was satisfactorily heavy.

'Oh, and the chestnut blossom bath salts,' said Dot. 'Miss Steinbach sent them. From America,' Dot added, impressed. 'And those books you wanted. Is there anything else, Miss?'

'Sit with me for a while, until Mr. Butler gets back from debriefing poor old Tom Ventura. I gather he isn't any happier.'

'No, Miss, but it's all gone well so far. Not even any injuries to mention. You haven't…you haven't found that poor little boy?'

'No, Dot, but I am at last seeing light at the end of the tunnel, and we must pray that it isn't an oncoming Cornish Express. What are the girls doing?'

'Drawing, Miss. Ruth found that paintbox she got for school and never needed, and now both of them are mad about watercolours. They're painting the sea today,' said Dot. 'Miss Eliza says that they can do whatever they like on Sunday, as long as it doesn't damage the house or wake her from her nap.'

'Another Godless heathen.' Phryne grinned at her worried companion. 'You're surrounded by them, Dot dear.'

'Actually I've been getting on with the mending,' confessed Dot. 'God forgive me, but those girls go through socks like a hot knife through butter.'

'And you like mending,' pressed Phryne.

Dot blushed as though confessing a grievous fault to a stern priest. 'I do,' she said. 'Oh, here's Mr. Butler.'

'Hello,' Phryne greeted him. 'How is your Mr. Ventura today?'

'Seems to be a bit more cheerful,' said the chauffeur, pushing back his cap. 'Mind you, couldn't have got any more doleful. But the party's nearly over, and nothing dreadful has happened. Yet, as he'd say.'

'All right. I'll keep in touch, Dot, and you have the phone number if you need to find me. Take care,' said Phryne as she watched Dot being handed into the red car. 'And I'll take care, too,' she promised. The Hispano-Suiza started with a roar and slid away, scattering gravel.

Presently Phryne roused herself and wandered down to the horse lines, where preparations for the polo match were feverish. She was just about to circumnavigate a huge elm when she heard a sentiment which made her stop, her hands on the rough grey bark.

'We'll pound 'em,' someone was saying in a fine upper-class accent. 'Pound 'em into the dust.'

'I say, steady on, Johnson!' murmured another voice. 'Brotherhood of the mallet, you know.'

'Brotherhood of the mallet my foot,' retorted Johnson. 'They've got girls on their team. It's an insult to the game.'

'They ride pretty well,' said Ralph Norton. 'I don't reckon there's any insult in them wanting to play our game. Trying to improve themselves. Hullo-ullo-ullo!' he carolled as Phryne came out from behind her tree. 'Hear you got on well with my Buttercup.'

'She's a darling,' said Phryne, as the little beast, hearing her name, tittupped forward to receive a carrot from her doting master.

'Isn't she though?' enthused Ralph. 'Johnson, this is Miss Fisher. Miss Fisher, this is Johnson.'

Johnson, a sleek lad with prominent teeth, evidently approved of girls who rode well but did not try to play polo. He shook Phryne's hand.

'Delighted,' he said.

'So, you are going to beat the Tigers?' asked Phryne, caressing Buttercup's silky nose.

'Of course,' said Johnson airily. 'I only hope they don't fall apart too fast. They might just be able to give us a game.'

'I see,' said Phryne. She nodded to Ralph, and passed on. She found Jill and Ann rinsing dust out of equine eyes and cleaning hoofs.

'Phryne! Good to see you! You haven't met our other mounts. This is Black Boy, named after King Charles,' said Jill. 'This is Rapide, and this is Ann's pony George.'

'Pleased to meet you,' said Phryne to the eager, questing noses, distributing some carrots which she had pinched from Ralph Norton's supply. He wouldn't miss them. 'Aren't you the pretty ones, though! No more now, neddies, you have to work hard today.'

'My old dad swears by a handful of sugar just before they go on,' said Jill. 'I reckon it works, too. How do they look?' she asked with pardonable pride.

Compared to the Grammar ponies, these were unkempt and homely. But they were clean and cared for and practically dancing in their horseshoes.

'They do you credit,' she told Jill and Ann, and walked on towards the lake.

Phryne, unusually, had time to waste and nothing to do so, in a spirit of satisfaction after she had ascertained that certain of her hypotheses were correct, she sat down on a rustic bench under a spreading monkey puzzle and opened her book. The polo match was at eleven. Plenty of time to find out what Hercule Poirot would make of the strange death of Roger Ackroyd. She lit a Sobranie.

A bleat and a strong whiff of goat, and she knew that her old friends were with her again. This time there were three goats, being walked on halters by the Goat Lady.

'Sorry, I haven't a leaf on me,' she apologised to Mintie.

'But you could give your butt to Willie, here,' said the Goat Lady. 'This is Willie and this is Wayland,' she introduced two billy goats of fearsome aspect. 'Willie got a taste for tobacco, somehow. I'm going up to the house for the breakfast leftovers. Never ate so well in all my puff.'

Phryne could believe it. Madge the Goat Lady had certainly filled out since the Last Best Party had been going on.

'How are you going to manage when we've packed up and gone?' she asked, stubbing out the cigarette and allowing Willie to snuff it up from her hand. He chewed on it like an old sailor. Mintie nudged Phryne and solicited a scratch between the ears.

'Oh, I manage, Miss, I manage like I always have. I've got my goats and milk and cheese, and I've got all the vegies that they don't eat, and I pick up some work here and there. I got my pension. This party is just a treat, that's all.'

'Yes, so it is,' said Phryne. 'What does Wayland like to eat?'

'Just about anything,' said the Goat Lady. 'Got to go,' she added, and led the goats around the lake, towards the house and the kitchen and a truly succulent breakfast. Phryne was pleased that Mintie had not scorned her because she had none of her favourite herb.

She returned to her book. Time passed. Phryne stowed the book and stretched. On the way to the polo ground, she detoured through the knot garden. Fortunately, there was no one to explain the rules to Phryne as the two sides lined up. She already knew that the game was divided into chukkas of seven minutes each. The ponies danced and neighed. The riders, in the case of the Grammar Boys, glittered. Phryne put on a pair of smoked glasses. The sward was emerald green and well watered so perhaps falls might be soft. The umpires reported all was ready. Then the game began.

After a few minutes Phryne began to get the hang of it. Inasmuch as she ever got the hang of games. The ponies darted across the lines, the riders clouted the ball with their mallets, and the game rushed, amazingly quickly, up and down the huge ground. The odd thing was that neither side seemed to be able to score. Just as the ball got within thudding distance of the Tigers' goal, a Grammar Boy would sneak it away. Just when the ball approached the Grammar goal, Dougie on Mongrel or Murph on Moke would sidle in and steal it. Chukka after chukka passed and still no one managed to belt the ball through the goals. The Tigers were being run ragged. The pristine Grammar Boys were sweating. And everyone, Phryne included, was barracking.

'They're good,' observed Albert Green, the elderly stable-man, who was sharing Phryne's verdant bank.

'Who is?'

'Both of them. I reckon they're evenly matched. But the Tigers can't win,' he said.

'Why not?' asked Phryne. 'They're doing pretty well until now.'

'They got no remounts,' said Green. 'My young men can have a fresh horse every chukka if they want.'

'Ah,' said Phryne. But he was right. The Tigers were beginning to flag. Their ponies, willing as ever, were tiring. Still the Grammar Boys did not seem to be able to break through. Whenever they set up a long run down the field, Jill would be there on Rapide, turning on a sixpence, or Ann on George, or the ever present Dougie on Mongrel.

'Half-time,' said the umpire, and the horses streamed off the field. The Tigers slumped to the ground while their mounts were watered sparingly and rubbed down. Valets and stablemen attended the Grammar Boys. Tired ponies were led away and fresh ones brought up from the lines. Phryne saw that Ralph was going to ride Buttercup. Housemaids from the manor were passing through the riders, distributing sandwiches, fruit cup and tea.

Phryne could hear the Grammar captain haranguing his team. 'Are we going to be beaten by these up-country rustics?' he yelled.

Phryne did not hear any answer from the exhausted men. The Wonnangatta Tigers were drinking tea as though there might be a world shortage, but they were not eating. Jill was lamenting Rapide's knee, which was swelling, while Ann was moving the saddle onto Black Boy's back. She fed him a handful of coarse brown sugar. Phryne could see the pony relishing the taste.

'Here we go again,' said Albert Green. He had managed to corner a whole box of unwanted sandwiches and had a huge tin mug of tea. 'You watch, Miss, they'll score this chukka.'

But they didn't. Faint and flagging the Tigers might have been, but their ponies were used to wheeling cattle in high country scrub. They were as tough as old tree roots, and so were their riders. They might have limped behind the action, but when the ball was there, so were the Tigers.

The Grammar Boys were wearying. This was not how the game was supposed to go. They decided on a rush and barrelled down the ground, only to be met with a resistance so fierce that the ponies must have wondered what had come over their riders.

The last chukka. The Tigers were exhausted. Their ponies' sides were striped with foam. Albert Green, having mangled his way through all of his sandwiches, said, 'By God, they might do it, they might!' and Phryne found that against all inclination she was caught up in this contest.

But she did not see it when Johnson, maddened by this rustic and feminine defiance, decided to settle the matter by himself. Rushing beside Dougie when the play was elsewhere, he delivered a powerful blow to the pony's knees, and Mongrel went down. There was a howl of outrage.

'What happened?' demanded Phryne.

'The hound!' howled the old man. 'That's never sport! They ought to be ashamed! A foul, and no umpire could see it!'

'They cheated?' asked Phryne

'They did, by God,' swore Mr. Green.

Phryne opened her bag, took something out and squeezed it hard.

Mongrel was led off the ground. His legs weren't broken, at least. But Dougie had no other pony and the Tigers were now one rider down. Surely the Grammar Boys must win.

Then, drawn irresistibly by her favourite scent in the whole world, along came Mintie the goat. She was inoffensive, as goats go. She tripped carefully through the people. She did not cross the sacred boundary onto the polo ground. She was merely heading for a source of mint.

The Grammar horses had seen cars and planes and trains and bicycles, but they had never seen goats. As one pony, they stopped and stared at Mintie as she made her way around the ground.

'Now!' yelled Jill, passing the ball to Ann, and they fled down the ground, skirting hysterical ponies who had found that they really couldn't stand goats until, with a resounding thwack, Ann hit the ball through the goals and rode off the field as the bell sounded for the end of the match.

There was a sudden, vast silence. Mintie had gone from their sight, seeking her herb. Fallen Grammar Boys got up from the turf, feeling their bruises. Ponies nuzzled riders, unable to explain what had come over them. Johnson scowled. Wonnangatta Tigers stared at each other.

Then someone on the hill began to applaud and the air was filled with clapping and cheering. The captain of the Grammar Boys slapped the captain of the Wonnangatta Tigers on the shoulder as the umpire proclaimed them winners. Ralph Norton said 'Good show!' to Ann. Then, horses and all, they paraded back towards the house, arms around each other, Jill and Ann carried shoulder high by their peers.

And when they had all gone, Phryne Fisher fed a whole bunch of mint to an appreciative goat.

No one noticed her actions except Mr. Green. He never said a word, but chuckled, at intervals, for the next three days.

'This is the festival of…' Dot began.

'I'm tired of all these saints,' said Ruth. 'Tell us a nice miracle.'

'All right,' said Dot, taken aback. 'One day Saint Elizabeth of Hungary was warned by her cruel husband that she could not give any more of his bread to the poor. He told her if he caught her giving any charity again, he would kill her.'

'They made husbands really nasty in the old days,' said Ruth, embracing Molly.

'But she was a kind lady and the poor were starving. So she went on feeding them. Then one day her husband stopped her at the door. She was carrying a basket of bread, one of those baskets with a lid. "What's in here?" he roared. And she said, inspired by God, "Roses." And he shoved her to her knees and tore open the basket and what do you think he found?'

'Bread,' said Jane, a practical thinker.

'Roses,' said Dot.

'I don't understand,' said Jane.

'Of course you don't,' replied Dot. 'It's a miracle.'

Chapter Sixteen

To kill two birds with one stone.

Trad.

Luncheon was hilarious, with polo players replaying the game, and notable for Mongrel hopping up onto the bar table for his champagne as if he hadn't been felled by a blow which would have broken the knees of a lesser beast. His action in kicking Johnson on the way out was charitably put down to the un-accustomed wine going to the pony's head. Phryne found Ralph Norton deep in conversation on pony rearing with Jill, Ann and several other Tigers. She attracted his attention long enough to collect on her bet.

Phryne sauntered back to the house to find that Nicholas had just woken up feeling like a human again.

'Bourbon,' he told her, shuddering strongly. 'Never touch the stuff. Or that peach brandy called Southern Comfort. It's lethal. Is it lunch time? I might be able to eat a bit. Thanks to you, Phryne. Ministering angel and all that.'

'I've brought our boxes,' said Phryne. 'You missed a riveting game of polo. The Tigers won with the help of a passing goat. Have you got egg sandwiches?'

'No, ham.' Nicholas investigated further. 'And this one's tomato and lettuce and cheese and things.' He ate it. It stayed down. 'I am not going to die after all,' he announced.

Phryne poured them both a cup of coffee from her refilled thermos.

'Good, because I need my bed. I am proposing to conclude lunch with a nice nap,' she told him. 'Tonight is going to be testing. Are you armed?'

'Yes,' said Nicholas soberly. 'Are you?'

'I am. My companion brought me some extra ammo.'

'I've got enough for all the good it will do,' he said, eating another sandwich. 'This Joker is impossible to catch.'

'Nonsense. You're just saying that because no one ever has,' she told him. 'Stop being so discouraging. I just won five pounds on a polo team that no one would sensibly back, so you can see how foolish you are being. Now, you need some exercise. Go for a nice long walk and a swim and you will feel much better. The Feast of Fools starts at four on the Great Lawn. I shall be there. And if you do not know how to dance a pavane, I shall be delighted to teach you. Bye,' said Phryne, and Nicholas removed himself and his lunch box into the corridor. He heard the door shut and a chair-back being forced under the handle.

A little at a loss, he went to the hornbeam to finish his meal, and then decided on a nice long walk as Miss Fisher had suggested. He was getting stale with all these late nights.

Phryne Fisher, relieved of company, finished the biscuits (which were as excellent as ever) with a cup of coffee. Then she took off most of her clothes and lay down in her bed, cradling the pillow to her cheek, and willed herself to fall asleep. And did.

Three thirty and Phryne came awake, as she had arranged with her internal clock. Time for a wash and the donning of her very own costume. Phryne had been persuaded by a certain Orkney fiddler to attend several functions which required medieval dress, and she decided that she would have her own clothes made.

This was a rather tasty page's outfit in Lincoln green. She did not want to be encumbered with the long sleeves and flowing gown of a medieval woman on this night. And her instructions had told her that she was elected page for the night.

And while she was at it she needed to muster her troops. She needed to talk to Sam, Gabriel, the wharfies and Mrs. Truebody about the projected capture of the Joker. This took some effort and she scrambled into the tights and jerkin just in time to arrive at the Great Lawn before the Templars. The company was very decorative, as multi-coloured as a field of flowers. Gauzy veils floated from high hennins, sleeves dipped to the grass to meet the curly points of shoes, and Sylvanus Leigh was resplendent as the Lord of Misrule. He had a jester's costume and a reproving bladder on a stick. He grinned sardonically at Phryne in her boy's clothes and belted her with the bladder.

'Lost your nerve, lovely lady?'

'Joining the other side,' retorted Phryne.

Sylvanus laughed. Phryne sniffed. Somewhere, someone had lit a fire and was roasting meat. On a spit, perhaps? Very medieval. We must look like a Turkey carpet from the sky, thought Phryne. All these colours. All moving. Nicholas arrived in a knee length purple gown and surcoat, wearing a small round Piranesi hat.

'Pavane,' said Phryne, holding out her left hand. He bowed, kissed her fingers, and waited for instructions.

'The pavane was invented so that everyone, even the elderly and infirm, could walk around the hall and inspect everyone else—clothes, hairstyle, who they were dancing with. There-fore it is slow and graceful and even one in possession of two left feet can dance it. Thus…'

The company had lined up in a long snaking circle of couples around the perimeter of the Great Lawn. Three musicians stood in the middle. One had a pipe, one had a drum, and one was playing Phryne's particular detestation, the crumhorn, an instrument which sounded like a trodden-on trumpet with warped clarinet overtones.

'Bow,' said Phryne, bowing. 'Step, pause at the end of each step. You lift yourself onto your toes and down but you don't need to worry about that yet. Step, three small steps, pause. Forward again. Step, pause, step, pause, step, step, step, pause. Again. Then back,' she said, shoving him gently. 'The same thing. Step, pause, step, pause, step, step, step, pause. Then you drop to one knee and I go around you, clockwise, thus. Then I stand here and you go around me. That's it. And now forward...'

After a few repetitions of the figures, Nicholas began to enjoy the pavane. It did allow one time to look around, especially considering that most medieval dancers would have been pavaning since early childhood. Even the hearties and the horsemen were joining in, though some were miffed when Jill and Ann insisted on dancing with each other. Step, pause, step, pause, step, step, step, pause. Where was the Joker? Who was he? And who was his target? Am I going to live through tonight? thought Nicholas. He stumbled, and missed his step.

'Hold up,' said Phryne. 'Talk, if you're worried.'

'How did you know that?'

'I'm worried too,' said Miss Fisher. 'I'm not a soldier, trained to battle. In fact I bet soldiers worry as well, they just don't tell us about it.'

'Just the usual worries, Phryne: shall I eat breakfast tomorrow?' he said, smiling with some effort.

'Oh, yes,' she said, smiling with no effort at all. 'I am confident of that.'

Nicholas immediately felt better. He told himself this was silly, but he felt better all the same.

'And I can't imagine a world without you in it,' he said to the top of Phryne's green velvet cap, which was all of her that he could see when she moved closer to him. Her long pheasant's feather tickled his chin.

'Good,' she answered. 'Keep on imagining. With you imagining and Dot praying, we ought to manage.'

An hour later Nicholas was mastering the intricacies of the Officer's Bransle and wondering why he had ever classed himself as an inept dancer. Of course, there was no medieval version of the Charleston, for which he just didn't have the ankles. And instead of the sharp, jarring rhythms of modern dances, the medieval ones were energetic enough but designed for someone wearing approximately three times the weight in clothes of the average 1928 nightclubber.

He grabbed a stout acolyte around the waist and hurled her into the air. This was fun. Though he did wish Sylvanus would stop bashing him with that stupid bladder on a stick. And if those were authentic medieval jokes, the bawdry of his ancestors had been remarkable.

Phryne took a break while the musicians retooled their crum-horn. With any luck it would be permanently broken. The strange thing was that anyone could even tell when there was something wrong with it. She accepted a drink of chilled red wine cup from Minnie, who was quivering with excitement.

'Everything's ready, Miss. Your blokes brought the stuff out and it's all where you said it should be.'

'Good,' said Phryne. 'And Mrs. Truebody knows about getting everyone inside and the big doors shut? This is a dangerous person.'

'Yes, Miss. Just you give the signal.'

'Good work, Minnie.'

'Oh, and Miss?'

'Yes?' asked Phryne, holding out her goblet for a refill.

'Sam said I should tell you, Miss. About him and me. We're getting married.'

'That's wonderful,' said Phryne. 'Congratulations. He's a very nice man.'

Minnie blushed. 'I never would have known it except for the way he's looking after Marigold. I mean, he looks sort of rough. And, Miss? Is there any chance we could keep her for our own?'

'I don't know,' said Phryne. 'I shall have to see. Let's just get through tonight, Minnie, and then tomorrow will be another day.'

'Yes, Miss.'

Minnie carried her big silver jug through the recovering dancers, distributing smiles and wine. The girl was glowing with happiness. One person, at least, is unaffectedly happy in this gathering, thought Phryne. How nice. How very nice.

The Joker mopped his brow. Tonight was the night. He would know when the perfect moment was. It was worth all this effort, if the execution was at the peak time. Few things gave him pleasure. Killing was one of them.

Phryne met Nicholas as they filed in to dinner in the purple tent. The daylight was beginning to wane. Swans flew over, heading for their nests on the little island in the lake. Crows winged towards the highest trees, croaking their dismal summons to dark things. Phryne drew a sharp breath. The hunting alertness, which had been soothed away by wine and exercise, was back.

'Over the top,' whispered Nicholas. Phryne nodded.

The tables had been set up like a baron's hall or a university college. Across the dais was the high table, where Gerald, Isabella and the favoured courtiers sat. The rest of the company were ranked by costume: aristocrats first, clerics and religious next, then the others in order, above and below the salt, down to Phryne and several people in pages' costume, who had leave to move all over the hall, serving wine to their betters. Nicholas took his seat directly in front of Gerald, and Phryne took up her station behind him, ewer in hand. Then the servers began to bring in the feast.

Phryne had never really thought about how important a feast was to a medieval person, especially in the middle of one of those English winters which seemed to go on for aeons: weeping skies, icy winds, blighted landscapes, perpetual cold nose, cold feet, cold in the head. To those poor souls, Christmas must have been a blessed festival indeed, a bright patch of food, wine and joy to both anticipate and remember as solace for the chill, monotonous months. Thus a spit roast of pig was a good thing, and a spit roast of mutton. And raised pies, game pies, apple pies, bitter sallet and fruit soup.

Phryne folded back her sleeves and flourished the carving knife in order to carve for the high table. There was a mountain of food. And this was only the first remove. Luckily the feast was to last for hours and hours, or no one would survive it. Would the Goat Lady get some of the leftovers? Phryne wondered what Willie, Wayland and Mintie would make of bitter sallet, composed of dandelion, purslane, wormwood leaves and lemon juice.

A minstrel with a lute begged leave to sing and to her astonishment Phryne knew the song. It was not 'Gaily the troubadour' or 'Greensleeves', it was 'The Lark' by Bertrand de Born, a famous troubadour.

'When I see the lark
'enfolding with his wings
'the warm ray of the sun
'until drowned in honey,
'he swoons with delighted joy:
'Ah, possessed am I with envy!
'Of all joyous ones so jealous.
'That my heart breaks not within me
'I find most marvellous.'

Phryne kept carving. The tune was odd and almost off-key and very, very sad. She found herself longing for a full chorus of anything cheerful. 'Round the Marble Arch' was what she was humming.

◇◇◇

The singers had begun on rounds, songs and madrigals, which Phryne loved. She was standing next to Gilbert, who was a page for the evening, along with Jonathan, Marie-Louise and Sabine. Gerald and Isabella were dressed, or rather clothed, in mystical, wonderful white samite in the form of flowing druids' robes, crowned with mistletoe, which ought to make kissing them a sacred duty.

'Who would have thought that Sad Alison would wash up so well?' asked Sabine.

'It's amazing what a vinegar rinse and a few kind words can do,' said Marie-Louise, straightening her jerkin.

'Really can't call her Sad Alison anymore,' commented Sabine. 'Amelia's put a lot of time into finding the right dress, too. That cooling blue calms the red of her complexion.'

'Amelia's looking stricken,' said Marie-Louise. 'I wonder what she's hiding?'

'We all have secrets,' said Jonathan profoundly.

'Shut up,' said Gilbert. 'I'm listening to the music. Don't you think that Bennet is wonderful?'

'I do,' said Phryne. Though she could think of more cheerful songs for them to be singing. 'Weep o mine eyes, weep o mine eyes and cease not,' they sang. Why not a brisk chorus of 'Philip my Sparrow' or 'Fyer Fyer' or even one of Phryne's favourites, 'When Celia was learning at the spinet to play...'

'But I prefer John Isum.' As though they had heard her, the singers regrouped, had a drink, and leapt into '*Laudate Nomen Domini*', one of the most cheerful exhortations to prayer in existence.

Phryne carried another platter of roast lamb to the high table as the next song repeated: 'Up and down he wandered, up and down he wandered, up and down he wandered...while she was missing. When he found her, o then they fell a-kissing, a-kissing, o then they fell a-kissing.'

That was more like a merry Christmas feast, thought Phryne. She sneaked a piece of the roast pork. It was smoky and crisp.

The upper classes lived well in the good old days. Except, of course, for the famines, the pirates, the bandits, the plagues, the shortness of life and the imminence of ever present death. And no medical treatment, no antiseptic childbirth, no hot baths, no coffee, no chocolate and no tobacco. The last four decided her on the advantages of the twentieth century. Her childhood had been so poor that Phryne still got a vague thrill when she turned on a tap and hot water came out.

The company lounged and lolled. The pages poured more wine. Phryne knocked off for a plate of roast meat, a slice of game pie, and a couple of goblets of the chilled red wine cup. It had slices of orange and lemon in it and the recipe owed more to Mrs. Beeton than the Goodman of Paris, but it was very refreshing. Nicholas joined her and slumped down onto a seat.

'This page lark has got whiskers on it,' he observed, pouring himself a cup of authentic medieval lemonade. It would be a while before his system could tolerate any alcohol. 'My feet are killing me.'

'You've been dancing for two hours in costume shoes,' said Phryne. 'That can take it out of you. I'm going back into the tent. Apparently we are going to have medieval games.'

'If it's anything like those jokes...' grumbled Nicholas. 'Did he tell you the one about "When has the goose the most feathers? When the gander is on her back"?'

'No, but he told me the one about "Why doth a dog lift his leg to piss? For he hath never a hand to pull out his prick". How they must have roared in the fourteenth century over that one. Then again, this is a man who knows all the words to "Abdul the Bul-Bul Amir", which is worrying in itself.'

When Phryne got back the singers were pronouncing that their man John had a thing that was long and their maid Mary had a thing that was hairy and their man John was about to put his thing that was long in their maid Mary's thing that was hairy when Phryne realised that it was a broom head and a broom handle, and nothing like as rude as it sounded. Another riddle. She had been encompassed by riddles from the moment she arrived at this strange party and she swore a small private oath that she would never countenance so much as a very clean and proper riddle in her house again.

Medieval games appeared to be simple enough. To allow the company some digesting time, this was the old pass-the-parcel of everyone's childhood.

A sole tootler, back turned to the assembled guests, tootled on a wooden recorder as a very large parcel, wrapped in cloth and tied with a ribbon, was handed along the table. The music stopped just as the parcel landed in front of a delighted Alison. She unpicked the bow and folded back the red cloth. Inside was another parcel, wrapped in green and tied with a green ribbon. A small gold dragon tinkled onto the table. Much prettier than anything Phryne had ever got in either cracker or pass-the-parcel. Alison took the red ribbon, threaded it through the ring on the pendant and allowed Jonathan to tie it around her neck. She was laughing. Phryne had never seen Sad Alison laugh.

The tootling began again and the parcel crept down the table. It stopped before a thin, pale acolyte in a clerical costume made for a large bass baritone or Chaucer's abbot. He undid the ribbon and revealed a yellow parcel and ribbon, and a slip of paper.

Sylvanus snatched it from him. 'Kiss the maid you love the most!' he roared, and bounced his bladder off the unfortunate youth's head. The boy blushed purple.

'These parlour games are hard on the shy,' Phryne said to Nicholas.

'All he has to do is kiss her,' Nicholas objected.

'Yes, easy for you or me, but very hard for him…'

The acolyte staggered up, approached the high table at a stumbling run, threw himself down on his knees and kissed Isabella's perfect toes. There was a roar of approval. He came back to his seat, tripping on his hem, on the verge of fainting. The parcel moved on.

The next victim had to stand up and sing a song. Fortunately this was a known singer and they obliged with a round of 'Sumer is y-cumin' in'. The next person got a bag of toffee. And so it went on, the parcel getting smaller all the time, Sylvanus capering and insisting on telling more riddles, and the forfeits becoming more biological. Finally the possessor of the tiny little gold wrapped parcel, Amelia, undid the gold ribbon and found a slender belt made of links shaped like leaves. It was a beautiful thing. The Templars did not play any games by halves. There they sat, like priest and priestess, shining in their white robes, beautiful and awe-inspiring.

To the tune of several tootlers, the next game was announced. As Sylvanus explained the rules, it seemed to Phryne that no new amusements had been invented since the twelfth century. For if this wasn't a medieval version of musical chairs, she was Wynkyn de Worde. She slipped out into the gathering darkness. The tent was close, though the great heat had not returned. The horsemen and hearties were gathered in an impromptu camp down by the lake, where the occasional splash showed that the 'throw a Chink in the river' boys were still at their nefarious trade. They had lit a bonfire and Phryne could smell roasting meat.

Phryne ignited an entirely unmedieval cigarette. She had a few useful objects in the pouch which was part of the costume. She sat down on an iron bench, smoking luxuriously, puffing the fragrant fumes at the mosquitoes who were gathered in a cloud, muttering and waiting for her citronella to wear off.

The gasper tasted so good that she had another and by the time she sauntered back into the tent, the musical chairs had concluded and the second remove was being brought in. More meat—of course, meat was such a luxury in the Middle Ages— more fruits of all sorts. And some entertainment, in the form of a very solemn boy who escorted a very solemn other boy and were accompanied by the singers.

'The Boar's head in hand bear I
'bedecked with bays and rosemarie
'And I pray you my masters be merry
'Quot estis in convivio!

'Caput apri defero
'Reddens laudes Domino.'

Isabella had probably considered the nauseating impact on a
modern diner of being presented with the head of a real boar, and
had ordered one made of marzipan. It was magnificent, likelife
in colour, the tips of its marzipan tusks gilded. It was surrounded
by a cornucopia of marzipan fruits and vegetables. The company
hopped into these as though there was no next Wednesday but
Phryne refrained because she did not like marzipan's texture or
taste. No matter what it was shaped like it still tasted very much
like marzipan. And because she had marked down a dish of apple
snow as her own. Also, she had to serve the Lord and Lady, as did
her fellow pages, who were recalled to their duty by the Lord of
Misrule, who made great play with his bladder and threatened to
tell them more riddles. That got everyone moving.

Wine was poured, marzipan was nibbled. Phryne secured
the dish of apple snow, which was a marvellous concoction of
apple puree and beaten egg white. No one else seemed to fancy
it so she ate it all.

'Any messages, Miss?' asked Minnie, disguised for the event
in a sober gown and wimple.

'Nothing yet,' said Phryne. 'Tell Mrs. T that the food was
magnificent. Particularly the apple snow.'

'I never thought anyone would eat that,' said Minnie.
'Uncooked meringue! I'll tell her,' she said, and withdrew with
the rest of the servers as the singers formed up again.

'Never weather beaten sail more willing bent to shore
'Never tired pilgrim's limbs affected slumber more
'Than my weary sprite now longs
'To fly out of my troubled breast
'Oh come quickly oh come quickly oh come quickly
    sweetest lord
'and take my soul to rest.'

'We don't seem to be able to get away from death, do we?' remarked Gilbert, wiping at a wine spill on his sleeve.

'It was always very close in the old days,' murmured Phryne.

The wine servers went around again and the next game was called. About half the company, she noticed, were either actually asleep or half asleep, their heads pillowed on their arms. Several had just curled up on the tent floor and gone bye-byes with the complete innocence of children. The wine cup wasn't that strong, Phryne thought. It could only have been about eight o'clock, quite dark. This sleepiness must have been the product of alcohol and exercise. Phryne herself had never been more wide awake in her life.

'Blind Man's Bluff!' announced Sylvanus. 'Hoodman's Blind! Who found the bean in their bowl?'

'I did,' said the druid.

Gerald was led forward, his eyes swathed in a white cloth.

The candles were put out and darkness flowed into the tent. Phryne had the same thought as Nicholas and a fraction of a second sooner. Fool, she told herself as she ran, idiot, it isn't during karez that he is perfect, it's when he is blinded and in the midst of his acolytes, perfectly trusting, perfectly vulnerable.

She shoved Sabine aside and dived towards the lone figure turning his mistletoe crowned head from side to side, trying to understand the flurry. And again in one of those instantaneous flashes, Phryne thought of the sacrificial human under the white robes, waiting meekly for his holy death that would bring back the sun for his tribe.

Phryne was behind Gerald as he stood blindfolded in the middle of the floor. Nicholas was in front, which was why the thin knife aimed at Gerald's heart went instead through Nicholas' shoulder. There it stuck. The assailant wrenched at it unavailingly for a moment and then took to his heels and ran, and Phryne ran after him. Nicholas sank slowly to the floor.

The Joker was examining Miss Fisher very carefully. In the riddle game going on, in connection with the missing boy, she appeared to be winning. She was beginning to look dangerous. And she would be so very beautiful, dead.

Chapter Seventeen

Here life has death for neighbour,
and far from eye or ear
Wan waves and wet winds labour,
Weak ships and spirits steer;
They drive adrift, and whither
They wot not who make thither;
But no such winds blow hither,
And no such things grow here.

A.C. Swinburne
'The Garden of Proserpine'

The killer was dressed in a page's costume. He was fast. So was Phryne. She was almost near enough to tackle and grab when he threw a bench down—she had to jump over it—and then he was racing for the back of the house.

Behind her Phryne heard screams. People and light spilled out of the Templar tent. That ought to act as a signal, she thought, but all her elaborate preparations had been predicated on the attack happening in the dark, at the love-feast. This half-light was confusing but would not hide some of the means she had hoped to use to catch the Joker.

Phryne excluded from her mind her concern for the stabbed Nicholas and her burning desire to find out who the Joker actually was. He was rounding the house, now; she heard his soft shoes scuff on gravel. Her own made an identical noise.

No one seemed to have noticed the two runners. Out of the corner of her eye Phryne saw Gabriel and some footmen issue forth from the front door, armed with various weapons. If she so much as paused to scream at them she would lose the Joker. Where was he heading? The area behind the house was a maze of washhouses, drying yards, back kitchens, sculleries and sheds for tools, coal, and miscellaneous gardening requisites. There he would hope to lose Phryne, and she did not mean to be lost.

Her breath was shortening. Her heart was pounding. Joker and avenger slid a little as they came into the cobbled space behind the laundries, where a hundred years' continual leakage of water had given rise to a fine fresh green growth of moss. The red page's jerkin vanished round a corner and Phryne hared off in pursuit. She had a gun in her pouch, she realised, and a fat lot of use it was. She couldn't free the thongs while she was running. At least, she thought, the murderer had left his knife in Nicholas. Must have stuck between bone and bone.

The red jerkin darted into a space between two huts and Phryne dived after it. He had not spoken a word, and she had made no challenge. Now she didn't have the breath to do so. If he can't lose me in this collection, she thought, he'll have to—

She stumbled and fell full length across someone's foot. All the remaining breath was knocked out of her.

'Ambush me,' she concluded the thought. There was a thin knife poised over her breast. The Joker had pulled his hood down so low that she could not see his face.

'Why?' she asked.

'Wrong question,' the Joker informed her. His voice was light and strangely characterless, with almost no accent.

'So it is,' said Phryne, allowing her breathing to become slow and deep, a technique taught to her by Lin Chung. 'The only answer is, why not? I don't suppose you'd like to tell me who hired you?'

'I might,' he returned. 'I do need something from you, as it happens, which is why I let you chase me all this way.'

'And what can I do for the Joker?' asked Phryne, matching tone for tone. 'Are you comfortable in English, or would you prefer to speak French?'

'English is my native tongue,' he protested.

'Is it, indeed? Tell me, do you like killing people?'

'It is one of the only realities,' he said. The knife had not deviated by a sixteenth of an inch from its place over her heart. But he wanted something and while he was talking he was not stabbing Phryne to death. This would not be a salubrious place to die, bleeding her life away on the slimy cobbles between two ruined buildings. Phryne resolved not to die there. Somehow.

'There are other realities. Birth, perhaps? Love?'

'I never loved anyone,' he said, as though it was a matter of no importance. 'I don't know how. It got left out of me, I suppose. My mother always said I was an unnatural child, and my father favoured his other sons. I killed them all, one night, in a fire. As the house burned, I felt pleasure. I never had before. I was fifteen.'

'How very interesting,' said Phryne. 'Did you take part in the Templar love-feasts?'

'I did,' he said. 'They were very boring. I had to lie still while people kissed me. I did not find it pleasurable. But death—now death is never without interest.'

'Tell me,' requested Phryne. Her muscles were beginning to tremble from staying so still for so long.

'If I was to push this knife into your breast, just there, it would slide in like butter,' he said eagerly. 'The blade is very sharp. It would meet no resistance. Then, as long as I withdrew it carefully, there would be no visible bleeding. It is unlikely you would feel much pain. You would become sleepy and then collapse, and the people who found you would never notice the little puncture. So while they were bringing the smelling salts you would exsanguinate and die. Just pass away, under their hands.'

'I see,' said Phryne. 'But Gerald…'

'That Nicholas interfered,' protested the light voice. 'Not fair. He leapt in the way, spoiled my stroke, and then my favourite blade Eleanora got jammed in his shoulder.'

'Eleanora?'

'I name my knives. Eleanora was my mother's name.'

Phryne bit back a comment about filial loyalty and tried a small flinch.

'It's cold on the ground,' she suggested. 'And you want me to do something for you, before you kill me?'

'Oh. Oh, yes,' said the Joker, slightly disconcerted. 'Perhaps you should get up, then. I will walk behind you,' he said, allowing Phryne to feel the prick of the blade in the middle of her back. 'And if I stab you here, you will be paralysed for quite twenty minutes before you die.'

Phryne believed him. She got to her feet carefully, shook herself, and dusted down her costume. Her hands went to the strings of her pouch.

'May I smoke?' she asked coolly. 'Even the executed are allowed a last cigarette.'

'No,' he said waspishly. 'I don't approve of ladies smoking. Shall we go?'

'Where?'

'Something I need to make sure of,' he said. 'Just walk, Miss Fisher.'

Phryne's fingers worked at the thongs of the pouch as she strolled, slowly, into the main drying yard. It was strung with lines made of all substances from string to galvanised wire. The Joker, however, divined that Phryne might try to trap him and forced her away from the middle of the yard and into the black shadows at the edge.

Damn, she thought. And these strings have chosen a hellish time to make themselves into a knot. He is going to kill me. Without a thought. Without a qualm. He is a true monster. And I really will miss Lin Chung. And Dot. And coffee.

'Left or right?' she asked at a corner.

'Left, please. I say, Miss Fisher, you are taking this well. I hope you aren't expecting to be rescued. I doped the Templars' followers. That will be attracting a lot of attention.'

'Did you poison them?' asked Phryne.

'No, just chloral hydrate in the marzipan. You seem very alert, though.'

'I don't like marzipan,' Phryne responded.

'That would explain it,' he agreed.

His muscular control was remarkable, Phryne thought. That knife had not moved, even though both of them were walking. It was about an eighth of an inch into her back, and one movement would sever her spine. She dragged at the knotted thongs. They did not budge.

'Now, where is the place?' he muttered. 'These old houses are so confusing. Not built, you know, but just "growed", like Topsy. Where is the kitchen from here?'

'If I gesture, will you impale me?' she asked, and he laughed, a light boy's laugh full of good humour.

'That's for me to know,' he chuckled, 'and you to find out.'

'The kitchen, I believe, is to your right and somewhat behind you,' she said, deciding not to risk the gesture.

'Then we will go that way,' he said.

Somewhere in a suppressed part of Phryne's mind terror ran round like a mouse in a wheel. She let it run.

'I believe I know what you are looking for,' she said.

'Indeed?'

'The child,' she said. 'The little girl.'

'Saw me sharpening my knives,' he said. 'I put her out of the way until this was all over. Now I will have to remove her as well, and you, of course, Miss Fisher.'

'Of course,' Phryne replied. Hope leapt in her heart. The old scullery where Marigold had been imprisoned was on the direct path to the kitchen door, and some preparations must have been made there by now. 'Satisfy my curiosity. How do you mean to get away? The place will be swarming with police-men any moment now.'

'No, there are only two of them at Werribee. They will have to telephone Melbourne, which is half an hour's journey even if they set out right away and use one of the new high speed cars. By the time they arrive I shall have clothed myself in my own riding garments, borrowed a pony and got to my car, which is hidden some miles from here.'

'And if you can't steal a pony? Those horse lines have valets and stablemen camped beside them and they can't all be drunk.'

'Then I shall take Templar's horse,' he said promptly. 'Acorn is a nice steady beast, unlike that demon Miss Isabella rides.'

'I see. Did you have an agreement about both of them, or was it just Gerald?'

'Just Templar,' he said. 'Not that I mind killing women. They are only disappointing in that they are so easy to kill.'

This one won't be, vowed Phryne grimly. One knot slipped under her frantic tugging. What she really needed, of course, was a knife. How foolish of her not to carry one at all times.

But of course, she did have a knife. All medieval persons had eating knives. Hers was in a decorative sheath hanging down from her belt. With great care she began to draw it up. It might not be sharp, but it was a weapon. Phryne's teeth ached from keeping her jaw and thus her voice steady. And they were approaching the back scullery where Marigold had been imprisoned. Marigold was gone, which might give Phryne a moment of inattention in which to avoid being skewered.

'I believe this is the place,' she told the Joker, grabbing for the sheath and extracting the blade. She jagged it across the thongs. It did not cut. She tried again. It was as blunt as a bottle and not even half as much use.

The Joker's attention was diverted for just a moment as he considered the prison, which was littered with broken planks. Phryne flung herself to one side and screamed 'Help!' His casually brutal slash cut a streamer from her long sleeve.

The kitchen door crashed open. Sam shouldered out. Ted and Rob sprang into the half-lit yard, armed with an axe and a shovel.

'Ah,' said the Joker. 'You surprise me, Miss Fisher.'

'Oh, I do hope so,' said Phryne. 'Sam, Ted, we need to disarm him. Be careful—he's really good with that knife.'

'Years and years,' said the Joker in a singsong voice, the knife making patterns in front of their eyes. 'I trained for years for my profession. If you think I am going to end it here, in this godforsaken country at the end of the world, you are wrong.'

'Don't watch the knife, block the exits,' said Phryne practically. 'Tell me, did you send the coral snake?'

'Yes, I went to some trouble to deter you,' he said, the knife still making patterns, a snake hypnotising birds. 'I like snakes and it was rather expensive. What became of it?'

'I'm sorry,' said Phryne. 'My cat killed it.'

The Joker gave an angry hiss. 'I hate cats,' he said.

'Yes, I thought you might. Now, tell me who hired you to kill Gerald. You promised,' she reminded him.

'I was paid by a blind trust called Adventures Limited,' he said. 'Is that enough for you?'

'No,' said Phryne. They weren't out of the woods yet. This was a dangerously slippery person and even now, as Ted covered one exit and Rob stood guarding the kitchen door, he could kill and get away, striking like the snakes he loved and slipping into the undergrowth of huts and sheds. 'Oh, and incidentally, did you really expect Marigold to still be alive? You shut her in that old laundry five days ago now. She wasn't exactly well fed to begin with.'

'So she's dead? That is a relief,' he said, and Sam roared and charged.

The Joker stabbed him in the upper arm as he was gathered into a gorilla embrace. Sam didn't seem to notice the wound.

'You bastard,' bellowed Sam, holding the Joker around the waist, shaking him as a dog shakes a rat and slapping the knife out of his hand. 'You left my little girl in there to die? You mongrel bastard!'

He snapped the Joker in mid-air like a snake and threw him away to lie crumpled against the smashed boards of Marigold's prison.

Phryne ran to the body. The head lolled on the broken neck. He was still warm. But he was completely dead. Dead in an instant. And his hood had slipped back from his face.

'Oh dear,' said Phryne to the corpse, even now hearing that detestable light voice discussing her imminent death. 'And I let you share all those baths, Gilbert.'

'Jeez,' said Sam shakily. 'I never meant to kill him.'

'You don't know your own strength, mate,' said Ted, removing his hand rolled cigarette from behind his ear and relighting it.

'Much better this way,' said Rob, reaching out to help Phryne up. 'Did you hear what he said about Australia? God-forsaken, he said. Foreign bastard.'

Phryne's teeth began to chatter. She was flooded with cold. Her knees were now entirely failing to support her. She leaned on the wall.

'It's all right,' said Phryne to Sam. 'Pure self defence. There will not be a charge. You just saved all our lives, Sam, and Marigold's as well.'

'Here, Miss,' said Sam, worried by her pallor. 'I think you'd better take me up on that free carry I offered you once.'

'I think I should,' said Phryne, and was borne into the kitchen in strong arms.

Mrs. Truebody was a veteran housekeeper and thought she had seen it all: hunting accidents, fowl pest, hysterical pregnancies, carriage accidents, and even that Patent Steam Pressure Cooker which had patently exploded so impressively, taking out all the windows of the kitchen and leaving everyone hard of hearing for three days. But a murder, a mass poisoning, and several stabbing injuries were trying her patience and extending her expertise. She had turned the back kitchen into her dressing station, and the Werribee doctor, McPherson, was there now, swabbing and stitching, assisted by Minnie.

As soon as Sam had been stitched, he had put on Gabriel's shirt (which was unbloodied) and gone to fetch Marigold.

Then—of all things—he had shown her the body of that terrible young man and said, 'That's him, Marigold. He can't hurt you no more. He's dead.'

And Marigold, instead of screaming and weeping, had just touched Sam very gently on the face and gone back of her own accord to her room, where she was now, apparently, soundly asleep.

'It doesn't seem right somehow,' complained Mrs. Truebody to Miss Fisher, who was also patched with plasters on two small wounds. Miss Fisher was dressed in her page's costume with the addition of a soft cotton blouse as her jerkin was soiled with mud, slime and blood. She was drinking strongly sedative valerian tea and smoking a gasper.

'It is necessary for the child to know that the monster is dead,' she said soothingly. 'Now she knows that, she can sleep. You are doing a wonderful job, Mrs. T.'

'The old lady used to call me that,' said Mrs. Truebody. 'What she'd think of these goings-on! Half the guests doped and sleeping on the ground!'

'How are they?'

'Doctor says they're just asleep,' said Mrs. Truebody. 'They arranged them comfortably and left them where they were. Except Mr. Templar and Miss Templar, of course. They got carried to their beds. The doctor says that none of the injuries is serious. Even your young man, Mr. Booth. He's in the front parlour with the police. He asked if you could join them at your convenience, Miss Phryne.'

'Which will be when I have finished this tea. I have had a strenuous evening.'

Mrs. Truebody approved of this attitude. Miss Fisher's face had regained much of its colour but the cigarette smoke betrayed a faint tremor in her hands. Mrs. Truebody applied her best remedy for anything short of actual death. 'We've still got lots of food. How about a tiny little slice of my game pie?'

'It's very good game pie,' conceded Phryne. 'Just a sliver, then. Or maybe a bit more than a sliver. And perhaps some of that fruit salad? And did I tell you that you make wonderful apple snow?'

Mrs. Truebody preened. Phryne ate her supper with the relish of one who had been unsure whether her future would hold any more game pie, cigarettes or, indeed, life.

The doctor reported most casualties had been attended to and was, it seemed, offering Minnie a job.

'You've got a nice neat hand and you aren't squeamish,' he said. 'Call on me when you finish this task. Nurse attendant pays a bit better than housemaid,' he added.

'Good,' said Minnie. 'I'm saving up to get married.'

Dr. McPherson left to attend to others. The kitchen gradually emptied of staff, as Mrs. Truebody sent them to bed.

By midnight, Phryne Fisher was presiding over a miscellaneous feast into which Jack Robinson, his sergeant Hugh Collins and a bandaged Nicholas were tucking as though they had not eaten for days. Phryne joined them.

'Good pies these,' remarked Robinson with his mouth full.

'Not as good as Mrs. Butler's, but good,' said Phryne, brushing crumbs off her blouse.

'Now, what have you been up to, eh?' asked Robinson indulgently.

'Well, since you ask, I have been threatened, nearly bitten by a venomous reptile, and chased all round the houses by an internationally renowned murderer with a knife. Other than that, it's been quiet. Now tell me something—have you ever seen that man before, Jack?'

'No,' said Robinson, looking, as directed, at Nicholas.

'He's Secret Service, isn't he?' she asked. 'I kept inserting your name into the conversation and he kept not reacting to it. But I knew he must be something in the policeman line, because of the things he was able to find out.'

'Ah,' said Robinson, taking another piece of apple pie and dousing it in cream.

'You didn't think I might be the Joker?' asked Nicholas.

'No,' said Phryne. 'Not after I saw you in that tree with the rifle. You had a perfect shot. The Joker would not have been able to resist it.'

'Probably not,' said Nicholas.

'So, what is it—are you in the Secret Service?'

'I can't tell you,' he said uncomfortably. 'Neither confirm nor deny.'

'He's high up,' said Robinson. 'His letter of accreditation isn't from Scotland Yard. Anyway, he's never a police officer. I'd know.'

'Right,' said Phryne. 'Are you staying for the rest of the party?'

'Phryne, you and Sam between you managed to catch and kill an assassin that no one else has been able to even identify, and because I was here being useless, I'll get the credit. Honourable wounds and all. I don't need to go home just yet.'

Jack grunted. 'I spoke to that huge bloke. They build 'em big in Werribee! If you can vouch for what he said, then it's a clear case of justifiable homicide.'

'I can vouch for every word. I never got so close to death, Jack, not even in France in the Great War. Gilbert would have killed me without a thought.'

'He must have been a kind of...' Jack groped for the word, '...those lizards that change colour and go insane when you put them on plaid?'

'Chameleons,' said Sergeant Collins. 'Though I believe the story about the plaid isn't true, sir.'

'Never mind that. Chameleon. He just fitted into the company he was in.'

'He was a very convincing artist in an artists' colony,' Nicholas said, sipping his whisky. 'A believable mechanic in a motor yard.'

'An aesthete who likes scent,' said Phryne. 'For a while I thought that Sylvanus might have shut Marigold up, because he always wears that dire freesia scent. But Gilbert smelt sweet because he wanted to blend in—he even used to borrow my baths.'

'He ran out of Rose de Gueldy,' Sergeant Collins informed Phryne. 'There was an empty bottle in his bag. Plus a lot of other things,' he added.

'Like an address book and diary which I handed to the correct authorities…and a lot of drugs, weapons, knives. Beautiful knives, sharp as razors,' said Robinson.

Phryne did not want to think about the sharpness of the Joker's blades.

'The one that stabbed you was called Eleanora, after his mother,' she informed Nicholas. 'And he kept a diary? Have you read it?'

'No, it's in code. I don't even know what language it's in.'

'Never mind. Tomorrow morning I will give you the person who hired the Joker. Now, I am going to bed. Are you staying here, Jack?'

'Yes, Miss, the housekeeper gave us a couple of rooms.'

'Good, then I'll see you in the morning,' said Phryne, and no appeals to her sense of honour proved strong enough to make her tell Nicholas or Robinson what she knew.

'She's like that,' said Jack Robinson, holding out his tea cup for a refill.

'And nothing to be done about it, I suppose,' sighed Nicholas.

◇◇◇

'This time I am going to read you the saint's life,' insisted Dot. The girls agreed, rather mutinously. They much preferred miracles to boring old bishops. 'This is the feast of Sylvester,' said Dot.

Jane and Ruth attended as she recounted Sylvester's blameless life. Jane pricked up her ears when she heard that he had cured the Emperor Constantine of leprosy. But they privately considered Sylvester a bore, and hoped that the next saint would be more intriguing.

Chapter Eighteen

It was meet that we should make merry,
and be glad, for this thy brother was dead,
and is alive again; and was lost, and is found.

Luke 15: 32

Phryne slept late. When she woke, she limped to the bath and flung in a whole handful of the chestnut blossom bath salts, one scent which the unlamented Gilbert had never shared. She was soaking luxuriously and just beginning to feel her muscles unknot when someone tapped on the door. The sound was disturbing. As she suppressed her start, she realised that she had thought it was Gilbert, asking for her bath as usual. He had fooled her completely. But now that she analysed it, for Gilbert to have been right there when she emerged from the Iris Room, he must have been watching her like a hawk. She banished this meditation with alacrity. Gilbert was dead, and it had enormously improved him.

'Go away,' said Phryne firmly.

'If you can open the door, Miss Fisher, I have coffee,' said Nicholas.

'Oh, very well,' said Phryne grumpily. She hauled herself out of the bath and unbolted the door, leaving it to swing wide as she returned pointedly to the foam and felt the perfumed heat draw the pain from her bones once more.

'I have Mrs. Truebody's best Arabica,' said Nicholas. 'And a little of the green chartreuse to act as a tonic.'

'You're almost forgiven for interrupting my ablutions,' said Phryne, drying her hands on the towel he held out and taking the coffee cup. 'How are you this morning?' she asked after a blissful interval, having drunk the coffee and the chartreuse in alternate sips.

'Bit stiff,' said Nicholas, wriggling a shoulder under his blue shirt. 'Stitches are pulling, I expect. And you?'

'Sore to the heels,' confessed Phryne. 'I never ran so fast or stayed so still in my whole life. I suppose you are used to this sort of thing?'

'Well, no, I don't know, this was my first mission. I'm very junior, you know.'

'Yes, they must have picked you up straight out of university. What did you read?'

'Humanities,' he said. 'Languages. At Cambridge, as you say. Wasn't much on offer for me except teaching. No friends of the family to get me into the diplomatic service. So when they offered me the chance, I jumped at it. And I owe you a great deal, Phryne. Pity they didn't recruit you, too.'

'Who says they didn't?' asked Phryne, and watched with pleasure as Nicholas' cornflower blue eyes narrowed. 'More coffee,' she requested. He refilled her cup.

'No, I really can't tell,' he said. 'Did they?'

'Neither confirm nor deny,' said Phryne smugly. 'How are the rest of the people this morning?'

'All of the acolytes who got the micky in the marzipan slept like logs and have woken refreshed. The ones with the hangovers are the ones who missed out on the marzipan but subsequently drank themselves catatonic trying to absorb the shock of someone wanting to kill Gerald. He and his sister appear to be well. I find it very hard to tell with those two.'

'Yes, they are something straight out of Mr. Wells' books, aren't they?'

'Indeed.' Nicholas could not help noticing that more and more of Phryne was being revealed as the bath foam oxidised and slid down her admirable shoulders, her champagne breasts, her…he dragged his mind back to the subject. 'Or maybe a Greek myth. Or a Teutonic one. The house staff are still a bit jumpy, but Mrs. Truebody has them well in hand. What a slave-driver that woman would make! The little girl Marigold is still asleep.

'Who else? Oh yes, the horsemen and the others, they never noticed a thing until the screaming began. Actually until it had been going on for some time. Then they all hotfooted it up to help and carried bodies and refreshments and ended up deciding that they ought to guard all those sleeping acolytes. So they set up their camp just outside the tent, which attracted the attention of the jazz musicians. So they had an all-night party, along with the acolytes who were still awake and the medieval musicians, and are presently indisposed for interview. They tell me that the New Orleans jazz version of "*In Dulci Jubilo*" has to be heard to be believed.'

Phryne laughed. 'I'd love to hear a jazz crumhorn,' she said. 'Help me up and give me my gown, please. I'll go and get dressed. Has Dot arrived yet? Send her to me, will you? All this adventure is very hard on the wardrobe.'

Not even trying to avert his eyes, Nicholas helped Phryne onto the bathmat and wrapped her in her terrycloth bathgown. Then he conducted her, step by step, to the Iris Room, where an anxious Dot was already waiting with fresh clothes and a scolding.

'Miss, you said this wasn't dangerous,' she complained as she whisked Phryne inside and sat her on her bed. 'Let me just replace those plasters, they're peeling. I've brought you some clean clothes. Will you wear the rose or the cornflower shift?'

'The cornflower,' said Phryne. 'It wasn't really dangerous, Dot. The ones who got wounded weren't me. Those little pin-pricks didn't even need a stitch.'

'That's not what that Sam has been telling Mr. Robinson,' Dot said severely, dropping to her knees to make sure that Phryne's feet were properly dry before fitting on her sandals. 'He says that you ran the killer ragged and then trapped him and never turned a hair.'

'Actually I think I must have turned handfuls of hair. Just look and see how many grey ones there are, will you? And if you wouldn't mind, Dot, my hair really needs attention.'

Dot sat Phryne in a straight chair and began a punitive brushing, muttering to herself.

'Where is Mr. Butler?' asked Phryne.

'In the kitchen talking to his old friend. This hair's in a shocking state. Dry as a broom. You're going to need a proper egg shampoo when you get home, Miss.'

'I know, I was just thinking that,' responded Phryne. The brushing was very soothing. This is how a stroked cat must feel, she thought. I might even purr.

Finally Dot was satisfied with Phryne's appearance and allowed her to stand.

'You'll do,' she said, flicking off some dust. 'What can I do now?'

'Come with me,' said Phryne. 'We'll collect our policemen on the way.'

Mr. Butler set down his tea cup. Mrs. Truebody made very good tea.

'Nearly over now, Tom,' he said to his disconsolate friend. 'Just the one more night and it'll all be done.'

'No,' said a voice from the door. 'It's not over yet.'

'Miss Fisher!' Mr. Butler rose respectfully to his feet. So did Mr. Ventura.

'It's no good,' said Phryne gently to the quivering man. 'Gilbert told me all about it before he died. Adventures Limited? Who else could it be? Why did you want to kill Gerald Templar, Mr. Ventura?'

Tom Ventura cast a panicky glance around the kitchen. Mrs. Truebody was standing by her small stove, frypan in hand.

Gabriel was sitting by the back door, sharpening a kitchen chopper with a whetstone. In front of him were three police-men. Nowhere to run. He let out a huge breath and sank down into his chair.

'It was Tom?' asked Mr. Butler, staring. 'Tom, did you do this?'

'Yes, yes I did,' snarled Tom Ventura. 'I'm proud of it. He was wasting the money, wasting it, and he was never pleased. He called me a small man who didn't understand magnificence. When I found out about the Joker and realised that he was an artist in his way, I told him to take away everything from the pompous bounder Templar and then kill him at the perfect moment. I was there to witness it. I saw the knife. Then you got in the way,' he snarled at Nicholas, who was standing with one hand on a concealed pistol. 'And you bitch,' he sneered at Phryne, 'you caught him and that mammoth Sam killed him. And there went my sweet revenge, all wasted. And I paid him two hundred pounds, and passage money and expenses!'

Tom Ventura began to cry. Mr. Butler reached out an uncertain hand and patted his shoulder. For a while nothing was heard in the kitchen but the gritty sliding noise of the whetstone and the sobbing of Tom Ventura.

Then he made a fast grab for his inside pocket and Phryne pounced. She twisted his arm and a paper of tablets fell onto the floor.

'No,' she said. 'I'm sorry. It might be the neatest way, but we need to know some things. Where is Tarquin?'

'Get off me!' screamed Mr. Ventura, struggling wildly. Phryne could not hold him. Mrs. Truebody surveyed the situation, came to a conclusion, and brought her frying pan down hard on his head. He collapsed without a murmur.

'Might be more reasonable when he wakes up,' she commented, and put the pan back onto the stove.

'If I wasn't already married...' said Mr. Butler in sincere admiration.

Mrs. Truebody settled her apron with a pleased hand. 'I take that as a compliment, Mr. Butler.'

'So you may, Mrs. Truebody.'

Sergeant Collins gathered up the body during this exchange of old-world courtesies.

'What shall we do with him, sir?'

'Take him along to my room and sit with him,' ordered Robinson. 'I'll send the doctor along. He's still attending to one of those idiots who fell into the campfire. He's just scorched but he's creating a treat. Search him first,' he added, as the policeman carried Mr. Ventura out of the room. 'Don't want him leaving us too soon.'

'I'll go as well,' said Nicholas. 'In case he feels chatty when he wakes up.'

'Now we have got to go and find out about Gerald's affairs,' said Phryne. 'We'll need all the papers from Mr. Ventura's room. I don't think we have good financial news for him and Isabella.'

'Lucky if he's got a penny left,' agreed Jack Robinson. 'What with Ventura spending all that gelt on assassins and fares and expenses and probably trousering a reasonable amount for himself as a commission.'

'I expect so,' said Phryne. 'How are you at balance sheets?'

'I'm a shark,' said Jack Robinson. 'I was in the fraud squad before I got sent to homicide.'

'Wonderful,' said Phryne. She looked with affection at this unremarkable policeman. 'Let's go, then.'

'So he even spent my money on trying to kill me?' said Gerald, wrinkling his perfect brow. 'But why?'

'He hated you,' said Phryne.

'But why?'

'Because you told him the truth,' she said gently. 'You said he was a small man who lacked magnificence. And he was. He probably would have been all right,' she added, 'if he had never met you. He had the making of, say, a small town accountant.

He would have married a small town princess and been very happy as a big fish in a little pond. But he could never match you, Gerald, and he knew it, and it rankled, and then it festered. He heard about the Joker from some of Paris' more dangerous underworlders, and from then on the whole thing has an air of Greek tragedy.'

'He was a small man, but I need not have told him so,' mourned Gerald. 'I lacked kindness and have been punished for it.'

'I reckon you have,' said Jack Robinson. He had spent an illuminating morning with the ledgers and invoices, fuelled by moral outrage and tea. Robinson liked accounts. Although they might lie, they never hid around corners and fired guns at the investigator. Mr. Ventura had kept two very clear sets of books.

'You might be able to get some of your gelt back from Adventures Limited, though you'd need a court order,' he said, taking off his glasses and rubbing his eyes. 'And perhaps a good accountant might find some of the money he's squirrelled away in various bank accounts. But as it stands at the moment, Mr. Templar, your remaining capital is—' he scribbled a few calculations—'three hundred and seven pounds five shillings elevenpence ha'penny.'

Gerald looked crushed for a moment. 'That isn't a lot,' he said, 'to keep all these followers. Yet I can't turn them away. They have been faithful. Some will manage by themselves, I am sure, but some won't. Isabella has no money of her own. What am I to do?' he asked rhetorically.

The parlour was silent. Phryne had nothing to suggest, though selling some of the younger acolytes did occur to her. Jack Robinson was sorry for Gerald. The description of the bloke did not convey what a nice man he was.

'Never mind,' he said. 'Something may turn up. I mean, you're still alive,' he told the disconsolate victim. 'The smart money would have been on the Joker, you know. You would have been skewered if it weren't for our Miss Fisher here.'

'That is true, and very wise,' Gerald replied. 'If only I could find Tarquin I would not be so easily discouraged. Cautious optimism, then. We still have tonight's New Year's Eve party, and all of the rest of the time is paid for and arranged. One thing to be said for him, Tom Ventura is very efficient.'

'He was,' agreed Robinson, using the past tense deliberately. The blanket-wrapped, foam-flecked and screaming lunatic who had been carried out of the house into the waiting police car had not been even marginally recognisable.

And the slight body of the Joker, carefully photographed for the first time in his career, had been taken off to the Coroner's Court for an autopsy. The coroner thought that evil people had organic brain damage or some other physical disease. Phryne did not think so, and neither did Robinson. Some coots were just naturally evil, was his view. And Sam's action had just saved the state the expense of a trial and hanging. Not to mention that the Joker had a talent for escaping. No, a good result all round.

Robinson closed the ledgers and shuffled the papers into order, with his neat handwritten summary on top. Someone would have to take over to pay the remaining staff. Phryne said she would send him the replacement accountant.

When Sylvanus Leigh appeared, pale as cheese with his hunting hangover, Robinson lent him his indelible pencil to make his own notes. Sylvanus came to the same conclusion. The Templars were, effectively, broke.

Phryne Fisher had used that same pencil to inscribe doggerel verse on her gummed pink paper, and Nicholas accompanied her as she went around the camp site and house, licking and gluing them at eye-height to trees, tents and walls.

'Tarquin alive not Tarquin dead/Or Phryne Fisher breaks your head,' read Nicholas. Under that was 'Hornbeam, noon'. He shrugged. 'You are trying to flush the kidnapper out?' he asked.

'Evidently,' she replied. The next one read: 'Tarquin lost or come to harm/Phryne Fisher breaks your arm/Hornbeam, noon'. This was to be attached to the bar tent.

'Hornbeam at noon and I'll find means/So we don't have to spill the beans', warned another. 'Tarquin hurt or in disgrace/

Phryne Fisher breaks your face,' she added, securing it on a monkey puzzle tree. 'Return the boy to me I beg/Or Phryne Fisher breaks your leg.' She gummed that threat to a tree near the horse lines.

'Yes, but if you know who it is, Phryne, why all these threats? Nice scansion, though,' added Nicholas.

Phryne looked at him. He was not as well as he was pretending. His face was flushed, his golden curls crisp with sweat. That knife had almost gone right through his shoulder and stuck in his scapular. He must have been in agony now that the excitement had worn off.

'You,' she said, in a voice which totally refused to believe that things could be otherwise, 'are going to Dr. McPherson for a change of dressing and a morphine injection, and then you are going to lie down in my bed again. You want to be in good form for the party, don't you? Well, then…' She stifled his muted protest with a kiss. 'Here's the key. Are you going by yourself or do I have to get a nurse for you?'

'I'll go. Provided you promise not to do anything dangerous.'

'I promise,' she said blithely.

He was deeply suspicious, but he went. Phryne watched him until he was safely in the house and proceeded to gum her last label: 'At noon under the hornbeam tree/Who loves to lie with me?'.

It was almost eleven. Phryne had her book. She sat down under the hornbeam tree to await events. She had just got to the part where Hercule Poirot lines up all the suspects and harangues them in fractured English as to their degrees of guilt when the kidnapper came in under the low boughs and sat down at her feet. She closed the book, put it in the Pierrot bag, and laid her hand on her little gun, which would never again be placed in any purse where the catch might tangle or jam.

'Well, here we are,' she said.

'*Viciste*, Galileae!' he quoted in an exhausted tone. 'You have conquered. I saw your riddles. Not as good as mine. Glad to find some way out of it.'

'This way we can do it quietly,' she told him. 'You tell me what happened.'

'I really can't,' he said. 'I don't know a lot of it.'

'Well, let's start with Marigold. Gilbert grabbed her and shut her in the old laundry, meaning to come back and finish her off later. She had seen him with his knives—you know, those knives all had names? That's why Marigold vanished. But Tarquin was snatched on orders to remove from Gerald every-thing that he loved. I found the place where he dropped the tray he was carrying and all the glasses broke. Also I found his shoe. But that wasn't you, was it?'

'No,' said the sad voice by her knee.

'No, you found the boy where Gilbert had hidden him. Is he alive?'

'Yes.'

'Good. Gilbert did rather enjoy a drawn-out gloat. So you freed Tarquin from wherever he was…' she stopped invitingly.

'The coal cellar. I heard him screaming. I let him out and sent him into a bathroom for a wash. Poor boy was filthy with coal dust. I got him some clean clothes and washed out the gold suit. But when I went back I couldn't find the other shoe. So you had it! While he was washing I…'

'Thought of a scheme to extract money from Gerald.'

'Well, yes, but not for me. For the others. Ventura said that Gerald was spending his fortune hand over fist and there would be nothing left.'

'He certainly tried to make it so,' Phryne conceded.

'So I talked to Tarquin, and we agreed that he should hide until the banks open on Wednesday, and then he could come forth, and I would have the money to get everyone home.'

'So you're Triceratops?'

'My brother. I have two brothers in Melbourne and a sister in Brisbane. But then this Gilbert thing happened and it doesn't seem fair on the boy…but I don't know how to get him back.'

'There once was a lady of Niger/Who smiled as she rode on a tiger,' said Phryne.

'Exactly. "At the end of the ride the lady was inside and the smile on the face of the tiger". I really do love Gerald. I wouldn't hurt the dear fellow for the world. And if he finds out that I betrayed him, he will be shaken. Can you get us out of this, Phryne?'

'Certainly, Sylvanus. If you do exactly as I say.'

'When did you know it was me?'

'I suspected you all along,' said Phryne. 'No one else has the right kind of mind to make up riddles. Gilbert wouldn't have the patience. I was rendered more suspicious when I saw you carrying two lunch boxes. Then I saw you rowing on the lake when I know you can't swim. Everyone else played con-sequences but you, and the riddler's neat script wasn't in the consequences, though that's negative evidence and might not have meant any-thing. But finally, I just saw the riddler's hand-writing on those notes in indelible pencil on the Templar accounts.'

'Oh,' said Sylvanus. 'Well, what shall we do?'

'Can Tarquin swim?'

'Yes, why?'

'This is what you do,' said Phryne, and gave careful, clear instructions.

'And this will work?'

'It will,' said Phryne.

Sylvanus kissed her hands, and left the tree. Phryne got up. She had to interview Isabella, and this was probably as good a time as any.

◇◇◇

The Lady was lying back in a hammock, listening to Sabine reading French poetry, when Phryne, Sam, Minnie and Marigold came in. Marigold was dressed in a cut-down and re-sewn shift with roses on it that Phryne had never really liked. Phryne attracted Sabine's attention and pointed to the door. Sabine's eyes widened as she saw the girl. She closed the book and went. Isabella became aware that the soothing voice had stopped and opened her ice blue eyes.

'I've found Marigold,' said Phryne. Isabella sat up in the hammock and swung her feet to the floor. Marigold went to her and hugged her briefly.

'Phryne, you really are amazing,' murmured Isabella. 'Are you well, child?'

'Yes, but…I want to go and live with them,' blurted Marigold.

'Do you?' asked the Lady. 'Why?'

'They saved me,' said Marigold. 'And Sam killed the man who tried to murder me. And Mr. Gerald.'

'Oh, you are that Sam,' said Isabella, rising to her feet. She was almost as tall as Sam. She put both hands on his shoulders. He swayed. Being this close to a deity was overwhelming.

'You saved Gerald's life. Thank you,' she said, and kissed him on the cheek. Then she turned her gaze on to Minnie, standing at attention in her black dress.

'And you love this Sam?'

'Yes, madam,' said Minnie.

'For what you have done,' said Isabella, 'you could have asked anything of me. If Marigold wants to be with you and you will undertake to love her, then she may go. The Melbourne lawyers will arrange the adoption. Take this to remember me by,' she added, detaching a sapphire brooch from her shoulder and pinning it on Marigold's flat chest.

'Thank you!' said Marigold. Then she took Sam's hand in one grasp and Minnie's in the other and the three walked out of the tent, dazed but happy.

'That's good,' said Isabella unexpectedly. 'I'm glad the child is settled. They seem to be nice, solid, peasant stock. I'm glad she has someone else to love her.'

'Why?'

'Well, we are broke,' Isabella told Phryne. So much for Gerald trying to protect her. 'That worm Ventura has stolen every centime we have. I had thought of a Teutonic ending— Wagnerian, you know. Brunhild has always been one of my heroes. But I don't suppose Gerald will allow it, and I can't leave him. I am not going to enjoy being a *hausfrau*, Phryne. We have always eschewed the bourgeois.'

'Something may come up,' said Phryne.

'That's what Gerald says,' she responded, combing her pearly fingers through her flaxen hair.

'And sometimes it is true,' said Phryne, and went out, sending Sabine in to continue with her rendition of Verlaine.

'*Il pleutre dans mon coeur.* It rains in my heart, as it rains in the city…'

Fallen Angel

3 parts gin
1 part lemon juice
2 dashes of green crème de menthe
dash of angostura

Stir gently with ice.

Chapter Nineteen

Now the New Year reviving old Desires,
The thoughtful Soul to Solitude retires,
Where the White Hand of Moses on the Bough
Puts out, and Jesus from the Ground suspires.

Edward Fitzgerald
The Rubaiyat of Omar Khayyam of Naishapur

After lunch, Phryne decoyed Gerald down to the lake. Gerald swam as he did all athletic things, with style and grave efficiency. The water was cool and several people were bathing. Even Sylvanus was out in one of the rowing boats. There was a hat over his eyes and he was leaning back, apparently half asleep. Gerald swam into the middle of the lake and lay back in the water.

'This was a good idea, Phryne,' he told her. 'I've been inside too long. This is a nice place, you know, Australia. The horizon is so far away. I could afford a small farm, perhaps, the acolytes could learn to plough and sow, and we could have a cow and a few goats, grow our own vegetables. Isabella…'

His voice trailed off. No, Phryne couldn't imagine Isabella as a farm wife, either.

'If only I could find Tarquin…'

'Gerald, look!' exclaimed Phryne. Gerald sat up in the water. She was pointing towards the little island where the gold-fish swam. A boy was crawling out onto the land, out from the shell grotto. He was wavering. He was falling into the lake…

Phryne was shoved aside by the bow wave as Gerald powered past her with a fast overarm stroke. He churned through the water and arrived in time to secure the drooping figure as it flailed helplessly and went down for the second time.

Gerald grabbed and embraced.

'Tarquin,' he said tenderly. 'There now, don't grab. I've got you, you're safe. Lie on your back and I'll tow you to shore. I have been frantic with worry for you, boy, searched every-where. Were you locked in the grotto by that murderer? It's all right, he's dead, quite dead and good riddance…'

It is hard to babble while swimming and towing a child in a lifesaving chin-grip, but Gerald was managing it. Phryne waved to Sylvanus that his boat was not going to be needed. Gerald reached shore and wrapped Tarquin in his towel, lifting the boy gently into his arms. Tarquin stared into his face with absolute worship and snuggled.

Phryne's eyes pricked with tears. She looked around for something to distract herself. The escape of Tarquin had attracted watchers. The horsemen and hearties were present, cheering the rescue. Amongst them Phryne saw three faces that she had memorised.

'Rally round, chaps,' she said to the horsemen. 'I need a favour. These three brutes and bounders play a game which involves throwing people into the water. They once did this to a young friend of mine and almost drowned him.'

'And you think a little cold water would do them good?' asked Jill.

'I do.'

'Heave ho, then,' said Ann. Joined by Ralph Norton and even Johnson, the riders descended on Belcher, Beldham and Travis.

'No!' screamed Travis. 'I can't swim!'

'Neither could my young friend,' said Phryne relentlessly. 'You are to be reminded that it is a good idea to ask whether someone wants to join your rustic games before engaging them. He was a Chinese boy,' she said. 'Throw a Chink into the Thames, I believe you said at the time. Well, today is Throw a Bastard into the Lake Day. You may proceed,' she said to the horsemen.

'One, two, three,' they chorused, and Beldham went into the water with a huge splash.

'One, two, three!' they laughed, as Travis struggled and tried to run away and was entered into the lake.

'One, two, three!' they giggled, and Belcher joined his Brook. Phryne watched them struggling with vengeful pleasure.

'Don't let them drown completely,' she called to Sylvanus.

'Right you are, Phryne,' said Sylvanus, radiating relief from every pore. He had thought Isabella a goddess. He just hadn't known what goddesses were, before he met Phryne Fisher again.

Phryne went back to her hornbeam tree and her book. Nicholas was still asleep in her bed. The room now smelt of iodoform, which was not erotic. Everything was approaching 'well' in the Dame Julian sense in her world. The murderer was dead. Marigold had her chosen parents. Tarquin was back with Gerald. Sylvanus was saved from exposure. Even if the little ratbag returned to his waspish personality, he could not do anything to Syl without exposing his own acquiescence in the scheme. The only remaining problem was the Templars' finances, and that seemed insoluble.

Phryne dozed. She was still weary from the previous night's exertions. The hornbeam tree filtered light through its leaves and it fell as an enchantment on tired eyes. Phryne slept and dreamed of fairies.

Phryne was woken at five by a faun. He was not young, and the pursuit of nymphs over difficult country had shortened his breath and stiffened his limbs, not to mention what the consumption of nectar and ambrosia had done to his teeth, but a faun nonetheless, smiling a vastly relieved smile. Sylvanus was himself again.

'Hello, Syl,' yawned Phryne. 'What's the time?'

'Five, and karez is at six in case you want to attend. I'm going to.'

'How is everything?'

'I didn't let your brutes drown,' he said, grinning again. 'Though I did get a reasonable number of lucrative offers on that score from the polo players. But they were breathless and drenched and scared by the time I rescued them and they won't be flinging people into water for the foreseeable. In fact, I suspect that they will be hard pressed to accept water of any sort but Scotch-and- or bath-.'

'Excellent.' Phryne stretched. Lin's cousin was avenged.

'Tarquin is nestled into Gerald's bosom as though he has never been away. The imprisonment and waiting seem to have rubbed some of the edges off the dear boy's character, which is an improvement. We've both got the goods on each other but he doesn't seem to want to exercise any sway.'

'Super,' said Phryne.

'Owe it all to you,' said Sylvanus, kissing Phryne's hand. 'Anything I can do for you?'

Phryne thought about it, and expressed a wish. The faun's lecherous grin showed again, crinkling his bright eyes.

'Done and done,' he said. 'I'll put a girdle round the earth in forty minutes.'

'Well done, fair sprite,' murmured Miss Fisher.

Phryne returned to the Iris Room to see how Nicholas was feeling. He was sitting up in a chair, reading one of her detective stories. His eyes were clear and he did not seem to be feverish.

'Hello!' he said. 'I wish I had this Miss Marple on my team. She can see straight through any malefactor.'

'Yes, old ladies are mostly like that,' said Phryne. 'Do you feel like coming to karez?'

'Are you going?'

'If you are. Otherwise we can sit here and read detective stories.'

'Karez it is,' he said.

Phryne went to her bath and adopted certain precautions. She wore her cornflower shift, as she would have to change into karez garments. Nicholas in flannels joined her and they were absorbed into the buzz of acolytes, changing clothes, listening to the soothing, slow, erotic music in the main tent. Puffs of hash smoke were already scenting the heavy air. Phryne caught sight of Sylvanus. He winked at her. It was the most obscene wink of her experience.

She took the faun's hand and he led her and Nicholas into a corner of the tent where a fold of material carelessly slung from a rope hung down. Phryne had brought along her bag, which was not unusual. She settled herself down on a mattress and Nicholas lay down beside her, close to the edge.

Kissing began with a sigh and a rustle like birds nesting for the night. Nicholas surrendered himself to gentle kissing and touching. He could not lean on his left shoulder, but he did not even need to move. Phryne positioned herself so that he could reach all of her salient features, and as the drugged karez hour went on, he heard her sharp sigh several times.

Then he was conscious of cool air moving across his belly. Miss Fisher had imported a pair of scissors, and had cut through his karez undergarments with careful nibbles, so slowly that he had not felt it. She stood to remove her own. The tent was darkened and the moaning of the semi-orgasmic was becoming louder.

Phryne straddled Nicholas and they came together at last, slow and close and so fiery that he felt that his bones might dissolve. Careful of his wounded shoulder, Phryne rode him with thighs strong enough to control a hysterical horse. He melted, he groaned; his mouth was covered by Amelia, who lay head to head with him. He stiffened in every muscle and then fell back, spent, exhausted, and terribly happy. He closed his eyes, just for a moment. When he opened them again it was obviously later. He was conscious of time having passed.

'Come along,' Phryne whispered, pulling him by his un-wounded hand. 'We have to get out before the lights come up.'

He crawled into the dressing annex. Phryne found his clothes and arrayed him. Then they went out of the smoke and erotic fug into the cool night air.

'Oh,' said Nicholas, coming awake all at once.

'Indeed,' said Phryne, and kissed him lightly. 'Don't worry,' she told him. 'I have taken precautions. There will be no unfortunate results. But I just wanted you. And I never could stand karez for too long. My Sapphic friends say I'd make a perfect lesbian if I didn't have this strange yen for male genitalia. But there it is,' she added.

'Yes,' said Nicholas.

'Now, we are going to the horsemen's fire to get some coffee,' said Phryne. 'Then back to change for the party. Are you too tired?'

'Oh, Phryne,' he said, embracing her. 'At the moment, I could fly.'

'Good,' she said. 'Let's fly.'

The New Year's Eve Bal Masqué, positively the Last Best Party of 1928, was just starting as Phryne and Nicholas returned. She had donned her folly dress, a concoction of sunshine yellow silk gauze and a froufrou skirt edged in black maribou. It had a daringly tight bodice. It was to be worn with a feathery mask. Nicholas was in correct evening costume, his blue eyes heightened by the black domino. His black suit had been made in Paris. It had that faint air of the fantastical which Paris tailoring brings to a conventional garment.

Sylvanus bounded up, dressed as Harlequin. He was in competition with several Pierrots, who would be spoiled for choice amongst five Columbines. The smoke had been cleared, the tent sprayed with eau-de-cologne, and the buffet laid out against the far wall. Gerald was wearing a Savile Row suit, Isabella wore an indigo-blue evening dress icy with Waterford crystal drops. Sabine, Pamela (in gentleman's dress), Marie-Louise, Minou, Amelia and Alison were all at the bar. For this last party, the bar tent had been opened on one side and so had the Templar tent, so that the greensward enclosed between them was large enough for all the guests and available for dancing.

The music, Phryne saw, was going to be interesting. Not usually given to mingling, the brouhaha of the night before had brought all of them together: the belly dancers and Arab musicians, the choral singers, the medieval musicians, and the jazz people. They had sat together, played together and got drunk together, and now they saw no reason why they should be separated. Jazz players in a small place like Melbourne knew all the other jazz players in town, and the same went for every speciality. They hadn't had anything to say to each other before, and now wondered why.

'One in, all in,' explained Tabitha, escorting Nerine, who was bringing with her a nervous Terence carrying a large jug and Thomas carrying a tray of glasses. They reached Phryne and Nicholas with an inaudible sigh of relief and set down their burdens on the white-clothed table.

'Have a drink with me, my honey-lambs,' said Nerine.

'It's a new cocktail, invented in her honour,' said Tommy.

'Made of mint, sugar, bourbon and pineapple juice, and real toothsome,' drawled Nerine.

'Called a Nerine,' said Tabitha, filling glasses. 'Cheers!'

'Bottoms up,' said Nicholas, sipping even though he had sworn off bourbon forever. The bourbon was not stressed. The Nerine was, in fact, deliciously acid. He said so.

'Gotta go,' said Nerine. 'Enjoy the music, y'all. You ain't heard nothing like this concert's gonna be.'

They went, thoughtfully taking their jug. Masked figures were arriving from the polo set and the horde of hearties. The impeccable evening costume of the Grammar Boys was a joy to behold. The improvised costumes of the Wonnangatta Tigers were remarkable for their ingenuity. Ann, for instance, was

wearing a medieval undergown in bright red, a soft Japanese
kimono and a bunch of hibiscus in her hair, which was loose
around her shoulders. Jill wore a strictly tied kimono and trousers, in which she looked severe but decorative. Dougie and
Murph were wearing their own moleskins and the short gowns
and surcoats from the costume store. They looked a good deal
more like the knights of the time than the acolytes had, Phryne
thought, hard-bitten men who were used to the saddle and
knew which end of a sword was the naughty one. They liked
their new clothes, and swaggered as though they had just won
the Battle of Agincourt.

Seated on folding chairs (which they must have brought with
them as there were no folding chairs in the house) were three
gentlemen in grey suits. Their sole concession to the masqué
theme was a domino each. By the strong green tinge, they were
drinking Nerines, as absinthe was not on the barman's menu.

Phryne was about to go across and ask them who they were
when the music began and she had to stay put.

The players had tossed for their performing order, and the
Arabs had won. The three belly dancers came on, standing perfectly still as a tall man repeated verses from *Omar Khayyam*.

'Come, fill the Cup, and in the Fire of Spring
'The Winter Garment of Repentance fling:
'The Bird of Time has but a little way
'To fly—and Lo! the Bird is on the Wing.

'But come with old Khayyam and leave the Lot
'Of Kaikobad and Kaikhosru forgot:
'Let Rustum lay about him as he will,
'Or Hatim Tai cry supper—heed them not.

'Ah, Moon of my Delight, who know'st no wane
'The Moon of Heaven is rising once again:
'How oft hereafter rising shall she look
'Through this same garden after me—in vain!'

At the end of each verse, the dancers came awake in a jingle of bracelets, twirled their rounded bellies and curved their smooth brown arms. Now that Phryne was not feeling disgruntled, she could appreciate how erotic they were. And how skilled. How long did it take to get that sort of muscular control over the whole abdomen? They danced through the hearties, fighting off unwelcome grabs while allowing the well intentioned to stuff folded money into their garments.

'And when Thyself with shining Foot shall pass
'Among the Guests Star-scatter'd on the Grass
'And in thy joyous Errand reach the Spot
'Where I made one—turn down an empty Glass!'

'So, the theme is wine,' said Nicholas.
'I don't know that there are many jazz songs about wine,' Phryne replied. That theme was too facile for the air of suppressed excitement being generated by the musicians.

The jazz players were next. Nerine leaned into her microphone to croon.

'Take a sniff, take a sniff, take a sniff on me,
'Ev'body take a sniff on me,
'Cocaine all around my brain.'

'"The Cocaine Blues",' said Phryne. 'Not just wine, then.'
Nerine concluded and the whole ensemble began to play a quickstep: 'Sweet Red Wine'. The company danced. Phryne stayed where she was. She felt that her friend had had enough exercise for one evening. The next dance was a foxtrot called 'Rosy, My Woman Now', about rosé wine, and the next saw Nerine return to the microphone. 'My lady Morphine,' she sang. 'She a mean lady to me/My lady Morphine...'

The jazz players went on with various favourites as the company danced and Phryne went to the bar for another Nerine for herself and a sherry cobbler for Nicholas. Was the theme...

surely they wouldn't dare…but why not? She would know with the next bracket.

The choral singers joined the medieval musicians and Phryne winced at the sound of the crumhorn. However, the singing was deft and very sweet. 'Oh, metaphysical tobacco,' they sang. 'Fetch'd as far as from Morocco…'

'Aha,' said Phryne.

The next song was a rousing temperance hymn about 'the cup that cheers but does not inebriate', which they sang with the verve of those who did not have to drink tea except by choice. Phryne applauded.

The singers filed off, some jazz players came on, and the musicians, after a certain amount of argument about which instruments they were replacing with which outmoded old relics, began a familiar theme.

'Crutnacker,' said Gerald, by Phryne's ear. 'That's what the players call it. Aren't we lucky to have so many orchestral players amongst these people? And dancers,' he added.

Two dancers leapt onto the greensward and began to sway. Coffee, thought Phryne. Considering that they were trying to keep their footing on grass, they were very good. She sipped her drink.

Coffee leapt off the stage, to be replaced by several people in flat Chinese hats.

'And tea,' said Nicholas, recognising the theme even though it was played on a viola, a psaltery, a flat drum, two recorders, a clarinet and a crumhorn.

'Drugs,' said Phryne. 'That's the theme. Cheeky. Pity they haven't got a song about hash. I must get someone to write one.'

When the orchestra had concluded their excerpts from *Nutcracker*, Gerald rose.

'Dear people,' he said, holding out his hand to his sister, 'we have had a wonderful time and we would like to thank everyone who contributed to this entertainment. It lacks only ten minutes to midnight and the end of the party. But I have grave news and I want you all to—'

'Wait one minute,' said a man in a grey suit who had run to the dais. 'We have a proposition for you, Mr. Templar.'

'You have? And who are you?' he asked, still holding Isabella's hand so that she could not get away and do something Wagnerian.

'Why, you don't know me? Of course, you couldn't. I am Sol Weisenheimer of Weisenheimer Bild, and I want to take you to Hollywood. We need you.'

'Well, thank you, that's quite an honour. But I'm sorry, I can't leave all my friends,' said Gerald.

Mr. Weisenheimer danced a frustrated dance, waving his hands, his watch chain glittering.

'I'm not asking you to leave your friends,' he shouted. 'I want your friends and all, and Nerine the singer, and the young Adonis and the girl who looks like Louise Brooks.'

Phryne looked at Nicholas and chuckled.

'Why?' asked Gerald, bewildered. 'What do you want with all of us?'

'You explain, Carruthers,' said Mr. Weisenheimer, and his second in command tugged on his lapels.

'You know of the recent great innovation in cinema,' he said.

'Sound,' said Phryne.

'Give the lady a cigar. Sound. More and more people will come flocking to the movies to hear their favourite silent picture stars. And what will they hear?'

'The stars?' said Gerald.

'They will hear heavy accents, mumbling, shrill piping and scratchy old whisky voices,' said Mr. Carruthers. 'So what we need are—'

'Melodious voices,' said Phryne, adding in an undertone, 'Nicholas, go and get Sylvanus and bring him to Gerald right away. Don't let Gerald sign anything without his leave. This could be the solution we have all been hoping for and we don't want to undersell ourselves.'

'Another cigar,' said Mr. Carruthers, 'to the very clever and beautiful lady. We need a bank of voices. Young voices, older voices, accents, sweet voices, rough voices, all actors who can read a script and memorise it, like you do with your poetry. We need people who are dedicated to each other so that they do not compete and scratch and—pardon me, ladies—bitch like our voice casting do now. You and your group are perfect for our purposes, Mr. Templar. You and your sister will, of course, be stars. You also have one very talented comedienne. But all the others will be on contract for when we need them. Now I can't offer you more than a quarter-million for the package, the whole package, mind.'

'Not me, honey,' Nerine called out. 'I like it here and I'll go home when I wish. If'n I do, I'll call you first, Mr. Weisenheimer.'

'Deal. Jazz will take a bit longer to become generally acceptable in Little Rock,' said Mr. Carruthers.

'Really can't,' said Phryne regretfully, 'but give me your card, just in case.'

'You sure?' asked Mr. Weisenheimer. Up close he had the bright eyes of the fanatic and smelt sweetly of coffee and cologne.

'You already have one Louise Brooks,' she told him. 'You don't need another.'

'We could always do with another Louise Brooks,' he replied. 'And I suppose you're keeping young Adonis, too?'

'That's up to him,' said Phryne.

'Sorry,' said Nicholas. 'But you've got Gerald. He's magnificent enough for any movie.'

'So he is,' said Mr. Weisenheimer. 'The women of America will be swooning over him before the end of 1929, or my name's not Weisenheimer.'

'And it is,' said Nicholas.

'So,' said half of Weisenheimer Bild, revealing his origin.

'Come and talk to me, Mr. Weisenheimer,' said Sylvanus, dragging Phryne along as well. 'We need to talk about contracts.'

'You'll do it?' cried Mr. Weisenheimer.

'If the price is right.'

After an interval of ferocious bargaining, Syl settled for half a million dollars, contracts for all, and a clause in them which said that if any person wanted to go home, his fare would be paid by the studio. Phryne thought that she could have got more from the incandescent Mr. W, but it was a good deal and left both sides thinking they might have done worse, which was the sign of an equitable contractual negotiation.

Gerald and Isabella were sitting on their thrones. The acolytes were discussing America. The musicians were working out who was going and who was staying. The rest of the gathering was treating their bemusement with more beer.

'Well, Gerald, this solves your troubles,' said Phryne.

'What a bolt from the blue!' murmured Gerald. For the last time he pulled Phryne into his loving, charismatic embrace. Tarquin, who was at his feet, did not even bother to bite her ankle. Everyone was excited, laughing, embracing.

'Charge your glasses,' said Gerald. 'It is now midnight. Happy New Year!'

Fireworks went off over the polo ground and lake. Phryne drew Nicholas close as a cool wind sprang up. She was supremely content and not a little amused at the turnings which fate had taken at the Last Best Party of 1928.

The singing of 'Auld Lang Syne' was conducted with especial fervour as the company knew that they were leaving. Some wanted to return to Paris. Most wanted to go to America. Contracts were being signed in a flurry of paper. Skyrockets went off in the pure, dark blue midnight sky.

'Didn't I say this was a marvellous idea?' cried Mr. Weisenheimer.

'Yes, Mr. Weisenheimer,' said Carruthers.

The third man grinned, seemed about to speak, changed his mind and nodded.

Late that night, after the sturdiest party girl had gone to bed, Phryne stood alone in the garden. She was still recovering her nerve and did not want to sleep quite yet. She was sleepy, but not sleepy enough.

It might have been the angle of the remaining lights, it might have been the hash smoke she had breathed earlier, but suddenly Phryne could see the manor house as it had been before it was uglified. Lights streamed from porch and windows. The front door was open, showing fine delicate decoration, green and pink and blue, gilded and shining. Gas lights burned with a fine glow from chandeliers made of rock crystal, like waterfalls of ice. Music sounded from inside, a string quartet playing Handel's *Water Music*. Phryne could not see any guests, but she could hear the drag and rustle of the trains of many ball gowns and the padding of many feet in dancing shoes which would be worn through by morning. Glasses tinkled. There was a murmur of voices. The whole house shone with welcome, with hospitality, with pleasure in its own society.

Phryne was entranced. She held her breath, knowing that the vision was as insubstantial as a soap bubble and could vanish at any moment. She strained her eyes but still could not see any people, though she could hear them dancing. She heard a girl laugh lightly and almost saw the flirt of her fan as she tapped her beau on the wrist for his impudence. Little points of red light on the balcony must have been gentlemen smoking their after dinner cigars. A scent of hair powder and shoe polish and silks cleaned with lavender water wafted her way from the shining house, and before she could prevent it, she sneezed.

And it was all gone into the darkness.

After that, there was nothing else to do but extinguish her own gasper, finish her Nerine, and put herself to bed.

Chapter Twenty

And if the Wine you drink, the Lip you press,
End in the Nothing all Things end in—Yes—
Then fancy while Thou art, Thou art but what
Thou shalt be—Nothing—Thou shalt not be less.

Edward Fitzgerald
The Rubaiyat of Omar Khayyam of Naishapur

Not having to pay her army, Phryne distributed her money to anyone to whom she owed a favour. The crowd waiting to see her off in the morning was considerable. Mrs. Truebody, having confided her recipe for passionfruit biscuits, beamed. Sam, Minnie and Marigold stood protectively together. The musicians gave her a fast rendition of 'Auld Lang Syne'. Nerine squinted in her general direction. Gerald, Isabella and Sylvanus stood with Nicholas and Tarquin. Jill and Ann had shaken hands. From the herb garden came the cries of Madge the Goat Lady being conducted against her will to a source of mint. All three goats seemed to have ganged up on her this morning, and three goats cannot be resisted by any earthly force.

The big red car slid to a halt. Mr. B got out and loaded the baggage into the boot. Phryne was helped into her seat by a tall and elegant Chinese man, who slid in beside her.

The car started. The Sapphic girls waved. The house began to recede into its forest. Phryne leaned back into Lin Chung's embrace.

'A good party?'

'Like the curate's egg,' she replied. 'In parts. The rest was stark murder and very frightening. Your cousin, by the way, is avenged. I'm amazed that you didn't hear the splash from St. Kilda.'

'That was kind of you,' said Lin gravely. 'And the pretty young man?'

'Pretty,' said Phryne. 'But he's a spy, and that makes him an unreliable lover. Anyway, Lin dear, I did say I would find my own amusement.'

'I know,' he said. 'I'm glad you were only amused.'

'Fairy floss,' said Phryne, closing her eyes. 'Just like fairy floss. Very sweet, but melts on the tongue, and leaves the deep hunger unsatisfied.'

'Ah,' replied Lin Chung, pleased.

By the time the car got to the Werribee road, Phryne Fisher was fast asleep, and the New Year had to get on with it without her.

Maiden's Prayer

3 parts gin
3 parts Cointreau
1 part orange juice

Shake with ice, decorate with orange peel.

Afterword

I would like to state very strongly that I am not in favour of drugs, not even the nicotine to which I am personally addicted. But in the twenties, governments, possibly learning from the terrible effects on crime and social order of the Great Experiment of Prohibition (the Mafia, the gangsters, corrupt police, politicans and judges and corrupt society—since getting a drink meant breaking the law, it fostered contempt for the law), did not prohibit anything much.

My own grandfather was prescribed stramonthium and cannabis cigarettes for his asthma. Cocaine, morphine and laudanum (alcoholic tincture of opium) could be bought over the counter as we buy aspirin today. No one thought much of cannabis smoking or hash-eating, as it was a strange habit only indulged in by foreign people. It was not until the 1930s that drugs began to be proscribed as poisons and we entered the present phase of prohibiting all of them. Which has been as successful at suppressing drug use and as productive of crime as ever Prohibition was at removing the taste for alcohol from the American public.

I have taken liberties with Chirnside Manor, and with the formation and depth of its lake. There is no point in sending me reproachful letters about this. I read all the history, and some of it I changed. Narrative has its prerogatives and I am not going to spoil a good story or the fairies may not give me any new ones. I remind my American readers that biscuits in England and Australia are crispy flat things such as you call cookies, and the soft doughy things you call biscuits are what we call scones. And they say we speak the same language...

Weird as it may sound, I did not invent karez (spellings differ—it is also called karezz or karetz). It was quite in vogue in the early years of the twentieth century, when it was thought that the emission of semen weakened a man, and that any system which allowed him to pollinate himself to a standstill without spilling any seed was strengthening. This might have been the case—who can tell? If my readers want to try it, I shall be fascinated to hear...or possibly not. It has some things in common with what is now known as Tantric sex.

The absolutely best book I have found on cocktails is by the charming and erudite Anthony Hogg (see Bibliography). My copy was found by my redoubtable mother in an op shop but other copies must exist somewhere.

You will find medieval jokes in *The Demaundes Joyous* and a delightful and practical guide to all those animals that someone thought that Australia needed (sparrows, foxes, rabbits, thrushes, sky larks, pigeons, rats, deer, mice, etc) in Ian Temby's book, *Wild Neighbours*. And also how to live with them.

My email address is kgreenwood@netspace.net.au and I would love to hear from you.

Translation of 'The Sky Above the Roof' by Paul Verlaine

Translation: Ben Pryor

Above the roof the sky is
So blue, so calm,
Above the roof the tree
Cradles its branch

In that sky the bell
Softly rings
In that tree a bird
Complaining sings

My God, My God, life is there
Simple and easy
That peaceful sound
Comes from the town

Oh you there, what have you done
Endlessly weeping
Say, you there, what have you done
With your youth?

Bibliography

Anonymous, *The Enquirer's Home Book*, Ward Lock, London, 1910.

Beeton, Isabella, *Cook Book*, Ward Lock, London, 1901.

Black, Maggie, *The Medieval Cook Book*, British Museum Press, London, 1962.

Blake, William, *Poems and Prophecies*, J.M. Dent and Sons Ltd., London, 1975.

Burt, Alison, *The Colonial Cook Book*, Summit, Sydney, 1970.

De La Mare, Walter (ed.), *Come Hither*, Constable and Co, London, 1950.

Farmer, David, *The Oxford Dictionary of Saints*, Oxford University Press, Oxford, 1992.

Grahame, Kenneth, *The Wind in the Willows*, Methuen, London, 1908.

Hogg, Anthony, *Cocktails and Mixed Drinks*, Hamlyn Publishing Group Ltd., London, 1979.

Kiddle, Margaret, *Men of Yesterday*, MIP, Melbourne, 1961.

Kipling, Rudyard, 'The Maltese Cat' from *The Day's Work*, Macmillan, London, 1904.

Lawler, James R., *An Anthology of French Poetry*, Oxford University Press, Oxford, 1960.

Nin, Anais, *Delta of Venus*, W.H. Allen and Co., London, 1978.

Temby, Ian, *Wild Neighbours*, Citrus Press, Sydney, 2005.

Wardroper, John, *The Demaundes Joyous of Wynkyn de Worde*, Gordon Fraser, London, 1986.

Various instructive maps, leaflets, booklets and visitor guides to the Mansion at Werribee Park produced by the National Trust and by Parks Vic.

To receive a free catalog of Poisoned Pen Press titles, please contact us in one of the following ways:

Phone: 1-800-421-3976
Facsimile: 1-480-949-1707
Email: info@poisonedpenpress.com
Website: www.poisonedpenpress.com

Poisoned Pen Press
6962 E. First Ave. Ste. 103
Scottsdale, AZ 85251